KV-364-886

Contents

Alfie, Stella and the Poachers

by Carolyn May

Alfie, Stella and the Poachers

Copyright © 2024 Carolyn May

All rights reserved. No part of this publication may be produced, distributed, or transmitted in photocopying, recording, or other electronic or mechanical methods, any form or by any means, including without the prior written permission of the publisher, except in the case of brief quotations embodied in critical reviews and certain other non-commercial uses permitted by copyright law.

All characters and events appearing in this work are fictitious. Any similarity to actual persons or animals, living or dead, is purely coincidental.

First Printed in United Kingdom 2024

Published by Conscious Dreams Publishing
www.consciousdreamspublishing.com

Edited by Elise Abram and Daniella Blechner

Cover Design and Illustrations by Laura Liberatore
https://liberatorelaura.wixsite.com/lauraliberatore

Typeset by Oksana Kosovan

ISBN 978-1-915522-58-0

Dedication

For Chris, Mum, Jeanette, Isla, and Truffle,
my dearest humans and animals, who cooperate and play
together in life. Always thinking of you, lovely Dad.

CHAPTER 1

White Rhino and Dent

IT WAS EARLY EVENING in the tropical grasslands of Africa, and the sun seemed to have settled for a moment on the far-off horizon. The night animals were beginning to awake and prepare themselves to hunt, whilst the day creatures started to gather their young around them to return to their homes.

White Rhino and her young son were grazing alone by a little acacia tree, browsing over the tender green grass, which was lush after the recent rain. They had travelled many miles to find a new area with plenty of food. The two grey shapes blended into the background so well that only when one of the animals moved could you see they were alive.

An oxpecker and his mate had gathered on White Rhino's dusty back and were busy picking at her skin for any ticks they might find.

'You're a long way from the rest of the group, aren't you?' remarked the male oxpecker, cheekily nibbling on the rhino's ear. 'You ought to be careful of poachers, being out here all alone. There are groups of humans who come to shoot at animals such as you.'

White Rhino tossed her head back, and the oxpecker flapped upwards in alarm before landing near her feet. 'Don't bite my ear,' White Rhino said irritably.

'It's not really any of your business, but we aren't part of a group. It is just my son and me now. I haven't seen another white rhino for a whole season.' She snorted and added scornfully, 'But really, why are you so concerned about poachers? Every animal seems to think humans are going to do something terrible to them, but humans are friendly creatures. I've seen them arriving in those noisy vehicles, stopping to shriek in delight when they see Dent and me.' She nodded towards her little son, who was pulling determinedly at a bunch of grass.

'They just set their machines off to clicking and talk excitedly to each other. They don't pose any threat at all. I can't see why everyone is so worried about them.'

White Rhino paused for a moment and then added daringly, 'It's not as if humans could do anything to animals like us. They are so weak with such tiny jaws and teeth. They don't even have horns to defend themselves.'

The oxpecker frowned at her remarks. 'You wouldn't say that if you'd seen some of the sights I've seen,' he said. He dropped his voice as if someone might be trying to overhear. 'It was humans who killed Hero not so long ago, the famous bull in the elephant herd. They have these terrible weapons called guns that can blow a hole through a hide as thick as an elephant's. Believe me, you should be very wary of humans, even if they seem friendly.'

White Rhino turned her head away, refusing to believe what the oxpecker had said. 'You are just a cowardly bird who flies away from everything,' she said rather rudely. 'I can understand why *you* have to be so careful – you have no way of defending yourself like us rhinos. We have our powerful horns.'

She stopped talking and bowed her head so the bird could better see her two white horns from his position on the ground. White Rhino smiled knowingly at him. 'Now, who would try to hurt me when they'd have to get past these horns? Even Lion, with all his strength, knows better than to confront me.'

She turned to look at Dent – so-called because he had a tiny dent in the little stump on his nose where his front horn would grow – and called him over to her. 'Come here, my son. Let us go and graze in the open, where there are juicier mouthfuls to be had.

'Good evening, Oxpecker. Thank you for your well-meant words, but I'm afraid we'll have to agree to disagree when it comes to our opinions of humans. I think they are a friendly and harmless species who obviously love animals like us.'

The bird watched the pair move away, the young rhino eagerly darting around in front of his mother and sighed.

'You did try, dear,' his mate said to him. 'That silly animal doesn't want to be told things for her own good. Let's just hope she doesn't come to regret her boastful words.'

♦♦♦♦♦

White Rhino and Dent plodded on towards the sunset, stopping to eat the fresh grasses they came across. The sun had disappeared beneath the horizon to mark the end of another day, and the big sky glowed a vibrant red and orange.

After a while, Dent stopped grazing and faced his mother. 'Mum, are humans really dangerous?' he asked. 'Shouldn't we always take cover when they are around, just in case?'

White Rhino rubbed her nose against his in a loving gesture. 'I would never let humans hurt you, my darling,' she said tenderly. 'Trust me: humans mean us no harm, but if it makes you feel safer, we can go into the bushes before it gets completely dark.'

She stopped suddenly and raised her head. Her sensitive ears picked up the sound of a vehicle in the distance. Her eyesight was too weak to make out the van, but she heard it coming closer, and her nose caught the scent of humans. White Rhino's instinct was to turn and flee at the growling sound of the engine, but she was stubborn and decided not to move.

Dent looked at her with wide, fearful eyes. 'Mum, what's that noise?' he asked. 'We should go and hide!'

The oxpecker's words echoed inside White Rhino's head. Though everything in her knew they should run to safety, she stood obstinately still.

'No, Dent,' she told her son, 'there's nothing to be afraid of. It will only be humans wanting to look at us. We shall stay and let them admire us. Besides, the grass is far better here than in the bushes, and I want you to eat your fill, so you grow as big and strong as I am.'

The noise came nearer and soon White Rhino could make out the dim shape of a van approaching fast on a dusty track. She heard voices, but, like all wild animals, she didn't understand human languages. Despite her earlier defiance, she suddenly felt afraid as their tones sounded low and threatening.

One of the men in the vehicle spoke rapidly to the others. He was standing and leaning over the edge of the open roof, looking keenly at the pair of rhinos in the grass ahead. Three other men were also in the van, and they all seemed excited to see White Rhino. Two of them pointed at her and Dent as if estimating the size of something with their arms.

The vehicle drew up close to the animals and stopped abruptly.

White Rhino stood completely still, watching what she could see of the men. She listened for the familiar sounds of happy voices and clicking machines, but all she could hear was whispering. The first man seemed to be telling the others what to do whilst the others looked around anxiously, as if afraid of being overheard.

Slowly, all four men got out of the van and crept towards White Rhino and Dent. They walked silently; their backs bent over as if trying not to be seen. White Rhino could just make out that they were all carrying something in their arms, but still she stood there, watching, and trusting, not realising what was about to happen.

The men were within a few metres now. The one who seemed to be in charge hissed at the other three, and they halted. They hoisted their guns to their shoulders, took aim at the watching rhino, and waited.

White Rhino shifted a little, puzzled by their behaviour. Then, at last, she understood what they were about to do. She turned to Dent with wild eyes and screeched, 'Run, Dent! Get out of here as fast as you can. Don't wait for me!' She charged towards him, nudging him in the direction of the bushes with her nose, and the little rhino sprinted off in front of her as fast as his legs would carry him. White Rhino hurtled after him, kicking up great clouds of dust as she tried to save herself, but she had left it too late.

All around the area, animals lifted their heads at the sound of guns exploding before they scattered into the bushes and lay low in fear.

The young rhino raced into the thorny scrub in panic. He couldn't think where he was or where he should go to hide. His whole body froze at the sound of the guns, and he stopped and turned to see his mother fall. Terror-struck, he stood still for a moment and waited for her to get up and come to him, but she didn't.

'Mum!' he yelled. 'Mum, quick! Run here!' He watched anxiously for any sign of movement and then called again, 'Mum, I need you. Please come. Don't just lie there.'

He watched the men run over to his mother.

In confusion, he started back towards her, but then he remembered how she had shouted for him to run away. 'Mum!' He gulped. Tears ran down his face when he realised she wasn't going to come to him.

He called out to her again, telling her, 'Mum, I'll go and hide. Don't worry. I'll come and find you later.'

Dent paused before adding, 'Perhaps the humans will help you stand up again,' but in his heart, he knew that wasn't true.

Dent peered out from behind a small bush, watching as two of the men took hold of his mother's horns and pulled her head into the position they wanted. A third man ran back from the van carrying something in his arms, but Dent's poor eyesight didn't allow him to see what it was. The fourth spoke rapidly at the others, scanning all around him.

Then came the dreadful whirring noise of an engine being started.

From where he was standing, Dent couldn't see what was happening, and he couldn't even begin to imagine what the men were doing. No longer able to listen, he hurried deeper into the bushes and paced around frantically. He tried to work out what he should do, turning over everything in his mind. Perhaps he should try to find other rhinos who might chase the bad men away from his mother to save her. Perhaps he should stay in the bushes until it was safe. Perhaps he should run out and rescue his mother from the men by butting them with his head. He knew he wasn't very strong yet, but he thought he might still be able to frighten the men a little. Then he remembered they had guns.

Dent didn't really know what guns were, but he suspected his small head might not be able to do anything if the men had them.

It was completely dark by then, and Dent felt afraid to be alone for the first time in his life. He gave up trying to work out what to do and threw himself on the ground. The little rhino nuzzled his head into the earth, trying to block everything out. He shut his eyes and pretended that he was asleep, safe and warm at his mother's side, but he couldn't stop himself from shaking. At last, exhausted by fear, he fell into a sleep disturbed by dreams about being chased by men with loud guns.

Dent was so tired that he slept the whole night through without waking once, and the evening's activities passed him by. He didn't notice when the jackal came sniffing around his face or when the lion cub patted his hide playfully. He was lucky the animals encountering him weren't hungry, as he was very vulnerable. He was, after all, a young rhino all alone on the African plains.

CHAPTER 2

A New Orphan

MORNING ARRIVED, AND AS the sun crept over the hills, a beautiful golden colour spread across the grasslands, rolling warmth into them. Everything was quiet. The only signs of life were a small herd of antelope grazing peacefully and two giraffes and their young wandering through the taller grasses. However, the peaceful scene was disturbed by the sight of a kettle of vultures high up enough to look like black dots circling in the sky. Every animal that saw them knew the vultures were looking for something to feast upon.

Dent awoke suddenly. He lifted his head, sniffed around, and listened for any sounds of danger. At once, he remembered the events of the previous evening. The morning air was cool, which helped to clear his head, and he felt better able to think than he had the night before.

The little rhino leapt to his feet and rushed from the bushes out into the open, but there was no sign of the men anywhere.

Dent was overjoyed to see his mother lying just ahead of him. He ran towards her and called out happily, 'Mum, you're still here. They didn't take you away from me. Mum! It's me, Dent. I'm coming!'

He urged his little legs on and sprinted flat out until he was just a few metres from where she lay. He nosed at her eagerly and was puzzled when she didn't respond. 'Mum, it's me, Dent,' he said again, afraid she might be cross with him for leaving her.

Dent pushed himself against her. Only then did he notice that she was completely cold. The world seemed to stand still when Dent realised that his mother was dead, and there was nothing he could do to bring her back. He was horrified to see that her majestic horns were also gone, leaving behind only tiny stumps of white.

Dent slumped down next to his mother's body in despair, no longer caring what happened to him and resolving to stay at her side, come what may. The little rhino had nowhere else to go. He had no mother and no other relatives. He pictured himself being an orphan forever, all alone with no one to help him. Dent had always found the other animals on the African plains frightening, but he'd had his mother to protect him until then.

He was hungry and thirsty, but he didn't know where to start to try to find water and the best food. His mother had always taken him to the right places before without him having to think about it. Dent felt completely dejected as he lay next to her with his eyes closed.

Meanwhile, the circle of vultures began to swoop towards him. It was not long before the birds grew brave enough to wheel down and land on White Rhino's body. Dent heard them, opened his eyes, and jumped up at once, charging at the vultures who dared to try to land.

'Go away! Leave her alone, you horrible birds!' He shouted with as much power as he could, although, unfortunately for Dent, the sound came out as the small, high-pitched voice of a baby.

The vultures laughed at him with cold-hearted cackles. 'It's too late for all that bravery, my little one,' a vulture told him with a mean smile. 'Do you honestly think you're going to frighten us away with your commands?' The vulture pretended to fly away in fear, and his companions sniggered. The other birds imitated Dent's voice and his charging movements, mocking him.

'Go away! Oh, go away, you nasty birds,' they shouted, laughing all the time. 'Oh, we're so scared!'

'Stop it,' cried Dent furiously. 'It's not funny! My mother is lying there dead, and all you can do is make fun of me. Just go away and leave us in peace.'

A large female vulture flew down and perched very close to Dent, looking at him straight in the face. 'There's no point in getting angry with us, sweetie,' she said. 'We don't do the dirty work. We just clean up after some scoundrel or other has done the awful deed. If you're looking for someone to blame, I suggest you look in the direction of the poachers. Perhaps you could charge at them instead.'

'I don't think they'd be afraid of a baby like him,' said another vulture, looking around at her companions with a jeering smile.

The other birds hooted with laughter again, and Dent felt his anger rise.

'I'll get my revenge on the humans,' Dent shouted. 'I'll show you! It's not right that they pretend to be friendly and then trick us.' He watched as the vultures circled around him again. 'And you're not going to touch my mum. I'll charge at you all if necessary,' he threatened bravely. Although he meant every word, he knew inside that he was no match for the large group of vultures now surrounding him.

Suddenly, the rhino's attention was taken by the scent of another animal nearby. It was strong and he turned his head to try to work out which direction it was coming from. Although he couldn't yet make out the skulking shape in the grass, he knew there must be a hyena close by. Dent had never encountered a hyena face to face, but his mother had pointed out their scent in the past. He remembered her telling him that hyenas often appeared soon after an animal had died.

Dent looked around nervously, knowing he was vulnerable now that he was alone. His ears picked up the telltale cackling sound that hyenas make. One animal called, another answered, and Dent realised there were at least two of them. He shrank backwards and crouched at his mother's side, afraid of what they might do to him. He remembered his mother saying that hyenas were mainly scavengers, feeding on the remains of animals hunted by other predators, but she had also said they would hunt live prey if the prey were weak or young. Dent realised he might soon be surrounded by a whole pack of hyenas, and that he was in grave danger.

Frightened, Dent tried to think about what he should do. Should he stay with his mum and defend her from the vultures and hyenas, or should he run for his life? If he tried to run, the hyenas might chase him. Or they might ignore him, as he was very little. Dent could hardly bear the idea of leaving his mother's body to the creatures that would come sneaking out of the shadows, but her voice kept coming back to him, and he knew she would have wanted him to get away. He suddenly felt strong inside when he thought of how he wanted to live on and keep his mother's memory alive. At that moment, he was determined to make his escape.

Dent brought his head close to his mother's, nuzzled her nose, and gently licked her beautiful face. He blew the flies away from her eyes and breathed into her nostrils. She felt so cold that tears came to his eyes, and the feeling of sadness nearly overwhelmed him. He wanted to throw himself down next to her and stay with her forever, but he willed himself to be strong. He rubbed his nose against hers one last time, whispered a loving goodbye, and turned away from her to face the world.

CHAPTER 3

Dent Finds the Waterhole

THE HYENAS MOVED IN closer all around him. Dent could smell them everywhere now and heard them calling to each other on all sides. He trembled a little, dreading what might become of him if they chose to attack. He knew he wouldn't stand a chance against a pack of hyenas.

His eyesight wasn't good enough to pick out where the hyenas were, but he felt sure they would never attack downwind. He thought he should be safe if he ran against the wind. He turned his head in the direction of the sun and listened quietly for a moment. Hearing nothing, he scuttled away at a pace that was not as fast as he could go as he thought that might attract attention. Nevertheless, it was a rapid pace as he was intent on getting away. He ran gradually faster and faster through the grass, hardly daring to listen for the howl that would mean they were coming after him. His heart thumped inside his chest, and his breathing became difficult, but fear wouldn't let him stop.

Dent raced on towards a small group of acacia bushes and hurried inside, letting his jelly-like legs rest under a small bush. He turned back to face the way he had come and sniffed the air cautiously. He almost shouted out for joy when he heard nothing but the gentle morning breeze hurrying through the grasses, making them rustle. The hyenas hadn't chased him. He was safe! He decided to rest there for a while until his breathing returned to normal, and he flopped to the ground in exhaustion.

The bushes hid him almost completely from any animals on the ground. Only the birds gliding way up in the sky, framed against the glorious blue, could have spotted him. The little rhino lay still, too tired to think about anything.

Some while later, Dent realised how thirsty he was, and he knew he needed to get to a waterhole or river to drink. He looked around, trying to work out where he was, but nothing looked familiar, and he didn't recognise any of the scents around him. Cautiously, he edged out of the bushes and hesitated, wondering which way to go. Eventually, he decided to wander down the gentle slope in front of him and Dent soon found himself in a huge open plain of green vegetation, where everything was lush and soft, and the ground felt moister to his hooves. He continued to follow the downward curve of the land, feeling the sun becoming warmer on his back as he grew increasingly thirsty. He felt tired again and nearly trod on a family of mice he hadn't even noticed were there.

'Hey, do you mind watching where you're going, mister?' squeaked one of the mice indignantly. 'What a typical blind rhinoceros. Some of us wouldn't fare very well under your enormous feet.'

Dent was startled by the angry voice. He saw the mouse below him in the grass and felt embarrassed. Dent tried to say how sorry he was, but he got tongue-tied. The mouse could see he was very young.

'It's all right,' the mouse said hastily. 'I can see you didn't mean to be so clumsy. Have you lost your mother or something?'

Dent's sorrowful expression was enough to tell the mouse that something terrible had happened. 'Don't tell me about it if you don't want to,' the mouse said kindly. 'I was only wondering if I could help you to find her.'

'Thank you, but I'm afraid not. She's dead now,' Dent whispered. 'She was killed by humans, and I don't even know why they did it.'

The mouse shook his head and said in his small, high voice, 'Nobody knows why humans do the things they do. Apparently, they don't even eat the meat of the animals they kill. They seem to just take parts of them away, like your mother's horns, I imagine?'

Dent looked surprised. 'How did you know that?' he asked.

'I've come across rhinos before with their horns gone and big wounds in their hides,' replied the mouse. 'If I were a rhino—or an elephant, come to that—I'd stay well away from any humans.'

'But my mother always used to say how friendly humans were and how they only admired us and wanted to look at us,' said Dent. 'Do you think she was wrong?'

The mouse shrugged. 'I couldn't really tell you,' he said. 'Perhaps it depends on the human in question. It makes them a very unpredictable species.'

Dent didn't understand what the mouse meant.

He realised how dry his mouth had become. 'Mouse, could I ask you for some help, please?' he said. 'I really need to get to a waterhole. It's been a long night and I'm very thirsty. Could you tell me if I'm going in the right direction?'

The mouse looked pleased to be asked. 'Yes, of course,' he said, 'and yes, you are headed the right way. There's a waterhole not very far off at all. Just carry on going down this slope, keeping the sun on your left, and you should soon be able to hear the splashing of other animals there. An elephant herd passed this way not that long ago on their way to the water. See how they have flattened the grass with their footsteps? Just follow the path they've made, and you will probably find them still there. Then it will be your turn to watch out for being trampled on by huge animals from above!'

Dent smiled and thanked the mouse for his help. 'I shall be on my way, then,' he said.

'Good luck,' said the mouse. 'You should try to join a group if you can, you know. It's dangerous for a young animal to be all alone. I wish you well.'

He watched as Dent walked away and sighed. 'Do humans realise the tragedies they cause, I wonder?' he questioned.

The rhino followed the trodden grass as the mouse suggested, and his acute sense of hearing soon picked up the sounds of animals in water. He hastened his steps, anxious to reach the drinking place as soon as possible. Winding his way around several fever trees, he arrived at a clearing. A slope thick with mud imprinted with numerous hoof and paw prints led down to a big waterhole, where many different species were drinking and bathing.

A small herd of zebras had gathered on the opposite bank and were drinking at the water's edge. Their tails swished from side to side to chase the flies away, and they lifted their heads frequently, watching and listening for potential danger. The whole herd jumped nervously, prepared to flee should even a single zebra take fright at something.

Near the zebras, several giraffes were drinking in their characteristic, awkward looking way. The legs of the giraffes were so long that the only possible way for their mouths to reach the water was to spread their forelegs wide apart. Their front legs then acted as a support while the giraffes bent their long necks down to drink. Three young giraffes were busy drinking whilst the adults kept guard. The adults knew their young were vulnerable to predators such as lions when in the difficult drinking position.

'As quickly as you can, children,' called one of the adults. 'We don't want to attract too much attention.'

Farther out in the water, several hippos rested with much of their huge bodies submerged. All anyone could see above the surface were their great, grey, rounded backs looking like smooth boulders and their heads from the nostrils upwards. Small ears and eyes set wide apart were also just visible, seeming almost to float on the water.

Various wading birds were also present, hunting for fish. A male heron stood at the edge of the water, his head bent over, watching for fish beneath the surface. When he spotted one, he plunged his magnificent orange beak into the water and attempted to catch it.

Dent couldn't make out the shapes very clearly, but his powerful nose picked up all kinds of scents, some of which he had never encountered before. He stood timidly at the top of the slope, not daring to join the other animals. Of course, he had been to waterholes before with his mother, but it had been different then. He had always felt safe because he knew she would protect him from any danger.

Just along the bank from where he stood, he could see a big herd of buffalo, and next to them were the elephants the mouse had mentioned. They seemed enormous creatures to Dent, who could have run underneath some of their bellies without touching them. There were at least ten elephants of various sizes, drinking from the waterhole with their long, grey trunks. Most had waded in up to their knees and were spraying water over their backs. Dent heard them talking, laughing, and enjoying their early morning bathe.

Only two elephants remained on the bank. The first was a huge female, who was the leader of the herd, and with her was her little son. Dent soon realised the female was trying to encourage her son to go into the water. However, it was plain to everyone watching that he had other ideas.

CHAPTER 4

Stella and Leader

ACROSS THE WATER, THERE came a dreadful noise. 'NNNNNNNNOOOOOO!!! I WON'T, I WON'T, I WON'T!!' shrieked the baby elephant. 'It's so cold. It's so muddy. I don't want to, and you can't make me.'

Animals all around the waterhole looked up, startled, and then laughed when they saw the frightened elephant. He was clearly very young, as his head still had some of his black downy hair.

His mother stood at his side and addressed him firmly. 'Now, darling,' she said, 'I think you're being a bit silly about this. You can see that the others are very happy in the water. I'm not asking you to do anything dangerous. It's really not that cold, and the mud is one of the best things about bathing. It's delightful to feel that lovely mud stick to your skin and cool you down.'

The young elephant gulped and stared wide-eyed at the water in front of him. He shook his head and shrank back even farther away from the waterhole. He thought for a moment and tried to bargain with his mother. 'Please, Mum, please don't make me do it today. I will be brave enough tomorrow, I promise.' He looked up at her and tried to adopt his most winsome expression.

His mother had to stop herself from smiling. 'I think I remember you telling me that yesterday, Leader,' she said. 'Don't you think a young elephant should be courageous enough to keep the promises he makes?'

'Yes. Come on, Leader,' called his sister from the water. 'Stop being such a coward and come in. Everyone's watching you embarrass yourself.'

The little elephant looked ashamed, but his fear was too great. He fixed his eyes on the water's edge and willed his legs to move, but they only trembled a bit, and he almost sank to his knees.

'It's no good. I can't,' he whispered, 'but I will go in tomorrow. I promise you, Mum.'

'I'm afraid too many unkept promises make another one sound doubtful, Leader,' said his mother. 'I can see I'm going to have to give you a bit of help.'

She walked around behind her son, so he was between her and the water. Before Leader realised what she was doing, his mother settled her head against his backside. She caught him by complete surprise when she drove forwards with her powerful legs to push him down the slope.

Leader squealed and tried desperately to resist her by pushing his front legs out straight, but his mother was far too strong for him. The other animals watched in amusement as she sent him flying head-first into the water, where he landed with a giant splash.

Leader floundered for a moment and sank before coming up again. He gasped for air and blew water furiously out of his trunk. The other elephants cheered, and his mother smiled. Leader stood on his own, still in shock and cross at the others for laughing at him.

His sister came wading towards him with a grin. 'You're going to make a fine leader one day, brother,' she said. 'I can see your group being the only one in the elephant world not to go bathing. You'll be known as the dirtiest group that's ever been.'

Their mother joined them in the water and overheard this comment. 'Don't be quite so sure of yourself, Bright,' she said with a twinkle in her eye. 'I seem to remember another baby elephant who wasn't so keen on the water the first few times.'

Leader's sister grinned in acknowledgement, and Leader looked happier.

All this time, Dent was standing nearby on the slope, watching the family with envy. He no longer had a mother to encourage him to go into the water or stand up for him if someone teased him. He felt very sad, and despite his thirst, he almost left the waterhole. He didn't want to see the happy elephant family playing with each other in the water, or the mother elephant gently squirting water over her son.

'I'll just take a very quick drink and ignore them,' he said to himself. 'I don't need a family around me like that anyway. I'm getting bigger now, and I think I can manage on my own.'

Unfortunately for Dent, his next steps showed just how wrong he was. He walked boldly down the slope to the water's edge without realising that the mud was slippery there and the slope much steeper than where the elephants had been standing.

He felt his hooves slip, and his stomach did a somersault as, for a split second, he thought he was going to tumble head-over-heels. The slide propelled him forwards, and he found himself having to run into the water, completely out of control. In the same way as Leader had done a few moments before, he landed with a big splash, finding himself very near to the young elephant and his mother.

Dent scrambled to his feet with embarrassment and looked at the elephants to see if they had noticed. Of course, they had, but to his surprise, they weren't laughing at him as they had at Leader.

'Are you okay?' asked Leader's mother, her gentle eyes full of concern. 'Are you hurt anywhere?'

Dent shook the remaining water out of his ears and smiled at the elephants. 'Yes, no, I'm sure I'm fine,' he said, although he had hit his right foreleg on a rock, and he suspected it was bleeding under the water.

'That slope's a bit slippery, isn't it,' said Leader with a giggle. 'I expect you saw me having problems a few moments ago.'

Dent thought he should be polite about Leader's misfortunes, but as he remembered the image of the elephant being heaved into the water, he couldn't help bursting out laughing. Leader could now see the funny side, too, and he joined him merrily. Together, they chuckled away, beginning what would become a firm friendship.

After a while, Leader's mother interrupted. 'I'm glad you find it so amusing now, Leader,' she said with a smile, 'but perhaps you should ask your friend his name.'

'It's Dent,' the rhino told them without waiting to be asked, 'on account of my front horn stump, which, as you can see, has a tiny dent in it. I know you're Leader, but why are you called that?'

Now it was Leader's turn to look embarrassed. 'I was named after my grandfather, Hero, who was thought to be the bravest elephant bull our herd has ever known,' he said. 'I'm supposed to follow in his footsteps, but I don't feel like a leader. I don't suppose my grandfather was afraid of the water.'

His mother brushed him proudly with her trunk. 'You've got plenty of time yet, my son, and you've shown that you're humble enough to laugh at your own mistakes. That's a fine quality in a young elephant.'

She turned towards Dent with a welcoming smile and introduced herself. 'My name is Stella,' she told him. 'I'm very pleased to meet you, Dent.'

Dent smiled in return, and something stirred at the back of his mind. Had he heard Hero mentioned before? He searched his memory, trying to remember. Slowly he recalled the conversation his ill-fated mother had had with the oxpecker, and how the bird had warned them to beware of humans, and suddenly, the words came back to him. 'It was humans who killed Hero, the famous bull of the elephant herd.'

'Was your grandfather the one who was killed by humans?' he blurted out to Leader.

Stella turned to him, looking very sad. 'Yes, he was. Leader's grandfather and my father,' she said. 'It was two dry seasons ago. We had seen humans following us around for a while, but they seemed harmless enough, just watching us and pointing at us. We didn't think they were any threat, as they seemed just like the other groups we see every day. But then, one day, when it was nearly dusk, the same group of humans arrived out of nowhere in their van. They jumped out, all of them carrying these weapons called guns, and took aim at the herd.'

Dent gasped, and Leader's eyes widened. He knew his grandfather had died, but his mother had never told him this story before. He realised how sad his mum looked and felt upset.

'My father went to speak to them,' Stella continued. 'He asked them why they were showing such unnecessary violence towards us, but of course, humans can't understand a word of our language, and it was as if he hadn't said anything. Father realised they might shoot the whole herd if they could, so he shouted to everyone to head for the trees. He knew the men's van wouldn't be able to follow us there.'

Stella looked down at the two young animals whose little faces were staring up at her. She wished she could protect them from the truth, but she knew her words were important for them to hear.

'Father showed enormous bravery as he walked towards the men,' she said as a tiny tear ran down from the corner of her eye. 'He knew he was sacrificing himself, but I think he hoped that if the men killed him, they would leave the rest of the herd alone. The heartless men shot at him with their guns, again and again without mercy. My dear, kind father remained standing for as long as he could bear the pain to protect all of us. I turned to look as we reached the safety of the trees, and the last thing I saw of my father was him falling to the ground.'

A little cry escaped from Leader's mouth, and Stella shook her head. 'The herd was devastated,' she told them. 'I don't know if you understand how elephants live, Dent, but we have very close family groups and all the female relatives live together with the young animals, both males and females. The older males live separately in their own groups or on their own. The female herds are led on a day-to-day basis by the oldest and wisest female, but our male relatives are often still nearby, even if they don't live with us. My father always came to help us if we were in any danger. Many times, he helped us to find the best food and defended our territory from other males. He also warned us always to be wary of humans, so it was terrible that he himself should die at their hands.'

Dent interrupted her, impatient to share his own story. 'Humans killed my mother, too,' he said breathlessly. 'It was yesterday evening, and it happened in just the same way. They came in their van, took out their awful guns and shot her.' He stood with his head bowed and felt warm tears trickle down his grey cheeks. They dripped into the water with a splash that sounded loud in the silence.

'She told me to run to safety,' he continued, beginning to sob, 'so . . . so . . . I did, but now I feel guilty. I should have stayed with her, and perhaps together we could have fought the men off. Then she might still be alive now.' Dent broke off, looking very upset.

'Dent,' said Stella softly, 'you wouldn't have been able to do anything against their guns. The humans have made those weapons so they can shoot through skin too tough for even the sharpest teeth of the biggest crocodile.'

Leader gasped as he considered this. His mother had warned him how dangerous crocodiles were, and yet, somehow, these guns were worse.

'The bullets come out at a speed fast enough to defy any cheetah,' Stella continued, 'and the aim they have is beyond that of any swooping hawk.'

Stella stopped and looked down at the little rhino. Don't blame yourself, Dent,' she said gently. 'I can tell you that what your mother would have wanted, above anything else, was for you to escape. You did exactly the right thing, and she would be incredibly proud of you.'

The big elephant reached out to Dent with her trunk and brushed it over his ears in a caring gesture. Dent smiled gratefully.

'Mum, why do the humans want to kill us?' asked Leader. 'Surely, they aren't afraid of us . . . are they?'

His mother's great ears flapped about as she shook her head. 'No, it's not that,' she said. 'For elephants, it has something to do with our tusks. Whenever humans kill an elephant, the first thing they do is take away its tusks.'

'They took my mother's horns, too,' said Dent.

'For some reason, they want horns and tusks,' said Stella, 'but I have no idea what they do with them. I can't believe they would kill us unless the horns and tusks were vital to them in some way.'

The elephant turned her attention back to Dent, who still looked forlorn. 'Are you all alone now, Dent, or is there a group of rhinos you could join if you wanted to?' she asked.

Dent hesitated for a moment. 'I've got no one now,' he admitted. 'We didn't see any other rhinos after my father died. My mum said there are very few of us around. She always warned me that I was only safe because she was there to protect me from other species. What worries me is that I don't think I am big enough to defend myself on my own yet.'

Stella thought for a while. 'Let me see,' she said. 'You're a white rhino, aren't you?'

Dent nodded.

'And that means you feed on grasses, doesn't it?' she continued.

The rhino nodded again.

'My dear, if you are happy to stay with our family, you would be most welcome,' Stella told him, this time brushing his nose gently with her trunk. 'I would look after your safety and protect you from danger as if you were one of my own calves. The herd sometimes ventures into trees and shrubs, but our diet generally consists of grasses and leaves, so you could easily graze with us.'

'That's a great idea,' shouted Leader, who had taken a liking to the little rhino. 'What do you say, Dent?'

Dent looked extraordinarily happy. Just a few hours before, he had imagined himself in the years ahead, being in constant danger and unbearably lonely, but now he had the chance to become an adopted member of a lovely new family. He felt both relief and delight.

'You are so kind. I don't know how to show you how grateful I am,' he said at last. He laughed when Leader cheered. 'I promise I'll never cause you any trouble,' he added.

CHAPTER 5

Dent's New Family

AT THAT POINT, LEADER'S older sister waded over to the trio and introduced herself to Dent. 'Hello,' she said, smiling. 'My name is Bright. I hear you're going to be a member of our family, too.' Bright was considerably bigger than Leader, although not yet as large as her mother, and unlike Leader, she had two quite sizeable tusks. Dent didn't know that elephants continue to grow taller and stronger until about twenty years of age, but it was evident to him that she must be a lot older than Leader. Stella also clearly treated her as a young adult elephant.

'I'm so sorry about what happened to your mother,' Bright told Dent. 'I think it's disgraceful the way humans treat us. Mum, can't we do something about it?'

Her mother shook her head. 'You know we always have scouts looking out for danger,' she said. 'The problem is that we can't always stay that close to cover. We have to go to the waterhole, and we have to be constantly on the move from place to place to find enough good quality food. We can't just live our lives in hiding, Bright.'

Bright lifted one of her big forelegs and plunged it back into the water in frustration, splashing water in all directions. 'Surely we have to do something, though,' she said. 'Are we all to fall victim to humans and do nothing about it?'

The conversation was interrupted by a cape buffalo, who was wallowing in the mud nearby. His huge, black body was covered in crusty mud, and even his horns looked brown as a result. 'From the sounds of it, I think you should try to do something before it's too late for all of you,' he said a little pompously. 'I've always thought elephants and rhinos are too naïve about what humans are really like. My species is related to the cows, whom humans keep imprisoned within their fences. We all know the stories about how humans pretend to be kind and feed our cousins, and then, one day, they are taken away and never seen again. The cows are resigned to never experience what it is like to live free in the wild, knowing all too well that one day they will just disappear.'

Stella tried to ask him a question, but the buffalo was rather fond of the sound of his own voice, and he was not about to be interrupted. 'Let me continue,' he said, ignoring Stella rather rudely. 'I am the leader of the buffalo herd—you can call me Buffalo. I think all of the animals should try to help each other, and if ANY humans are seen, we should charge them down. Of course, some of us might fall in the effort, but it would be worth it in the end because then, the humans would never dare to come again. It would be good for us buffaloes, too, as humans have also been known to shoot at members of my herd.'

Stella tried to be polite. 'That's a very good idea,' she said, 'but it might not be practical. After all, why should other species help elephants and rhinos? I'm also not sure that charging at humans would do any good. They would just shoot at us with their guns, and everyone would get frightened and run away.'

'Elephant, you are wrong,' Buffalo said bluntly. 'I have seen lions, leopards, and cheetahs also suffer at the hands of humans. Don't think it's only species such as yours that humans kill. They hunt the cats as well, so I think you'd find that they, too, would be keen on some communal defence. As for running away, I know all of us are brave enough to charge as a herd. I can certainly speak for the buffaloes and say that we would be happy to join your cause.'

Stella watched in amusement as some of the surrounding buffalo herd shifted uncomfortably and looked most unhappy at this remark. Buffalo steamrollered on, regardless. 'All we need to do now is coordinate our approach. I think—'

Stella had heard enough of what Buffalo thought, and she interrupted him. 'Thank you. You are obviously a courageous animal,' she said warmly, 'and I think you're right: it is time we animals joined together to fight back against the poachers.'

She drew herself up to her full height, and Dent realised what a huge elephant she really was. 'Ever since my father died, I've been determined to avenge his death,' she said. 'Now that I hear about other animals being mercilessly killed as well, I'm even more determined. We've got to start standing up for ourselves.'

'That's the spirit!' agreed Buffalo, looking pleased.

'And we'll help, too!' squeaked Leader. 'We'll charge at any humans coming anywhere near us.'

'We are not going to charge at them, Leader,' his mother told him firmly. 'If we charge at the poachers, they will simply shoot at us, and even more animals will be killed. We need to think of other ways to protect ourselves.'

Stella was silent for a moment, deep in thought. 'We have got to be clever,' she said. 'It's also important that we only target poachers and not the groups of humans who just come to look at us and mean us no harm. I believe they are called "tourists". It is only the poachers and their guns that represent a danger to us.'

Buffalo snorted. He was evidently not fond of the human species. 'ALL humans are dangerous,' he said. 'Frankly, I don't see why we should treat some differently from others. How are we supposed to discriminate between different types of humans? Do we have to wait until they shoot us before deciding which ones might be threats?'

Bright answered, 'I know how you can tell the difference,' she said. 'The humans who won't hurt us lean out of their vehicles and make a lot of noise. They have those machines and things that make strange beeping sounds, and they seem to wear funny-coloured objects on their heads and bright clothing.'

'Whereas the poachers arrive in silence,' said Dent, remembering how he and his mother hadn't heard the poachers' voices until they had been very close. 'And they wear clothes that make them difficult to pick out.'

'Poachers and tourists seem to act differently, too,' Stella continued, nodding. 'The tourists sound happy and relaxed, but the poachers appear anxious and look around as if afraid of something. I wonder if poaching is not allowed by other humans, and they are afraid of being caught. Humans really are such an odd species.'

Buffalo couldn't help but offer his opinion again. 'Well, I think we would all be a whole lot better off if there were no humans around at all,' he said. 'I am going to order my herd to charge at any humans we see, and I think you should do the same.'

Stella decided to take control of the situation and she called to the rest of the herd to gather round. It was the first time Dent realised she was the elephant in charge of the herd and that she must, therefore, also be the oldest and wisest. The other elephants stopped their bathing and drinking and plunged towards her through the water. From their obedience, it was clear they respected and trusted her entirely.

Great waves rolled off in all directions as their feet churned up the mud on the bottom of the waterhole, thickening the water and turning it black. The water battered Dent across his side, almost knocking him over. The noise of the wading was so loud that it was hard to believe it was only a small group of elephants moving towards him.

'Ladies and young elephants,' Stella began, 'let me first introduce you to Dent, who is going to be a new member of our family.' She gestured towards the rhino with her trunk.

One of the female elephants at the back of the group strained her eyes and whispered far too loudly, 'Well, that's the funniest looking elephant I've ever seen. What a square jaw and no kind of trunk to speak of. Just some tiny stump on its nose. Is there something wrong with it?'

Bright interrupted in amusement. 'For those of you whose eyesight isn't so good these days, Auntie, I'd like to point out that Dent is, of course, a rhinoceros.'

A chorus of exclamations came from the back of the group. 'Oh, it's a rhino.'

'What's a rhino doing joining an elephant herd, then?'

'Don't ask me. Perhaps he thinks he's an elephant.'

Stella continued in her imposing but kindly voice, and the elephants stopped talking at once. 'Sadly, Dent has been made an orphan by poachers,' she said. 'I would like you all to make him feel very welcome as a part of our family.'

Her tone grew firmer. 'I'm sure nobody needs reminding of how poachers cost our family a magnificent bull in his prime, and everyone knows that the threat of more deaths remains. My herd, it is time to defend ourselves from this danger. Enough of being timid and too gentle to fight back. From now on, we are going to give the poachers something to think about.'

The eyes of every elephant in the herd were fixed on their leader. There was a buzz of excitement, and Dent heard hasty, whispered conversations.

'But how can we do anything?' asked one of the older elephants, looking very doubtful. 'I mean, what can we do against those dreadful guns?'

Stella smiled. 'That's a good question, Mabel,' she said. 'Guns make it difficult for us, but there are other ways we can fight back. I'm going to call a meeting of all the grassland animals tonight at the waterhole. We need to discuss our tactics.'

The elephants spent the rest of the day passing on the message to the other animals. Stella told them to approach everyone they came across to ask them to attend the meeting. She was keen to get as many different species involved as possible, as all of them had skills that could be useful.

The elephants had no difficulty persuading the other animals to attend. Their leader was greatly respected by the creatures of the land, and when she called a meeting, everyone knew it must be for an important reason.

Dent and Leader raced around, calling to all the birds and small animals they saw. Stella had strictly forbidden them from speaking to any of the cats. Although she knew no one would dare to harm a messenger of hers, she was afraid the cats might tease young animals like Leader and Dent, so the elephant leader kept a watchful eye on the two youngsters.

The buffalo herd joined the elephants in informing the other animals, and the news soon echoed across the plains.

'Stella has called a meeting!'

'Tonight, at sunset at the waterhole. Everyone must be there.'

'It's very important. We've got to start standing up to the poachers.'

'We're going to show those awful humans what we're made of!' (That was Buffalo, of course.)

'I'll be there!'

'So will I!'

'Until tonight!'

CHAPTER 6

The Meeting

STELLA STOOD CALMLY AT the front of the elephant herd near the water's edge. It was sunset, and she watched the sun sink into its rosy bed far away on the horizon feeling her heart beating fast. It was nearly time for the meeting to start.

Figures of different shapes and sizes began to gather around the waterhole. In the dim light it was difficult to make them out clearly, but across the water, Stella could see the zebra herd packed together with dozens of wildebeests next to them. A herd of antelope soon joined the zebras, and between them, the three herds took up all of one side of the waterhole.

Stella turned her head to look at the animals to her left. The buffalo herd was standing nearest, just a few paces along from the elephants. Stella smiled when she heard Buffalo reminding his herd of the evils of humans. He was a fiery character, but she was glad he was on their side.

A little farther along the bank, Giraffe and his family were just arriving. Stella could see them looking around for her, and she waved her trunk in greeting. The giraffes preferred to stand with the elephants at meetings if they could. Otherwise, they tended to tower over their neighbours and feel rather awkward.

The elephant turned to her other side and was delighted to see the ostriches had come to the meeting. She looked hard at the smaller bird pacing by the ostriches' feet and realised it was Martial Eagle. Excellent! He would be useful to detect the poachers from above.

A sudden movement within the zebra herd caught her eye. Stella frowned, wondering what had upset them, but then she noticed the lion pride strolling slowly towards the water's edge. For many generations, the grassland animals had sworn an oath not to threaten any other animal during a group meeting called by any species. Nevertheless, the timid zebras couldn't help themselves backing away from the lions as they arrived.

Stella glanced across the assembly to see that almost all of the animals she had expected to attend were now present. Leopard and her two cubs sat slightly apart from the other animals near the waterhole. The elephant could just make out the form of the very shy Cheetah, who had taken up his place behind the giraffes. The baboon troop had also arrived and were sitting together with their backs hunched over and orange eyes staring out across the water. The moon's light glinted on the golden scales of a puff adder in the grass, and Stella thought she could hear scorpions hissing nearby. The elephant wasn't at all surprised to see no sign of the jackals or the hyenas, who were known to be selfish animals who would do nothing to help the other species. She reflected sadly that no black rhinos had joined the group either. They seemed to be so few in number now.

Across the water, the waiting animals talked, making the strangest sounds. Stella listened in amazement. It was rare for such a group of different species to come together.

Stella decided it was time to open the meeting. She raised her trunk high up in the air and trumpeted. The chattering stopped at once, and the animals fell silent. Stella took a deep breath and began to speak. 'Animals of the savanna . . . friends,' she addressed them, as loudly as she could, 'thank you all for coming here tonight to this important meeting. I know some of you don't feel very comfortable in each other's company, but I promise that you are all safe.'

Lion couldn't stop himself from leering at the zebras at this remark, and the herd looked nervously at each other.

Stella continued: 'Everyone here knows about the terrible poachers in this land who kill without mercy. My father lost his life at their hands, and only yesterday, a baby rhino was orphaned by their guns.'

The older elephants shook their heads in dismay, and dozens of animals looked sympathetically at Dent, who felt very sad.

'Species like the elephant and the rhino may eventually no longer exist if the poachers aren't stopped,' said Stella. 'Our numbers are dwindling, but the poachers don't seem to care.'

There was a wave of uproar at this. The animals cried out and looked at each other with angry expressions. How dare the poachers not care! Cheetah felt the tension rise and hid even farther behind the giraffes as Stella continued.

'Animals of the savanna, we must act now! Will you all join me to fight back against the poachers?'

The elephant was overjoyed to hear the audience break into a mighty cheer made up of dozens of different voices, knowing that she had managed to influence them with her words.

Silence fell again, and Lion's lazy drawl came across the water: 'I don't really see why the lions should get involved,' he said. 'No one in my pride has ever been targeted by poachers. We would only be putting ourselves in unnecessary danger if we tried to fight them on your behalf.'

Stella looked a little sad. 'I know it seems to be elephants and rhinos who are especially threatened by the poachers,' she admitted, 'but we need everyone to help us defeat them. You can't be certain the poachers won't come after you, Lion. We know that lions and other cats are also hunted, and the herd animals, too.'

'Yes, don't be so selfish!' said Buffalo indignantly after Stella had finished. 'My herd doesn't seem to be targeted so specifically either, but the buffaloes are going to help in every way we can.'

'Mmm, but lions hunt buffaloes,' said Lion, quietly licking his lips. 'I do feel rather hungry at the moment.'

The zebras gasped at this comment.

'What was that?' Buffalo demanded, but Lion pretended not to hear.

Stella moved on hurriedly, hoping to avoid an argument. 'The question is, how are we going to defeat the poachers?' she said. 'Obviously, we cannot hope to beat their guns.'

'That's it!' said Lion. 'I'm not going to put myself at the wrong end of a gun for a herd of elephants.' There were angry cries from the other animals. Many of them shook their heads in disbelief at Lion's remark.

'Lion, we need all the help we can get,' pleaded Stella. 'I know we will all be at some risk from the guns, but if my plan works, nobody will be hurt.

'Now, are you willing to help us or not?'

The assembly's eyes all switched to Lion, making him feel uncomfortable. He knew his reputation would never be the same if he appeared cowardly now. 'I suppose so . . . if it won't take up too much of my time,' he muttered.

'If l know you, it won't take up any of your time at all,' his mate said to him sharply. 'I seem to end up doing most things for you, and I suspect this won't be any different.'

Lion was annoyed to hear some of the zebra herd tittering at this comment. He thought about making a witty reply, but he couldn't think of one, so he just lay down and pretended to look majestic and amused.

'So, what, exactly, are we going to do?' asked Baboon, bringing the conversation back to the plan and frowning so hard that his eyes were almost buried beneath his furrowed brow.

'We are going to be ready for the poachers,' Stella replied. 'First, we need an excellent lookout system, so we always know when the poachers are coming.'

'Martial Eagle – I would like you to be involved in this, please. High up in the sky, you are in the best position to see them early.'

The bird hesitated. 'I will do my best to help, but I can't cover the entire area,' he said. 'Besides, I'm not always up in the sky.'

'Yes, you'll need some assistance,' Stella agreed. 'Does anyone have ideas about who could help with the lookout?'

'What about the meerkats?' suggested Puff Adder in his lisping voice. 'They never fail to spot me coming.'

The meerkats were famous throughout the grasslands for their watch brigade and its impeccable organisation. From an early age, all meerkats in the mob were trained up by their leader, the commander-in-chief, to keep watch for any threats or danger. Whenever danger was detected, it was reported immediately to the meerkat headquarters, and the commander-in-chief called up the troops from the burrows to prepare a defence.

'That's an excellent idea,' said Stella, after a moment's thought. 'Did anybody ask the meerkats to the meeting today?'

'Yes, I did,' said an older elephant from behind her, 'but the commander-in-chief was very rude. She told me to go away and not to interrupt their training sessions.'

'She does take the training of her troops seriously,' Stella told her. 'Don't be upset. I shall talk to her myself tomorrow.'

'It's all very well to see when the poachers are coming,' said Buffalo, 'but what are we going to do when they arrive? I still think we should charge at them.'

'I was just coming to that,' the elephant leader told him. 'This is where everyone has a part to play!'

CHAPTER 7

The Commander-in-chief

THE NEXT MORNING, STELLA left the herd early to find the meerkats. Buffalo saw her leave and insisted on coming with her. Privately, Stella thought she could handle the commander-in-chief better on her own, but Buffalo was so keen to help that she didn't want to discourage him.

The two animals headed in the direction of the meerkat base. In the distance, Stella soon picked out a group of meerkats standing on their hind legs and peering across the grasslands. Shortly, she saw one of them jump down and scuttle away, and she knew their presence was being reported to the commander-in-chief.

Stella had met the commander-in-chief before and found her very efficient, but she was difficult to talk to because she was always so busy. The elephant was, therefore, surprised when the commander was waiting for them as they arrived at the base.

She stood on a high termite mound and saluted them. 'Good morning, Elephant, Buffalo!' she cried, and she let her paw drop. 'Can I be of any assistance?'

Stella gave her a respectful return salute with her trunk before speaking politely: 'Good morning to you too, Commander,' she said. 'I have come to ask you an enormous favour.'

'Go on,' said the commander, who had been expecting as much. She already knew what had happened at Stella's meeting, thanks to her network of spies.

'As you may know, I held a meeting last night to plan our fight back against the poachers,' said Stella. 'Every animal in attendance agreed to join the cause. I have come to ask if the meerkats would be willing to assist us in the early detection of poachers. The whole animal kingdom is in awe of your outstanding vigilance, and you would be a great help in putting our plan into place.'

The commander-in-chief couldn't help but feel pleased with such flattery from the famous elephant leader. It made her feel proud and quite important. Nonetheless, she decided to be a little awkward. 'My troops follow a demanding schedule of watch duties,' she said, sounding doubtful. 'I don't want to ask them to work for longer than they already do.'

Stella smiled to herself. She would have been amazed if the commander had agreed straightaway.

Unfortunately, Buffalo wasn't so tactful, and he snorted rudely. 'What a load of rubbish—' he started to say, but Stella interrupted him in haste.

'I know your troops work very hard already,' she said, 'but all I am asking is for one of them to report it to me when poachers are detected in the area.'

The commander ignored Buffalo's comment and pretended to think. 'Well,' she said at last, 'I suppose I could add it to the list of one of the new trainees' duties. Number 23 is a young meerkat who has not yet undergone much training. He wouldn't be missed quite so much if he occasionally reported to you.'

Stella was delighted. 'Thank you very much,' she said. 'Of course, if I or any of my herd could ever be of help to you, you would only need to ask.'

The commander smiled briefly and gave a little nod of acknowledgement. 'Now, I'm afraid I must return to my duties,' she said. 'Watch brigades don't run themselves, you know.'

Stella raised her trunk in a mini salute. Even Buffalo had the grace to dip his head as the meerkat darted away, leaving the two animals feeling very pleased.

'Excellent,' muttered Buffalo as they turned to walk back. 'I think we handled that very well.'

'Yes, we did, didn't we?' said Stella, amused at Buffalo's self-praise. 'I'm glad the commander agreed to help us.'

'Now we'll know when they're coming, and we'll be ready for them,' said Buffalo, practising a delighted little charge.

Stella saw him and frowned. 'Buffalo! Remember what I told you,' she warned. 'Charging doesn't come into the plan, but yes, we'll be ready for them now.'

CHAPTER 8

The Poachers Return

THE ANIMALS WENT BACK to their normal lives after the excitement of the meeting. The herds grazed peacefully in the grasses, whilst the cats busied themselves hunting for prey.

Baboon and his family were too preoccupied with their frequent arguments to think much about the meeting and the plans that had been made. The ostriches raced across the plains from time to time, and Martial Eagle was often visible gliding across the sky.

Stella led the elephant herd some way away from their usual territory so they would all find enough food as the grasses became drier in the early winter months.

Dent was now an accepted member of the herd and went with them. The buffalo herd also followed the elephants to the new pastures. Stella was patient with Buffalo, but she sometimes wondered why he had to follow her everywhere. Although he would never have admitted it, the truth was that Buffalo greatly admired the elephant leader and thought it best to copy her decisions.

Meanwhile, the meerkats dutifully scanned the grasslands for any sign of the poachers returning, but they seemed to have vanished. Tourists came and went, but they were noisy and carried no guns. The meerkats knew these weren't the dangerous people they were looking for.

The animals began to forget their fears and grow bolder. Leopard and her cubs often roamed the savanna in broad daylight. Even Stella had to remind herself that the danger had not gone away, and she tried to ensure the herd was always close to cover in case needed.

Then, late one afternoon, the poachers came back, and as Stella had planned, the animals were ready for them. It was Martial Eagle who spotted them first. Flying way up in the sky, he was no more than a speck against the sun to the poachers below. The bird caught sight of the van and glided down to take a better look. His heart quickened when he realised the men were holding guns, and he shot off to find Stella.

Martial Eagle screeched as he approached the elephants, and Stella looked up at once. It was the signal she had been preparing for.

'The poachers are on their way now!' yelled the bird before he had even landed. 'They're coming on the road to the east, and they're no more than a bird's eye view away.'

'Right! All systems go!' shouted Stella. 'Please go and give everyone the signal to get ready. Thank you, Martial Eagle.'

Martial Eagle flew off like an arrow and skimmed over the land, calling out a warning for the animals to get into their positions. Just after he left, a young meerkat came running towards the elephant herd and breathlessly delivered the same message to Stella.

'The poachers have been sighted, Your Majesty,' the little animal gasped. 'I'm sorry it's taken me so long to find you, but I got lost. Please don't tell the commander. I'm very new to my training, you see.'

Stella smiled and promised she wouldn't tell anyone. 'Now, back to your troop, and keep a lookout,' she told him. 'Let us know if anyone else is spotted. Well done!'

The meerkat turned slightly pink in the cheeks and scuttled away whilst the elephant leader turned to face her herd. Despite her beating heart, she addressed them calmly. 'Ladies and young elephants—I'm sure you've heard that the poachers are on their way,' she said. 'Now, does everyone remember what you are to do?'

The other elephants raised their trunks in reply and whispered excitedly to each other whilst Leader and Dent danced around in anticipation. This was the moment they had been waiting for since the meeting.

CHAPTER 9

The Poachers Get a Shock!

THE ELEPHANT HERD SPLIT into two groups as planned. Stella and two of the other largest elephants in the herd hurried off towards the road to the east, where Martial Eagle had seen the poachers coming. The rest of the herd, including Dent and Leader, went towards the waterhole, plunged into the water until they were knee-deep, and waited.

'We must make haste,' panted Stella as the trio raced through the grass. 'We've got to get to the trees before the poachers arrive.'

Ahead, the elephants could see the road the poachers would use. There were several acacia trees with wide-reaching branches on either side of the road. Stella was relieved to see that Baboon and his family were already sitting and waiting in the trees. The giraffes were also in position, taking the opportunity to graze nearby while waiting. Stella caught sight of Leopard sitting just in front of the trees. The cat lifted a silent paw in greeting, and Stella raised her trunk in reply.

Stella knew there was no time to lose. The three elephants hurried to reach the trees and they arrived breathless and hot. 'Right, now, help me get this tree down across the road,' Stella commanded.

The elephants stood side by side, settled their heads against the trunk of the tree, and put all their strength into driving forwards against it.

'Come on...push!' said Stella through gritted teeth. 'Give it everything you've got!'

At first, the tree didn't move, but the elephants were determined as they knew how important it was to the plan. After a few mighty heaves, the trunk creaked slightly, and the whole tree swayed.

'It's nearly down!' Stella cried. 'One last effort, and we'll be there!'

The elephants pushed so hard that tears came to their eyes. Finally, there was a tremendous splitting sound, and the tree fell. It tumbled across the road with a crash, and one of the roots tore completely out of the ground. The baboons cheered from the other trees above, and the giraffes shouted out in delight from the grass.

Stella surveyed the scene with a critical eye. The tree hadn't quite fallen all the way across the road, but she thought it would be enough of an obstruction to stop the poachers' van. At least, she desperately hoped it would. The plan wouldn't work if the poachers stayed in their van.

'Right, now we've got to get to safety,' she told her fellow elephants, who nodded. Stella looked up into the trees at the baboons sitting in the branches.

'Good luck!' she said. 'Remember how important your part of the plan is. You mustn't make a mistake, or Leopard could be killed. Now, we must hide.'

The three elephants darted away from the road towards a nearby larger group of trees, thick with bushy scrub, where they would be completely hidden from view.

Stella took a last glance along the road before stepping into the trees to hide and saw there was still no sign of the poachers. She felt a buzz of satisfaction – the first part of the plan had worked!

As expected, it wasn't long before there came the sound of an engine. The three elephants looked at each other, not daring to make a sound. It was critical the poachers didn't find them.

The noise came steadily closer, and the baboons barked to give the signal the poachers were coming. The giraffes confirmed this by making their characteristic roaring sound, and the elephants stood silently without moving a muscle.

The animals waited as the van approached the trees. Stella heard the vehicle slow down as it neared the fallen tree. Then, just as she had hoped, the van came to a halt. She waited for what seemed like an agonisingly long time for the men to switch off their engine. If they managed to drive around the tree, the plan would fail.

The baboons peered at the van from the trees, watching in horror as it edged towards the grass. It looked as if the men were going to try to drive around the tree. Fortunately, the driver realised it was impossible. The ground was uneven, with a broad and deep ditch running alongside the road, making it too treacherous as the van might easily fall into the ditch.

The waiting animals felt a great sense of relief when the engine stopped. Now, to get the men out of the van.

As soon as Leopard heard the engine go quiet, she knew it was time to put her part of the plan into action. She summoned up all her courage, raised her head out of the grass, and shook the dust off her back to attract the poachers' attention. Her heart pounded as she waited for the men to react—had they seen her?

Leopard stood up a little further so her whole body would be visible. Then she knew the men had seen her, as she heard the sound of the van doors opening and the men jumping out. Knowing her job was done, she ducked back into the grass and ran off quickly, keeping her head well down.

Meanwhile, the poachers had their eyes fixed on where they had seen the leopard. Leaving the doors of the van open, they stepped hastily along the road under the other trees, each carrying an enormous gun. All three were so preoccupied with looking for Leopard that they didn't notice the baboons coming.

Three of the nimblest baboons in the troop leapt across from the trees on one side of the road to those on the other side, swiping the guns from the poachers' hands as they passed overhead. The men stopped in astonishment and looked up to see the baboons grinning down at them, holding their precious guns way up in the trees. Before the poachers could do anything to stop them, two more baboons jumped across the road, whisking the hats from their heads. Then, to their enormous disbelief, a second pair snatched their sunglasses.

The baboons hooted delightedly and passed the guns to each other in glee. Baboon put the men's hats on his head, one on top of the other, and danced along the length of the branch, making the others laugh. There was a resounding snap as one of the other baboons broke a pair of sunglasses in half. Meanwhile, the men stood under the trees, looking furious.

From her hiding place, Stella heard them talking angrily to each other. She didn't understand what they were saying, but there was no mistaking the tone.

The poachers seemed to be having an argument. Baboon peered down through the branches to see one of the men point up towards him. It was clear he was telling his companions to climb the tree and take back the guns, but the men did not seem enthusiastic about it. After a few irate exchanges, the smallest man stomped towards the tree and set about climbing up the trunk.

It was the moment Baboon had been waiting for. Stella had correctly guessed the men might try to retrieve their guns, but rather than put the baboons in the position of having to fight the poachers, the elephant had another plan.

Baboon screeched loudly. The noise was so terrible that one of the poachers covered his ears. Giraffe heard the signal and knew it was time to spring into action.

While one of the men struggled halfway up the trunk, several giraffes appeared, apparently out of nowhere, and cantered right up beside the poachers on the road. The men looked alarmed, but the giraffes ignored them, stopped, and stretched their necks high up into the trees.

'Quick—hand the guns over,' Baboon shouted to his family. The baboons tossed the guns from one to the other and finally to Baboon, who handed the weapons carefully down to the giraffes. Three pairs of giraffes took up one gun between two, each pair holding the gun at either end with their mouths.

'Now, run!' Baboon urged. The giraffes wasted no time cantering across the plains, gripping the guns between their teeth. They were slippery and difficult to balance, but the giraffes hung on to them with great determination.

The man slithered down from the tree, and the three poachers stared open-mouthed, watching their guns disappear at a tremendous pace.

The men stood to look at each other for a moment, each of them needing confirmation that the others had seen the same sight. They had another rapid exchange of words and made as if to hurry back to their van. However, their ordeal was only just beginning.

The poachers turned in unison. One of the men leapt sideways when he saw that, just behind them, positioned midway between the men and their van, was Lion. The other two men clutched at each other in fright when they saw the mighty king of the plains sitting tall, looking calm and unruffled as he carefully licked one of his front paws. Baboon was delighted to see that they had no idea what to do. The escape route back to their van was blocked, and they had no way to defend themselves.

Lion yawned, pretending to look bored, then deliberately turned his back on the men. He wandered back towards the van, and to the men's dismay, leapt up on to the bonnet, making the vehicle rock backwards and forwards. Now what could they do?

The poachers didn't have much time to think about it. Several ostriches rose out of the grasses on either side of the road and sprinted towards them as fast as their powerful legs would go. The men panicked and pushed against each other, desperate to get away. Then they turned from each other and ran faster than they knew they were capable of along the road, down through the ditch and across the plains.

The baboons and Lion watched the ostriches race after the enemy, laughing and laughing until they were quite breathless. The elephants heard their laughter and looked cautiously out of the trees before joining in.

Cries of fear came from the terrified men as they charged across the plains. The ostriches caught up with them easily, playfully nipping their bottoms as they ran. Stella laughed until she cried when she saw an ostrich rip a great chunk out of one of the men's clothes and heard the startled yelp that followed. At the same time, Martial Eagle and a few of his relatives appeared overhead and targeted them from above, dropping clods of earth from their talons with exceptional accuracy. The men yelled out again and again.

Meanwhile, Puff Adder and the scorpions were ready to play their parts. The men ran on in a frenzy, trying to shake off the ostriches, earth raining down on them from above. In their hurry, the men didn't notice the trap that had been laid for them. The meerkats had dug a big hole in the ground, large enough to hold several men. The herd animals had been summoned and tasked with producing a generous spread of manure to coat the bottom. Then, the ostriches had covered the pit with long strands of grass so the hole would be invisible.

The ostriches steered the men directly towards the hole in the ground, and the poachers toppled into the crater one after the other when the grass gave way under their feet. They cried out in dismay and then were silent. The ostriches came to a halt and stared down in satisfaction as three filthy faces covered in animal dung looked back up at them. The ostriches had to pull back slightly at the terrible smell.

A small moan came from one of the poacher's mouths. They had nowhere to go. They were at the complete mercy of the frightening wild animals, and they clung to each other in fear. However, worse was to follow.

As the trembling poachers stared up at the ostriches, Puff Adder slowly uncoiled himself from the corner of the pit. At the same time, the scorpions scuttled out of the other corners, holding their stingers up high.

The poachers swung their heads around at the sound of the snake's hiss, and then they saw the scorpions. The men shot up as if on a trampoline, leapt out of the pit, and pushed their way through the ostriches. The birds were thrilled–the chase was on again!

The ostriches charged after their targets, snatching at their now filthy clothes, whilst the men had no option but to sprint away. As Stella had planned, the ostriches gradually steered the men towards the waterhole. The men saw the water a little way ahead and shouted at each other as they ran. It seemed they were being driven straight towards it!

At the waterhole, a young meerkat announced to the waiting animals that the poachers were almost upon them. There was an enormous cheer from the watching crowd as the men arrived and plunged headlong into the water. The rest of the elephant herd was waiting there to drench the poachers with water from their trunks. Even Leader and Dent did their best to add to the men's discomfort by splashing them as hard as they could.

'Pooh, what a stink!' exclaimed Maud, one of the older elephants, as she stood over the poachers.

'Yes, don't these men ever take baths?' her sister Dorothy said with a wicked laugh.

'I think we need to give them a good soaking!' Maud added with a glint in her eye.

The trembling men shut their eyes while the water crashed down on their heads, perhaps wondering when their nightmare would be over. The force of the water almost knocked them off their feet. In no time, they were completely soaked, and the strange sound of the animals laughing together surrounded them.

CHAPTER 10

The Animals are Triumphant

MEANWHILE, THE BABOONS BUSIED themselves with the destruction of the poachers' van.

Once the men had raced away into the distance, Lion jumped down from the bonnet, stopped nearby, and continued licking his paws. The baboons turned their attention to the van, which was now standing alone on the road. The troop clambered over the vehicle, examining the different parts with interest. Baboon jumped up into the seat and turned the steering wheel left and right, pretending to drive. At the same time, another baboon was thrilled to find that the windscreen wipers could be easily pulled off. Three more animals bounced around on the roof, which began to sag beneath their weight.

Inside the van, Baboon could hardly hear himself think. He banged on the ceiling with his fists, shouting for the younger animals to stop jumping up and down, and with the greatest reluctance, they eventually did so.

Baboon turned his attention to the key he found on the seat, wondering if he could make the van move. He put the key into the ignition, turning it this way and that. He was close to turning the van on when he was distracted by a strange sound. Baboon looked all around, wondering where it had come from.

The noise came again, and he managed to track it down to the mobile phone sitting under the dashboard. Baboon put his ear to the phone and listened. There was a human voice on the other end, but of course, he had no idea what it was saying.

His mate swung in through the open window and dropped down on to the seat beside him. 'What is it?' she asked, looking at the phone with curiosity.

At that moment, the roof suddenly caved in after four of the younger baboons leapt on it at the same time. The two animals inside ducked and Baboon muttered angrily under his breath. 'That's enough!' he shouted to the youngsters. He was relieved to see them go running off into the grass, each of them carrying a different part of the van as a souvenir.

The van stopped shaking, and they listened to the voice on the phone again.

ALFIE, STELLA AND THE POACHERS

'That is a human talking, surely, but where are they?' said his mate with amazement.

'I don't know.' Baboon shrugged. 'I was wondering if that object can transfer human voices across long distances. It sounds as if there is a human here in the van, but there clearly isn't.'

'What a strange thing,' said his mate. She thought for a moment as Baboon played with the buttons on the phone, and a grin spread across her face.

'Wait a moment,' she said. 'Surely, if we can hear them, there is a chance that they can hear us, too.'

The baboons looked at each other and giggled.

'I think we have to give it a try!' said Baboon.

He brought his mouth to where the voice was coming from and hooted into the phone, making the most frightening set of noises he could think of. The younger baboons returned to the van, and they all joined in with delight. Meanwhile, a voice spoke sharply at the other end and in tones of increasing volume.

The baboons answered back with gleeful babbling until, finally, there was a click and silence at the other end. The baboons cheered and bounced up and down inside the van, making it rock.

At that moment, Stella banged on the windscreen with her trunk, and the baboons looked up, startled.

'Now that you've had your fun, can we continue, please?' said the elephant. The baboons looked a little shamefaced, having suddenly remembered the plan. They jumped out of the van at once and listened as Stella gave her instructions. Leopard returned from the grasses to join them.

'Right. First, we need to make quite sure the men can't drive their van anywhere,' said Stella. She reached into the van with her trunk and deftly pulled the key from the ignition.

'Good,' she said. 'Would somebody look after this, please?'

Cheetah appeared at her side, keen to do something useful. 'I will,' he said.

'Thank you, Cheetah,' said Stella, handing the key over to the cat. 'Now, we must move this van before the men get back. Would all baboons clear the way, please? Mabel, Ethel—are you ready? HEAVE!'

The three elephants pressed their heads against the side of the van. Stella counted to three, and they strained against the weight of the vehicle. The strength of the elephants was easily enough to overturn the van, which went tumbling off the road and across the ditch, rolling over twice before finishing on its roof. Dust flew up all around them, and Mabel sneezed six times in a row.

'Well, they won't be driving that away,' said Stella, and she looked at the wreck of the van with satisfaction.

The van had crumpled badly during the roll, and there was a hissing noise as one of the tyres quickly lost its air. The baboons danced around cackling, and the elephants entwined their trunks together and smiled at each other. Lion allowed himself a majestic smile, and Leopard grinned. Even the usually nervous Cheetah couldn't help but laugh.

'Right. Now all we need to do is to take the key far away so the men will never find it,' said Stella. She turned to Cheetah, who suddenly looked very uncomfortable.

'Do you have the key please, Cheetah?' Stella asked.

Cheetah squirmed and looked down at the ground. 'I don't know where it is,' he said, almost in a whisper.

'What do you mean?' asked Stella, looking puzzled. 'I only gave it to you a moment ago. You can't have lost it.'

'I'm afraid I don't know where it is,' Cheetah said again. He backed away from the elephants, and Stella thought he was about to run away.

Cheetah turned bright pink under his fur. 'I've got to go,' he mumbled. He turned to run off, and Stella's face broke into a huge grin.

'Cheetah, you've swallowed the key, haven't you?' she exclaimed.

The other animals turned to look at poor Cheetah, who tried to say something but was too shy.

Stella roared with laughter. 'Don't worry,' she told the cat kindly, 'it doesn't matter. Now I'm quite sure the men will never find it!'

'Will I die?' asked Cheetah, looking mournful.

'No, I'm sure you won't,' Stella comforted him. 'You might feel it inside you for a while, though.'

'I could reach down your throat and get the key out,' offered one of the baboons, suddenly looking interested.

Cheetah shrank back in horror. 'No, thank you,' he said. The prospect of a long, hairy arm being forced down his throat was dreadful. 'I'm sure I'll be all right.'

The cat felt embarrassed as he looked at each of the faces watching him. 'I've got to go,' he muttered again and bounded off over the plains. The animals watched him run, trying desperately not to laugh, but once Cheetah was too far away to hear them, they could contain themselves no longer, and the whole group burst into laughter.

'Poor Cheetah,' said Stella as tears rolled down her cheeks. 'Something funny always seems to happen to him.'

'Fancy trying to pretend he didn't know where the key was, though,' said Lion. 'I've always thought he was rather stupid.'

'He's just very shy,' Stella said, jumping to Cheetah's defence. Lion never missed an opportunity to criticise the other animals.

Stella changed the subject quickly. 'Well, that's our job done,' she said. 'I don't think those poachers will be back in a hurry. Perhaps now they will leave us alone.'

'Look—there they go!' said Leopard. She nodded her head, and everyone turned to look. In the distance, three figures leapt through the grass at a frantic pace. Large patches of bare skin winked at the sun, and shreds of clothing flapped as they ran. There were still smears of muck across their faces, and their hair was soaking wet. Even from a distance, the animals could hear the men's desperate gasps for breath as they urged their legs on.

Behind them, Buffalo was having the time of his life. He had organised his herd to chase the men out of the grasslands, and thousands of hooves now thundered behind the terrified poachers. Stella had strictly forbidden Buffalo from head-butting the men with his horns, but he couldn't resist the odd gentle poke, which made the men squeal and run that much faster.

The elephants from the waterhole, the ostriches, Puff Adder, and the meerkats joined the animals on the road in time to see the herd charging over the hill. All together now, the animals laughed and celebrated their triumph.

'Did you see their faces when they realised they had fallen into a cesspit?' shrieked one of the ostriches, shaking his head from side to side in laughter.

'Did you see the one trying to hold his clothes up?' hooted a second ostrich. 'I think I snapped something and made them fall down.'

'It's all very well for you to laugh,' lisped Puff Adder. 'You didn't have to spend ages down a hole full of manure waiting for them.'

'We'll be able to smell you coming now,' one of the meerkats said. The other meerkats sniggered.

Puff Adder was not amused and turned away, scowling.

'Didn't they run when they saw Crocodile in the water?' said Dent. 'I didn't know humans could move so quickly.'

'Yes, and then the buffalo herd was ready and waiting for them.' Leader chuckled. 'I almost felt sorry for them at that point.'

Stella interrupted the excited chatter by waving her trunk in the air. 'Friends, we have done magnificently today,' she said. 'I think you'll agree that we've shown the poachers we animals can look after ourselves.'

'Are we rid of the poachers forever now?' Leader asked his mother with hope, but the wise elephant shook her head.

'They'll be back,' she said. 'We've won the battle, but the war isn't over yet. We need to be just as alert and even more careful now.'

'I don't believe we'll ever see those poachers again,' declared Leopard. 'Who would dare to come back after what happened today?'

Stella started to remind them they still needed to be cautious when there was a sudden explosion, and the animals jumped in fright. There was no mistaking the sound of a gun being fired.

'They can't be back already,' said Dent, horrified.

Stella scanned the grasslands anxiously. The shot had come from close behind them, but she could see no sign of humans anywhere. The only animals nearby were the giraffes, who were making their way through the grass towards the group.

To Stella's relief, Giraffe called out, 'Sorry about that gun going off. I dropped it, and it made a big noise.'

'It was Giraffe,' murmured Stella, and she breathed again. The other animals sighed in relief.

'What shall we do with these awful things?' asked Giraffe, nodding at the gun on the ground in front of him.

'We shall bury them,' said Stella. 'Meerkats, could you lend your paws to the job, please? We don't want anyone finding them again.'

The commander-in-chief saluted Stella and ordered her meerkats into formation. They picked up the guns and carried them away in an impressive display of teamwork.

Meanwhile, Stella looked at the little group of animals with a serious expression. 'Well done to everyone today,' she said, 'but please do believe me when I say the poachers will be back. They won't give up as easily as that. We still need to be vigilant, and we must make plans for every possibility. The fight isn't over yet.'

Stella looked at Leopard, who was busy licking one of her cubs and not really listening. Leader and Dent weren't paying attention, either, as they chased each other around in the grass.

The elephant leader felt uneasy. She hoped their success that day wouldn't make the animals too confident, as that was exactly what the poachers would want.

CHAPTER 11

The Trap

THE ANIMALS WENT BACK to their normal lives, feeling jubilant. They had bested the poachers, and it felt like nothing could harm them now. As Stella had feared, many began to forget what a threat the poachers still represented.

The lion pride went back to their lazy ways, spending most of the hot days reclining in the grass. The ostriches dashed across the plains as a flock from time to time, and Martial Eagle soared across the clear blue skies. The herds spent their lives grazing, always keeping a watchful eye out for predators.

Meanwhile, Cheetah was relieved to see the key on the ground after his digestive system worked it out, and he ran off feeling happier and surprisingly lighter.

The meerkats returned to their watch duties and resumed their ongoing battle with Puff Adder. The commander-in-chief trained up her new recruits by pitting them against him, something Puff Adder found extremely annoying. The unfortunate snake never had a moment's peace. Just as he had given one of the irritating creatures the slip, another one arrived on the scene. The meerkats tormented him by darting in to nip his tail, and the snake was forced to coil around and fight them off. He never got near catching any of the little creatures, who were as quick as lightning. By the end of each day, Puff Adder felt quite exhausted.

The baboons went from one argument to another. It was a standing joke amongst the other animals of the grasslands that Baboon's permanent frown was because of his family disagreements. There was always a fight of some sort going on between members of the troop.

Not long after the defeat of the poachers, Baboon had to win one such battle of his own. One of his ambitious sons thought it was time his father moved aside and allowed him to lead the troop, although he didn't dare to say this openly to his father. Instead, he secretly enlisted the support of a few of his cousins, and together, they plotted to ambush Baboon one afternoon while he was sleeping. Baboon had no idea of the plan until one of his nephews betrayed the challenger, hoping to win Baboon's approval. Baboon was horrified to learn his own son had been plotting against him and quickly banished him from the troop. With their leader gone, the rest of the group backed down and humbly apologised to Baboon, fearing they, too, would be banished.

Baboon watched the nervous figure of his son leave the troop and sighed. He wondered why they always had to challenge him. Why couldn't the family just live in peace?

Meanwhile, the elephants and faithfully following buffalo herd were often visible across the plains. Leader and Dent were now best friends and rarely apart. Stella was pleased to see Dent looking so happy, although she sometimes had to scold the pair for their pranks. One of the friends' favourite tricks was to sneak up behind the older elephants and make the sound of a gun going off. All too often, the elephants failed to see the funny side of the joke.

Leopard spent her time looking after her cubs and teaching them the hunting skills they would soon need. The cubs were growing bigger, but they were young and often clumsy in their attempts to catch food.

It was during one of these hunting trips that something terrible happened to Leopard. The cat and her two cubs were stalking a young antelope that had become separated from its mother. Leopard suddenly realised the cubs were no longer keeping up with her. She looked round to see what had taken their attention and saw that both cubs had stopped and had their heads bent low, staring at something at the base of a small acacia bush.

'What is it?' she called over. 'Why have you stopped?'

'Mum, look at this! There's a huge piece of meat just sitting there!' cried one of the cubs with excitement.

Leopard frowned. No animal would deliberately leave its kill behind for another animal to eat. Her instincts told her she should be wary. 'Don't get too close,' she warned her cubs, who were licking their lips at the sight of the meat.

'Can we eat it, Mum?' asked the other cub eagerly.

'Wait until I've seen it,' answered Leopard, hurrying towards them. She stopped in amazement when she saw the enormous hunk of meat her cubs were referring to. Leopard snatched a quick look around her, but there wasn't a single animal in sight, no other leopard, no lion, and no cheetah. So, who did it belong to?

Leopard inched closer and sniffed cautiously at the meat. It smelled fresh, and her hungry stomach grumbled in anticipation, but the cat sensed that something wasn't right. The meat looked as though it had been placed there recently, yet there was no sign of the rest of the animal. There were no bones or skin, only one big piece of flesh.

Leopard made her decision. 'We're not going to touch it,' she told her cubs firmly. 'I don't know where it came from. It might be dangerous.'

'But Mum, you can see it's fresh,' said one of the cubs, looking bitterly disappointed, 'and I'm so hungry.'

'Me, too,' whined her brother, putting on a wretched expression. It made Leopard feel guilty for depriving her children of such a feast.

She looked at the meat again. As far as she could tell, there was no reason why they shouldn't eat it, although it might be dangerous to eat it on the spot as the killer could still be nearby. Leopard took another quick look around and saw no sign of another animal, so she relented.

'All right, children. We'll take the meat with us to a safe place,' she said, 'but we won't eat a morsel until we're up a tree.'

Leopard stepped in quickly to lift the meat with her jaws. It was a terrible mistake.

She howled in pain as something lashed into her front leg. Leopard struggled to pull away from the vicious grip, but she was caught. She looked down to see a wire with jagged hooks embedded deeply in the top of her leg. When she pulled against it trying to free herself, the hooks tore further into her thigh, making her bleed. Leopard whimpered and brought her mouth to the wounded part, licking the blood.

The cubs stumbled over to her. 'What's happened?' one of them asked.

'I'm trapped,' gasped Leopard, wincing at the tight hold the wire had around her leg.

She yanked at her leg again, trying desperately to free it from the wire, but it was useless. The more she pulled, the more she bled, but try as she might, she couldn't free herself.

Leopard stared at her cubs, ashen faced. She could do nothing for them now. She realised she must be caught in a poacher's trap. Soon, the men with the guns would come for her, and everything would be over. They would probably take her cubs with them and kill them, too.

What could she do?

The cat looked around frantically for someone who might be able to help her. If only the meerkats were nearby, perhaps they could gnaw through the wire with their strong teeth. Her own pointed teeth were useless, and completely failed to get a grip on the metal wire.

She couldn't see Martial Eagle, and there was no one around to take a message. For a wild moment, Leopard thought about sending her cubs, but she knew they would have no idea where to go. Despite her entrapment, she didn't dare to send the cubs away on their own.

Leopard flung herself to the ground, feeling utterly helpless. The pain in her leg was terrible, but there was nothing she could do.

The cubs clambered over her, nuzzling her face. 'Can we do anything to help?' asked one in a small voice. The sight of tears in his mother's eyes frightened him, and he realised she was in real trouble.

Leopard shook her head, gasping for breath and feeling incredibly hot. 'There's nothing you can do,' she whispered hoarsely. 'I'm completely trapped.' She swallowed hard, trying not to show the pain she was in. 'It must be a poacher's trap,' she said. 'I knew there had to be a reason why the meat was just left there.'

'You mean the poachers will come and find us?' cried the other cub in distress.

Leopard nodded. 'The only way I might escape is if one of our friends happens to pass by. Then, perhaps, somebody could help me to get free from this wire,' she said.

'We'll go and find someone!' said the cubs in unison. They jumped up at once and looked at their mother for her approval.

'No, you must stay here with me,' Leopard replied weakly. 'You aren't safe on your own. Besides, you wouldn't know where to look.'

Leopard broke off in horror as a sound came to her ears. It was the sound she had dreaded: an approaching engine.

'They're coming!' she said, frightened. She hadn't expected the poachers to arrive so quickly. For the first time in her life, Leopard knew what it meant to be hunted by another animal. Was this the end?

CHAPTER 12

Alfie and the Ranger

LEOPARD PULLED FRANTICALLY AGAINST the wire again to no avail – the sharp hooks only cut further into her, and blood ran down the top of her leg from the wounds. The noise of the engine came closer. Leopard saw a van bouncing along the road, and she lay down in defeat. It was all over.

'Mum, they're coming,' wailed one of the cubs. 'What shall we do?'

Leopard changed her mind. The cubs should try to escape while they still could. At least they might survive.

She raised her head from where she lay and cried, 'Run, my children. Run for your lives! You two mustn't be caught!'

The cubs looked at each other in confusion. They turned one way and then the other, not knowing which way to go, as their mother had always led them before.

Meanwhile, the poachers' van was now no more than fifty metres away. The vehicle bore down on the cats, and Leopard realised it was too late. The poachers would probably shoot the cubs if they tried to escape now. 'No, it's too late,' she told them. 'They're here now. We're done for.'

Leopard knew her position was hopeless, but she was suddenly determined not to give up without a fight. With an enormous effort, she raised herself to her feet, ignoring the dreadful pain of the hooks tearing into her muscles. She turned to face the evil man now walking towards them, carrying a gun across his shoulder. Leopard snarled and bared her teeth as viciously as she could, even though, in her heart, she knew it was pointless. It didn't matter how threatening she was when she was trapped and the poacher had a gun in his hand. Beside her, she was proud to hear her cubs hissing and growling savagely in their high, little voices.

Leopard crouched, ready for the chance to spring at the man and hurl him to the ground. That was when she got an enormous surprise.

Something else was padding through the grass, and her nose picked up an unfamiliar scent. To her astonishment, there was a black, hairy shape following behind the man.

'Mum, one of the baboons has come to save us!' one of the cubs squeaked in her ear.

Leopard shook her head quickly. 'It's not a baboon, it's –'

'A chimpanzee!' the chimpanzee finished for her. 'And don't worry – you don't have to be afraid of the man.'

The chimpanzee hurried towards Leopard whilst the man stopped and stood still, watching the animals. Leopard pulled away instinctively as the chimpanzee approached. He stopped a few metres away, seeing her discomfort.

'Don't worry,' the chimpanzee said again in a friendly manner, 'we aren't going to hurt you. We've come to release you from the trap.'

The chimpanzee smiled and pointed at the man, who was now squatting on his haunches.

'Let me introduce you to the new ranger of the National Park. His job is to protect animals like you from poachers. It's only his second week in the park, and he's more nervous of you than you are of him.'

The three cats looked at the man, who smiled and spoke softly to them. Although they couldn't understand what he said, the leopards somehow felt reassured by his gentle tone.

'What are you doing with him?' asked Leopard, looking puzzled. 'Surely, you should be living with your family in the forest.'

'It's a long story,' said the chimpanzee, 'and one I shall tell you later. First, we need to rescue you from that trap. I'm sure it must be painful.'

He looked at Leopard's bloodstained leg in dismay. 'I can't believe what poachers do,' he said, shaking his head. 'Shall I tell the ranger you will let him cut the wire away?'

Leopard hesitated for a moment and then realised she would have to trust the man. She had no other choice.

She nodded slowly. 'How should we address you?' she asked the chimpanzee before he turned back towards the ranger.

'Oh, I'm sorry,' the chimpanzee replied brightly. 'I didn't introduce myself. My name is Alfie, and I live with the ranger.'

The ranger spoke to the chimp in his human language, and whilst Leopard didn't understand anything he said, Alfie nodded and made strange signals with his hands in reply.

'What are you doing?' Leopard asked in amazement.

'I'm communicating with the ranger,' Alfie told her. 'I understand the language humans speak, but I can't speak it myself, so the ranger has taught me some sign language with my hands.

'He said to tell you not to worry. He's going to take you back to his house to clean up your leg properly. He'll bring you back to the wild when your leg is better.'

Leopard felt her heart race. 'But he can't!' she said in panic. 'My cubs wouldn't survive without me!'

Alfie laughed. 'Trust the ranger,' he said. 'Of course, we will take your cubs with us.'

Leopard felt hugely relieved. The cubs clung to their mother with determination as they had no intention of being separated from her. They peeped out shyly at Alfie, who winked at them and pulled a face. The cubs giggled and felt less afraid of the strange animal.

Meanwhile, the ranger took a pair of wire cutters out of his shoulder bag and walked slowly towards Leopard. He bent down in front of her and let her sniff his hand. Leopard still felt wary of him as he was a human being, after all. However, his gentle manner and kind voice persuaded her that perhaps she could trust him.

She watched as the ranger reached out to take her leg in his hand and trembled when she felt him touch her.

'It's okay,' said Alfie, seeing her discomfort. 'I promise you he won't hurt you. He loves animals.'

The ranger gripped the wire so deftly with his cutters that Leopard didn't even feel them against her leg. He paused for a moment to check that the tool was in the right place, and Leopard heard a loud click. Despite herself, she pulled away at the sound to find she was free of the terrible wire. However, her leg had several cuts deep into her muscles that were bleeding badly. It hurt so much that Leopard could barely put her leg on the ground, let alone place her weight on it. When she tried to stand up, she fell back to the ground with a gasp.

Leopard lay on the ground in pain and heard the ranger talking to Alfie again in that strange, foreign tongue. She watched as Alfie nodded in agreement and signed back to the man.

'Are you willing for the ranger to take you back to his house?' asked the chimp. 'He won't do it unless you feel happy about it, but I must say, I think you'd be silly not to let him treat that leg.'

Leopard tried to struggle to her feet again but found it was useless. She knew she needed help. 'That's fine,' she told Alfie, without hesitation this time. She looked the chimp straight in the eye. 'I am trusting what you say about the ranger,' she said.

Alfie smiled warmly. 'You're right to do so,' he told her.

Leopard got up tentatively on her three good legs, and Alfie and the ranger helped her into the van. She was a heavy animal, and they struggled between them, but they eventually succeeded in helping her inside and covering her with a blanket. The cubs followed, trying to scramble up into the van.

Alfie laughed as he watched them bravely attempting to climb up the big step on their own. He scooped them up, one cub in each arm, and placed them gently at their mother's side before shutting the door behind them. He and the ranger jumped into the front seats, and the ranger drove off without delay. Alfie could tell the ranger wanted to treat Leopard's leg as soon as possible.

Meanwhile, the ranger's arrival was noticed and reported by the ever-watchful meerkat network. Meerkat number 23 watched in horror as Leopard was carried to the van and immediately assumed the worst. It must be a poacher taking Leopard away! Number 23 hurried off to tell Stella the bad news.

♦♦♦♦♦

'The man took her away?' repeated Stella in dismay. She tried to hold back tears that seemed to come out of nowhere as the rest of the herd listened in shocked silence.

'At least he didn't shoot her, Mum,' said Leader, trying to be optimistic. 'Perhaps it wasn't a poacher.'

His mother shook her head. 'It must have been a poacher,' she said. 'Why else would he have taken Leopard?'

Stella turned back to the meerkat messenger. 'Did you see anything else we should know?' she asked.

'It looked like Leopard was caught in a trap, and she couldn't get away, Your Majesty,' explained the young meerkat in a high, squeaky voice, 'but it's very strange because the man went right up to Leopard and seemed to release her from the trap. She could have tried to bite him or run away, but she just sat there and let him carry her off. She didn't put up any fight at all.'

Stella frowned. 'I don't understand it,' she said after a while. 'Leopard would never just let a poacher take her and her cubs without trying to defend herself.'

'Perhaps the poacher did something to her to make her go quiet,' said Dent uneasily.

'Or perhaps she was in shock and couldn't move,' said Bright.

'The other strange thing, Your Majesty,' added the meerkat, looking puzzled, 'is that there was a chimpanzee with the poacher.'

The meerkat watched the confusion on the elephants' faces and felt extremely important to be delivering such an odd message.

'A chimpanzee?' echoed Bright, looking mystified. 'Why on earth would a poacher have a chimpanzee with him?'

'Was it on a chain or something?' asked Stella, trying to make sense of this new information.

'No, Your Majesty. It was wandering around quite freely,' the meerkat told her. 'I think it even spoke to Leopard at one point.'

The elephant herd and Dent looked at Stella, who shook her head. 'I don't know what to make of it,' she admitted after a brief pause.

'Well, one thing's for sure,' came Mabel's cracked voice, 'we'll never see Leopard or her cubs again. You mark my words.' The big elephant shook her head sadly as she spoke, and the other animals felt shivers go down their backs.

There was a short silence as each animal tried not to imagine what might be happening to Leopard at that very moment. Dent found himself thinking back to when his mother was killed, and he, too, had to fight back the tears. It was too bad the same thing should happen to a friend, especially after the animals thought the poachers had been beaten.

'Poor Leopard,' said Bright at length, gulping a little. 'I can't believe the poachers took her cubs as well.'

'I don't know any other leopards,' said Ethel unhappily. 'I think the poachers have taken the only ones left in the area.'

'I thought we had gotten rid of the poachers,' added Maud with disappointment in her voice.

'No, I knew those evil humans wouldn't give up that easily,' commented Buffalo, looking grim. He looked from one solemn face to the next. 'The question is, what are we going to do now?'

'Well, first we've got to spread the message around to avoid any traps,' said Bright, taking charge for a moment while her mother listened gratefully. Stella sometimes thought how difficult it was being expected to come up with ideas all the time. 'It sounds like Leopard would still be free if she hadn't tried to eat the meat in the trap.'

'I think you're right,' Stella agreed, 'and we need to keep being vigilant. I still think we can beat the poachers if we keep looking out for them. They can't shoot us if they can't find us.'

There was a chorus of agreement from the listening elephants, Dent, and the meerkat. Buffalo shook his head, looking angry, and wished for the umpteenth time that he could charge at the poachers with his magnificent horns. However, in his heart of hearts, he knew Stella was right: the hunted species had to keep hidden from the poachers for as long as they possibly could.

'I still think the herd animals should charge at the poachers when they come,' he could not stop himself from saying.

'Buffalo, you are very brave,' said Stella, 'but they would simply shoot you. I'm not prepared to ask good friends like yourself to sacrifice your own lives for us. Please, be sensible and stick to our plans.'

Buffalo scowled and decided to say no more, but he knew that when the opportunity came, he would take it.

CHAPTER 13

Poison!

THE STORY OF LEOPARD'S capture spread amongst the animals very quickly. The meerkats, Martial Eagle, and the elephants told the terrible news to every creature they encountered, and Stella sent word around to be even more careful than usual.

The animals were upset to hear that another of their friends had fallen victim to the dreadful poachers. Cheetah, in particular, was horrified. Now he knew for certain that the poachers came after spotted cats, too. He was so frightened that he hid inside the trunk of a huge tree for a whole day before realising he would have to go outside to find food.

A week passed. Soon, one week became two. The animals went about their business, doing their best to be careful. The elephants were exceptionally cautious and passed most of their days trying to keep hidden. The problem was that there was little tree cover on the plains, and try though they might, it was difficult to hide a herd.

Following Leopard's capture, the meerkats and Martial Eagle were even more conscientious in their watch duties. The meerkats reported every vehicle they saw to Stella, and the elephants moved quickly away from where the vans had been seen. Not a single tourist caught so much as a glimpse of the park's elephants, but they seemed to be followed around by an aggressive herd of cape buffalo, who looked ready to charge at them at any moment.

Martial Eagle spotted the tourists, too, but he knew the safari vans with their noisy humans posed no threat. Flying high up in the darkening sky one evening, he also noticed a van parked near the waterhole, and he plummeted towards the earth to investigate. He saw two men by the water's edge, apparently filling up their water containers, but as neither carried a gun, he thought nothing more of it and took himself off to roost for the night.

The next morning dawned beautifully, with faint blue light slowly spreading across the dark sky. The elephants awoke early, and Stella guided them down to the waterhole for their daily drink and bathe. It was the elephants' favourite time of day and they chattered with excited voices as they made their way towards the water. The sun was only just creeping over the horizon as they walked, and everything else was still.

Stella surveyed the area as they approached. The waterhole was unusually quiet. A small group of zebras had gathered along the nearby bank and were preparing to drink, but otherwise, the elephants were alone.

The elephant leader eyed the water cautiously for any sign of the crocodile living there. Although she was not afraid of him herself, she knew that Leader and Dent were vulnerable to his savage jaws. However, she couldn't see the reptile's long, brown shape. Stella stepped slowly down the muddy bank, paused, and as always, the other members of the herd waited a respectful distance behind their leader.

Stella hesitated at the water's edge. She didn't know why, but for some reason, she felt uneasy that morning. She looked around and waved her trunk in all directions to sniff the air, but there didn't seem to be any danger around. Stella decided she was becoming too nervous, and she spoke firmly to herself to keep calm.

At last, she turned her head and gave a slight wave of her trunk. 'I think it's safe to go in,' she called to the waiting herd, and she plunged into the water herself. The others followed her eagerly, lowering themselves into the cool water wearing joyful expressions.

Stella looked around again—why did she have the feeling that something dreadful was about to happen? She scanned the waterhole again, but all seemed well. She frowned—why did she feel so worried?

The elephant leader dipped her trunk into the water and let it soak there. For the first time, she noticed a slightly peculiar smell, but it was too faint for her to think anything of it. All around her, the elephants splashed themselves and each other, and Stella began to relax a little. Perhaps she was just being over-anxious.

A shout from Leader interrupted her thoughts and made her look up. 'Hey, Mum—there's something really strange down here under the water,' he called. 'I can feel it with my toes. It's hard, but I can squish it, too.'

His mother smiled. Leader was always getting excited about the things he found. She made her way towards him, wondering what he had discovered this time.

'It feels quite scaly,' said Dent at his side, feeling with his hooves.

Stella bent her head down and felt around on the bottom of the waterhole with her trunk. She soon realised what they were talking about. There was something very large with a lot of ridges down there. She wrapped her trunk around the object and tugged it upwards towards the surface. It was very heavy, and she almost dropped it.

Leader and Dent gasped when Crocodile's body emerged, whilst the other elephants looked on in horror.

'He's dead!' exclaimed Dent.

Stella saw what she had unearthed. Shocked, she dropped the reptile's body back into the water. 'My goodness!' she cried. 'Whatever happened to him?'

At that moment, there came a terrific disturbance from the zebras along the waterhole. The whole group whinnied together in panic and galloped away as if they were one. The elephants looked up at the commotion, and a terrible sight met their eyes.

Three zebras were lying at the water's edge. They were quite still, and it was obvious that they, too, were dead.

Stella stared aghast. What was happening at the waterhole? She looked from the zebras to the shady form of Crocodile near her feet under the water. That was when it dawned on her: there was something wrong with the water.

'Don't drink!' she shouted.

The elephants stood completely still and stared at her with wide eyes.

'Why not?' came Mabel's puzzled voice.

'You mustn't drink the water!' Stella repeated. 'I think it's poisoned!'

Some of the elephants squirted water violently out of their trunks, blowing all the air out of their lungs to expel any remaining droplets. Their leader had spoken only just in time.

'Did anybody drink the water?' Stella demanded, looking around the group anxiously.

The elephants shook their heads, and Stella breathed a sigh of relief. 'Thank goodness,' she murmured. 'That could have been even more catastrophic.'

'Now, everyone out of the water at once!' she commanded. The herd picked up their feet and charged towards the banks, sending waves crashing in all directions.

Once out of the contaminated water, the elephants stood on the banks, looking in dismay at the poor zebras who had lost their lives. Their three sad bodies lay at the water's edge, and a dreadful silence surrounded the waterhole.

'This must be the work of the poachers,' Stella said to Bright. 'They've found another way to threaten us. If we take away their guns, they poison our water supply.'

'Where are we going to drink?' Bright asked in concern.

'We shall have to travel to another waterhole I know,' Stella told her. 'I only hope they haven't poisoned that one, too. If they have, I don't know where we'll go.'

'We must stop any other animals from drinking at this waterhole,' said Bright.

'Yes, you're right,' Stella agreed. 'We must spread the word around at once. I'll ask the meerkats and Martial Eagle to tell every animal they see, and we shall leave a message here as well.'

The elephant stood on three legs and drew a huge 'X' in the mud with one of her front feet. It was a signal the savanna animals knew meant danger. The other elephants saw what she was doing, and they moved around the waterhole doing the same. Meanwhile, vultures started to gather around the bodies of the zebras on the bank. It made Dent feel sick just to see them there.

'That should be enough of a warning,' added Bright, pointing her trunk towards the scene. 'Three zebras don't just fall down dead for no reason.'

Stella nodded and thought for a moment, looking serious. 'We can't live like this,' she said. 'We might be able to hide from guns and avoid traps, but there's nothing we can do if they poison our water. I think we need to have another meeting to discuss ideas. I've got to do something, or every animal on the plains could die at the hands of these humans.'

Bright nodded. 'It's not up to you to solve the problems of all the animals, Mum,' she comforted. 'Don't take so much responsibility on to yourself.'

Stella smiled at her, silently thanking her for her support. 'But I am partly responsible,' she said after a while. 'If it weren't for the elephants, rhinos, and spotted cats, the poachers probably wouldn't have poisoned our water supply. We few are endangering all the other species. It is up to me to do something about it, and quickly, before it is too late for all of us.'

'Call another meeting then,' agreed Bright. 'Perhaps someone will come up with an idea we haven't thought of.'

And so, another meeting was arranged. Word spread to the animals that the waterhole had been poisoned, and they kept well clear. The reaction was one of fury and despair.

'I'm going to charge those evil humans down!' was Buffalo's instant and angry response. 'How dare they poison the water supply that so many animals depend upon?'

'Poisoned?' echoed the secretary bird when Martial Eagle shouted the news across to her as she flew. The bird dropped to the ground at once in a state of panic. 'Oh, goodness me! Oh, goodness gracious – what are we going to do?' she flustered. 'This really is terrible. Whatever is to become of us all?'

Even Lion was shocked out of his usual lethargy upon hearing the news. He stood up slowly and shook his great golden mane, making the meerkat messenger tremble and feel very uncomfortable. The huge cat stepped softly towards the little animal and stared down into his eyes, making him back a few quick steps away. 'This isn't some kind of joke, is it?' he demanded, and the meerkat shook his head in silence, finding that he was unable to talk. Lion continued to stare at him, waiting for an answer.

'Nnnnnnno, Your Majesty,' the meerkat stuttered at last. 'I would never play such a joke on you, I promise.'

'I hope not,' said Lion with a threatening snarl. 'I'm not some stupid snake the meerkats can tease and torment all day.'

Most of the animals knew where they could find another water supply, and Stella was able to direct those who didn't to the place she knew. It was several miles from their usual drinking place, and it took the elephants a long time to reach it. Stella wondered how some of the smaller animals would fare travelling such a long way to drink. They might be forced to leave their homes and live nearer to the new water supply. She had no idea whether the water in the poisoned waterhole would ever be safe to drink again.

At the second waterhole, Stella ordered the others to stand well back. She sniffed the water suspiciously for a long time before accepting it was safe to drink. In her usual selfless way, she proceeded to drink some of the water herself before allowing anyone else to touch it. To her relief, the water tasted clean and fresh in her dry throat. It seemed the poachers hadn't touched this waterhole.

The elephants spent the rest of the afternoon ferrying some of the smaller animals back and forth to the new waterhole so they could drink. Stella knew creatures such as Puff Adder would otherwise never have been able to travel such a great distance.

'He wasn't very grateful, though,' said Mabel, who had been unfortunate enough to have Puff Adder wrapped across her back as a passenger. 'He complained the whole time about having to travel in such an uncomfortable way. He kept saying it would ruin his reputation, and everyone would laugh at him. I almost felt like leaving him there to die of thirst.'

Stella looked at Mabel's wrinkled face full of indignation, and she couldn't help laughing.

'What's so funny?' the elephant demanded, wondering if her beloved leader was making fun of her.

'Nothing, Mabel, nothing,' said Stella, who would never have dreamt of upsetting her cousin. 'I find I have to laugh about things these days, or I'd start to feel unhappy. We are facing an enemy we aren't equipped to deal with, and it is sometimes more difficult to feel cheerful.'

A message was passed around about another meeting that evening at sunset, this time at a new venue. Stella feared the poachers would be likely to return to the waterhole, hoping to pick up the bodies of any animals they'd killed. Although she felt desperately sorry for Crocodile and the zebras who had died, she couldn't help feeling relieved their bodies were the only ones the poachers would find. The elephant asked for the animals to meet at a particular, curiously shaped baobab tree far away from the waterhole, where she hoped everyone would be safe.

While the other members of the herd munched on leaves and Leader and Dent played chase across the plains, Stella spent the rest of the afternoon deep in thought.

'What are you thinking about?' asked Bright, wondering why her mother wasn't eating anything.

'I'm thinking about Leopard,' replied Stella, looking sad. 'With our problems at the waterhole, we have all forgotten that Leopard is still missing. I was wondering if we will ever see her or her two cubs again and what else we might do to try to find her.'

Bright looked serious. 'Mum, you can't do this all yourself,' she told her mother. 'You can't be with all of the animals every day to make sure none of them is caught. It's a near impossible battle for us animals to fight day after day against humans and their weapons, traps, and poisons. You have to accept that we can only do our best and hope that we get some luck.

Stella was staring at the ground in front of her, but now she turned to face her daughter. 'Bright, I don't think it will be enough,' she said. 'We need some help, but there's no one who can help us. I think we may be in trouble.' The elephant leader let her gaze drift into the distance, and she knew she was out of ideas.

Something had to change, and soon.

CHAPTER 14

What Was Happening to Leopard?

LEOPARD WAS, IN FACT, having a wonderful time. Never in her life had she been waited on in such a manner, with enormous plates of food appearing every few hours. Her eyes grew wide in disbelief when the ranger presented her with her first meal. The plate was full of delicious-smelling, fresh meat, with the fur and skin removed and only the best parts left behind. She didn't even have to wait while her cubs took what they wanted first as there were separate, smaller plates for each of them. The three leopards were ravenous, and they scoffed down the food in no time, half afraid that otherwise the ranger might take it away.

The ranger also tended to Leopard's leg. He removed the remaining hooks and cleaned up the wound, and now Leopard wore a white bandage around the injured area. She found that she could walk around, although it was with a bit of a limp, and her bad leg soon got tired.

The three leopards were being kept in a large room at the back of the ranger's house. It had three brick walls, and the fourth wall, facing the garden, was made of crisscrossed wire. It meant Leopard could look out towards the grass and bushes, and she could hear the calls of the birds in the trees. She felt safe in the knowledge that the wild she loved wasn't far away, and she now trusted the ranger implicitly, knowing he would release them all when she was ready.

One evening, the ranger came in to fill up the leopards' water bowl, and Alfie bounced in behind him with a cheery smile. 'Hellooooo, how are you all?' he asked. Leopard smiled while the cubs hid behind her nervously.

Alfie saw two little faces peering around their mother with curiosity and grinned. 'Don't be shy,' he told them. 'I know I've got big ears, and I'm extremely hairy, but don't hold it against me.'

The cubs giggled and dared to move a little way out from behind their mother. Their wide-eyed, innocent expressions and slightly clumsy movements made Alfie want to laugh.

'How is your leg feeling now?' Alfie asked Leopard.

'It's better than it was,' said Leopard hesitantly, 'although it still hurts a bit when I walk.'

'The ranger said it's getting a lot better, and you should be back in the wild within a few days,' Alfie told her, expecting her to be pleased.

To his surprise, Leopard looked slightly disappointed. She paused for a moment, unsure how much she should confide in Alfie. 'I'm not sure I want to go back to the wild,' she eventually confessed.

'Why not?' asked Alfie. 'I thought you would be longing to run across the plains in the fresh air. You can't enjoy being cooped up in this little room, and your cubs need to learn how to hunt and survive on their own.'

'I know that!' snapped Leopard, who felt she didn't need a domesticated chimpanzee to tell her how best to look after her cubs. 'I'm worried the poachers are going to come back, though. We've beaten them once, but we might not be as lucky in the future.'

'What do you mean you've beaten them?' asked Alfie. 'Who's we?'

'The animals in the savanna have made a pact to help protect each other from the poachers,' Leopard explained, wondering if Alfie would laugh at her. She waited for him to say something, but he just nodded, encouraging her to continue. Leopard rather reluctantly recounted the tale of how Stella's plan had worked to frighten the three poachers away. Alfie listened in delight, laughing his loud chuckle when Leopard described how the ostriches had torn the clothing from the poachers as they ran. He clapped his hands when he heard how the men were drenched, and hooted when Leopard told him the fate of their van.

Leopard finished her tale and watched rather suspiciously as Alfie rolled around on the floor in laughter.

'I'm sorry!' he spluttered. 'I'm not laughing at you. I'm laughing at the poachers. That must have been the shock of their lives.'

Leopard allowed herself a smile as she remembered the terrified expressions on the men's faces, but it soon faded. 'It's all very well,' she said to Alfie, who was still shaking his head and wiping his eyes, 'but the poachers must have been back since to set the trap. We obviously haven't beaten them yet.'

Alfie's face grew more serious, and he nodded. 'It's time to stop them, once and for all,' he agreed. 'You can't live your lives in constant fear of being killed or horribly wounded by poachers.'

'I don't understand why they hunt us,' said Leopard. 'We don't pose any threat to humans in their cars and vans—why are they so anxious to kill us?'

'Don't you know?' asked Alfie in surprise. 'They shoot you for your fur. Humans want your fur so they can dress up in coats made of leopard skin.'

Leopard couldn't believe her ears. 'They dress up like leopards?' she repeated. 'I don't believe you. Why would they want to do that?'

'Apparently, it's regarded as attractive in certain human societies,' said Alfie, shrugging his shoulders. 'It's beyond me, I must say. The ranger doesn't understand it either.'

'What about elephants and rhinos, then?' demanded Leopard. 'Don't try to tell me that humans like to dress up in grey, crusty skins, too?'

Alfie frowned. 'No. Humans like other parts of the elephants and rhinos,' he said. 'They use elephant tusks to make little statues and other objects, and rhino horns to make medicines. Some humans believe rhino horns are very good for treating sick people, although the ranger told me it isn't even true. Really, the horns have no magical powers at all, but some people still believe the myth, so the poachers go on killing rhinos in return for money. In human society, they give each other money in exchange for whatever they want for themselves.'

'So, that's it?' stormed Leopard. 'That's why the poachers threaten us, making us live in constant fear?' The cat prowled around the room, feeling as if she wanted to meet some poachers right now and take out her fury on them.

The cubs watched her timidly, realising she was very angry.

Alfie sat quietly in the corner of the room. 'I'm afraid so,' he said. 'It's hard to believe, isn't it? You do realise quite how serious it is, though?'

Leopard stood still for a moment and looked at him. 'What do you mean?' she asked.

'The survival of species such as elephants and black rhinos is threatened now,' Alfie explained gravely. 'If more isn't done soon to stop the poaching, some species might be wiped out completely. African savanna elephants are described as endangered, and black rhinos as critically endangered. That means they face a very high risk of their species becoming extinct. Lions, leopards, cheetahs, and even giraffes in Africa are described as vulnerable, which means that they too face a high risk of extinction.'

Leopard's anger collapsed, turning to horror. She gasped and sat down. 'That can't be true,' she whispered, turning a frightened expression towards Alfie. 'Does that mean every single leopard could be gone forever? Does that include my cubs?'

Alfie nodded again. 'That's exactly what it means,' he said. 'That's why the ranger is employed, to protect animals like yourselves. Otherwise, you could all be killed, and species such as yours may never walk these plains again. It's the same situation for hundreds of different species across the world. Your cousins, the tigers, are also on the endangered list, as are chimpanzees. As well as poaching, humans are destroying the habitat of many species, which is another big problem.'

'I think it's terrible!' cried Leopard, who still couldn't believe what the chimp was telling her. The eyes of the two animals met, and each knew what the other was thinking.

'We've got to do something else to stop the poaching,' voiced Alfie.

Leopard nodded. 'Yes, we have,' she said, 'but the question is, what?'

At that moment, the ranger came in to give the leopards their dinner, and the conversation paused.

'Speak again later,' Alfie said. He looked meaningfully at Leopard as he left the room.

CHAPTER 15

Never Give up

ONCE THE RANGER HAD taken away the empty dinner plates, Leopard and Alfie resumed their conversation.

'I'm prepared to do whatever I can to help you,' said Alfie, 'and I know the ranger will feel the same. It's his job to catch the poachers, but it's more than a job for him. He loves all animals, and he'll do anything he can to protect you. He really is a very kind man.' Alfie's face was full of pride as he spoke, and Leopard realised how attached he was to the ranger.

'He seems lovely to me,' agreed Leopard, 'but I'm not sure what he can do to help us. The poachers can come at any time, and the ranger can't always be there to stop them. We have lookouts to warn us when poachers are coming, and we could send a message to the ranger when they are spotted, I suppose.'

Leopard looked hopeful at this, but Alfie shook his head. 'Unfortunately, the ranger would never get there in time,' he said. 'The poachers would have come and gone by the time he arrived. The National Park is a huge area, you know. The poachers also know to look out for the ranger's van, and they would see us coming and vanish.'

'What else can the ranger do?' asked Leopard, thinking the task seemed hopeless. She started to feel anxious again. The prospect of her cubs being killed was more than she could bear.

'I think we should have a meeting between all the animals and the ranger,' said Alfie. 'I'll speak to the ranger before the meeting and ask him for his ideas. I'm sure that if the ranger and the animals work together, we can stop these poachers.' Alfie had a determined expression on his face, and Leopard felt her spirits lift slightly.

'Yes, we must have a meeting,' she agreed. 'I'll speak to Stella as soon the ranger releases me, and she'll gather the other species together. The animals all respect her, and if she asks them to attend, they will.' Leopard licked each of her cubs fondly. 'We've got to do something at once,' she said. 'I don't want my cubs to be in danger any longer.'

There was a solemn silence, which Leopard eventually broke to ask something that had been puzzling her. 'Alfie, why do you live with the ranger?' she asked. 'Wouldn't you too be happier in the wild?'

The chimp looked sad for a moment, but then his usual sparkle returned, and he replied brightly, 'I did use to live in the wild,' he said. 'All of my family lived together in the forest until one terrible day when a group of men captured us. They came sneaking through the woods, and we hid way up in the trees, but they shot at us, not with bullets but with tranquilisers.'

Leopard looked confused. She had never heard the word tranquiliser before.

'Tranquilisers are used to make animals go to sleep very quickly,' Alfie explained, seeing her blank expression.' He continued, looking glum, 'The next thing we knew, we found ourselves crammed into tiny cages, with three or four animals in a space barely big enough for one.'

Leopard gave him a sympathetic look, and the cubs stared wide-eyed as the chimp told his story.

Alfie paused for a long moment and then began again with effort. 'The men gave us virtually nothing to eat and just a little water. Some of my family died in the cages, and they just left their bodies there with us living animals. Other members of my family were taken away, and we never saw them again.'

'But why did they do it?' asked Leopard. 'Did they want your fur, too?'

Alfie shook his head slowly, and Leopard realised how upset the memories were making him. 'I don't know,' he said. 'The ranger told me they might have captured us to take us to zoos or dress us up as pets for human children.'

'What's a zoo?' asked Leopard, feeling ignorant. There seemed to be so many things she didn't know.

'It's a place where wild animals are kept so humans can go and look at them,' Alfie explained.

'Why would they want to do that?' asked Leopard in surprise.

'Some humans are apparently very interested in animals,' Alfie told her, 'and they like to look at different types of animals that don't live in their own part of the world.'

Leopard thought for a moment, trying to get to grips with the idea. In her view, other animals were only important if they were friends, prey, or dangerous. Otherwise, why take such an interest in them? Then, it seemed, there were other humans who spent their time trying to kill animals. She decided humans were a very peculiar species, and she gave up trying to understand.

'What happened to you?' she asked. 'Were you taken away to a zoo?'

'I was very lucky,' said Alfie. 'There weren't many of us left alive, and I'm sure I would have been one of the next animals to be taken. Fortunately, one day, the ranger came to rescue us. He was working in a different place then, which is why you've never seen him before. He arrested our capturers and released those of us who were left from those awful cages. Then he gave us the chance to go back to the wild, and many of my family returned to the forest.'

Alfie paused and shook his head. 'I just couldn't go back,' he said. 'The forest reminded me too much of my relatives and friends who had died or were taken away. The ranger tried to persuade me to go with the others, but I stayed in the van and refused to move. I think he understood me even then. He let me stay and brought me back to his house, and I've been with him ever since. That was nearly two years ago now, and when the ranger moved to patrol this part of the National Park a few weeks ago, I came with him. I do miss the wild sometimes, but the ranger is the kindest of men and very interesting because he teaches me everything he knows. He calls me Alfie because his grandfather was called Alfred, so he named me after him.'

Leopard looked sad when she realised what a terrible experience being captured must have been for Alfie and his family. The chimp saw her expression and realised it was time for a lighter topic of conversation.

'Mine is a tale with a happy ending,' he began brightly. 'Although I actually have an ending without a tail!' He turned his back on them, bent down to look through his legs at the leopards and stuck his tongue out at the cubs, sending them into fits of giggles. It was the only encouragement Alfie needed to play the entertainer.

The chimp jumped up and took a bow. He cleared his throat and sang in a growly voice, jigging around in time to his words. The cubs stared in astonishment. Even Leopard found herself watching Alfie with wide eyes.

'Yes, I'm so happy. This is where I want to be,' he sang.
'The bold adventures of the wild are not for me.
'There's warmth and light. I'm completely safe from danger.
'I spend my time with the most delightful ranger.
'Then, Sunday is my day for acrobatics,
'Whilst Monday I do amateur dramatics.'

Alfie stopped singing, and with an exaggerated, solemn expression, declared loudly, 'To be or not to be, that is the question.'

Alfie looked at Leopard as he spoke, and the cat wondered if he expected her to answer. 'To be what?' she started to say, but Alfie launched himself into an acrobatic display.

The cubs giggled as the chimp rolled over and over across the room, going from feet to hands to feet again in a flash. He stopped when he reached the wall at the end and returned, doing the same routine backwards.

The cubs looked at each other and tried to copy him. Leopard smiled as they attempted to flip over, but only succeeded in rolling across the floor as clumsy bundles of fur.

Alfie watched them for a moment, a grin across his face. He loved the little leopards.

Meanwhile, Leopard looked at Alfie in disbelief. She had never heard of chimpanzees doing amateur dramatics, whatever that was. However, the cubs drank in every word.

'Can you really do all that, Mr Alfie?' asked one of the cubs in a high, little voice, overcoming his shyness for a moment.

'Can you teach us how to do acrobatics?' the other asked eagerly.

Alfie grinned from ear to ear. 'Of course,' he said. 'I can teach you lots of other things, too. Have you ever played a piano?'

The cubs shook their heads innocently. 'What's that?' asked the braver one, too interested to be shy.

'It's a musical instrument I play every day,' Alfie told them. 'As well as that, I do paintings, and the ranger is teaching me how to play chess. Oh, and I nearly forgot to mention that I'm about to start flying lessons.'

The cubs gazed at him in awe. They were desperately impressed, although by then, Leopard didn't believe a word Alfie was saying.

'Do you mean to say you'll be driving those flying machines we see in the sky?' asked one of the cubs.

'Oh, yes,' said Alfie, winking at Leopard. The chimp walked across to their side of the room and beckoned for the cubs to come closer to him. 'In fact,' he whispered confidentially, looking from one face to the other, 'one day, the ranger and I are going to fly to the moon. It's a long way away, but we think we can get there. The ranger is busy building the machine now.'

'You're going to the moon?' echoed one of the cubs in amazement.

Alfie looked so serious while nodding that Leopard almost burst out laughing. The cat opened her mouth to set her cubs straight, but Alfie brought a finger to his lips, and she said nothing.

'You can do anything if you really want to,' said Alfie, while the cubs listened intently. 'You can play the piano, you can fly to the moon, and you can certainly beat poachers. You must never give up on anything, even when it seems impossible.'

The cubs nodded. Alfie threw a glance at Leopard, and she realised that the last point had been aimed at her. 'I still don't see what else we can do to beat the poachers,' she said.

'Wait and see,' said the chimp. He pointed through the crisscrossed wire at the silvery crescent of the moon, which was just beginning to appear in the darkening sky. 'It might seem impossible,' he said, 'but if we're really determined, we can do it.'

CHAPTER 16

The Next Meeting

MEANWHILE, THE ANIMALS WERE preparing for their next meeting.

As sunset approached, Stella and Bright led the herd towards the narrow valley that would be the meeting place. The elephants were unusually quiet as they walked. For once, Mabel and Ethel could think of nothing important to gossip about, and even Leader and Dent felt too subdued to play. Bright looked at Stella's determined face as they walked side by side, marvelling at how strong her mother was. It was impossible to guess that only a short time earlier, the elephant leader had been in near despair. Now, she walked proudly and with an air that showed she had not given up. Not for the first time, Bright thought how fortunate the elephant herd was to have her mother at its head.

The herd descended the sloping plain and were in the coolness of the valley within a few minutes. They were early, and the sun was still hovering above the horizon. Nonetheless, they were not the first to arrive.

A lone figure stood shifting impatiently from hoof to hoof, and even Stella allowed herself a smile. Of course, it was Buffalo. It had been decided that other than the elephant herd, only the leaders of the various species and perhaps their mates would attend that evening's meeting. It became too large a gathering when all of the animals attended, making it difficult for everyone to hear and participate.

'Good evening!' said Buffalo, his voice sounding unnecessarily loud in the silence. He had been waiting for some time and was now in a state of irritable excitement.

'Good evening, Buffalo,' said Stella and the elephant herd obediently chorused a greeting.

'Why is everyone else always so late?' grumbled Buffalo without really thinking. 'We've got something important to discuss tonight, and nobody can even be bothered to turn up on time.' He stamped one of his back hooves and scowled.

Leader giggled but quickly subsided when Buffalo swung around to look at him.

'Be patient, my friend,' said Stella. 'It's not yet sunset. The others will come in good time. I can see the lions on the brow of the hill now.'

Everyone looked up to where Lion and Lioness appeared as two golden specks moving slowly down the slope in the distance.

'Hmm, well, perhaps we could do without the lions coming at all,' Buffalo couldn't help saying. Under normal circumstances, the lions were his arch enemies and, although he would never have admitted it, he felt vulnerable in their presence, especially away from the rest of the herd.

Giraffe and his mate soon appeared from the other direction. Their necks were bent low, and they nodded from time to time. For a while, it looked as though they were talking to the ground.

'What are they doing?' asked Dent.

'It looks like they've gone mad,' said Leader with a chuckle.

'They're talking to the commander-in-chief,' came a voice at their side. Martial Eagle had flown in without a sound, his sharp eyes picking out the meerkat's little body hurrying along below the giraffes and keeping pace with her giant companions.

'Hello, I'm so glad you could make it,' said Stella with a warm smile.

Martial Eagle nodded, looking pleased at the greeting. 'Have you had any ideas at all?' he asked her.

Stella grimaced. 'It's not easy,' she began. 'No, I'm feeling rather desperate,' she admitted. 'I can't see how we can fight an enemy like this.'

'Perhaps someone will think of something,' said Martial Eagle, trying to sound as comforting as he could. Privately, he thought the animals were in real trouble. Personally, he didn't feel in such danger from the poachers, and he didn't need to rely on waterholes for his drinking water. However, he admired the elephant leader tremendously and was prepared to do all he could to help her in her battle. In turn, Stella greatly appreciated the bird's support. His powerful wings and exceptional eyesight were so useful when looking out for poachers, and Martial Eagle was always calm and unflustered, which, Stella realised, helped to give her confidence.

The animal leaders began to arrive from all around. Baboon and his mate looked exhausted. They slumped down on the ground a little way away from the others.

Mabel poked Ethel with her trunk and indicated in the direction of the baboons with her head. 'What's the betting they've had an argument?' she whispered with a grin.

'He does look tired,' agreed Ethel. She moved a step closer to her sister and hissed confidentially, 'Apparently, one of his nephews tried to take over the troop this time, and Baboon nearly died defending his leadership.'

Mabel's face lit up at this interesting piece of news. 'Who told you that?' she asked, but Ethel only nodded wisely, as if she knew a lot of secrets that she didn't tell.

'Here's someone else who's had an argument,' she said, changing the subject. It wouldn't do to give away her sources to Mabel.

The two elephants watched Lion and Lioness walk stiffly towards the gathering, several metres apart. Lioness greeted the other animals warmly, but she refused to look at her mate. For his part, Lion stood aloof, pretending to stare into the distance.

'Is everything all right?' the elephants heard Stella ask Lioness quietly.

Lioness made no attempt to lower her voice. 'My mate is the laziest creature in the entire savanna,' she said loudly enough for all of the animals to hear. 'Well, that's going to change. I'm not going to do all the hunting for him to just dive in and take the best food.'

There was an awkward silence during which none of the animals knew where to look. Lion continued to stare in the opposite direction as if he hadn't heard. Buffalo looked uncomfortable. He didn't like the references to hunting and felt glad some of his nervous herd members weren't with him.

'Good evening, everyone,' said a quiet voice, breaking the silence. The animals looked up in relief to see that Zebra had arrived. Lioness suddenly thought of the three zebras who had lost their lives earlier that day and realised she should say no more. She took herself off to sit with Cheetah, who had crept in at the back of the group.

Zebra had arrived with the leaders of the antelope and wildebeest herds, who had come mainly to support their friend. One of the zebras who had died had been Zebra's own daughter, and poor Zebra was still in shock. His mate had been too upset to come to the meeting.

'Thank you for coming tonight,' said Stella. She patted his back gently with her trunk. 'You have my heartfelt condolences, Zebra. I'm so sorry. We are here for you, my friend.'

Zebra nodded and had to look away. He couldn't trust himself to speak.

Stella understood, and she turned to cast her eye over the group. She was pleased to see that nearly all species were now present. The shadowy figures of Ostrich and his mate were coming towards them across the plain. The moon glinted on a scaly shape in the grass, and Stella felt glad that Puff Adder was still supporting the group. Yes, Cheetah was there, although she hadn't noticed him arrive. The only creature she could see who was missing but due to join was the secretary bird.

The sun had left them, and a large moon shone hazily in the darkening sky. Stars started to appear like tiny, far-off lamps, and Stella decided it was time to open the meeting. She looked at the faces of the animals and realised how upset they seemed. She had never seen Baboon look so miserable, and it was unusual for Lioness to speak out against her mate. Stella realised the threat of the poachers must be affecting the animals' spirits. Even the normally cheerful ostriches looked sombre, the commander-in-chief serious, and Stella hardly dared to look at poor Zebra.

'Leaders, thank you all for coming,' said the elephant, looking around the little group from one face to the next. 'It has been a terrible day for all of us and especially for Crocodile and Zebra. Leopard and her cubs are also still missing. I'm sorry to say that it looks as if everyone is involved in the fight against the poachers, whether we like it or not. It is no longer a case of a few species being targeted, as we all need to drink. Friends, what are we going to do?'

There was silence as the animals looked at each other, wondering who would speak first. Buffalo saw his chance and jumped in eagerly. 'It is time to give the humans a real shock,' he urged. 'We must frighten them all away from the savanna in the same way as we frightened the others away. We should charge at them from all directions!'

'Buffalo, how can we do that when we can't always spot them coming?' said Stella wearily. She had had to listen to Buffalo's preferred plan too many times.

'Did anyone see the poachers at the waterhole?' asked Zebra, who had been thinking about this.

The meerkat commander-in-chief shook her head. 'My scouts were occupied with the changing of the meerkat guard,' she said a little apologetically. 'There were no lookouts on the plains yesterday evening, I'm afraid.'

Martial Eagle took a breath and hesitated. 'I did see some men at the waterhole late last night,' he admitted, 'but they didn't have guns, and they didn't seem to be doing any harm. I'm sorry if I've let you all down. I had no idea they might be poachers.'

The bird tried not to look at Zebra, but he couldn't help it. Zebra looked completely lost in thought. The sad expression in his eyes was terrible to see, and Martial Eagle felt awful.

'It wasn't your fault,' Stella told him kindly. 'Any of us could have seen the men and thought they were harmless. How could you have known that what they were doing was dangerous?'

Martial Eagle looked grateful, but he felt sick inside. If only he'd flown down closer to see what the men were doing, perhaps

Crocodile and those three zebras would still be alive. He shuffled backwards to the outside of the group and felt relieved that no one seemed to be looking at him.

'So, you see, Buffalo, how can we frighten off an enemy we can't always identify?' Stella explained.

'Suppose they poison all of our water supplies?' asked Dent. 'What will we do then?'

'There's nothing we can do, is there?' said Giraffe. 'We all have to drink somewhere.'

'We could dig down until we find water,' said Mabel. 'I've heard you can't fail to find water if you dig deep enough.'

Buffalo snorted. 'What a stupid remark—' he started to say, but the meerkat commander-in-chief cut across him in her usual, matter-of-fact manner.

'As I represent the species who is probably the best burrower of us all, I think I am qualified to answer on this,' she said. 'It would take us a very long time to dig deep enough to find even a drop of water in this dry land. That is not a viable suggestion.'

'Never mind. I thought it was a good idea,' whispered Ethel to Mabel, who looked a bit crushed.

There was silence again as the terrible truth began to sink in. The poachers were in complete control. If they chose to poison all of the waterholes, there was nothing any of them could do about it.

'I think Buffalo's right,' broke in Lion, to Buffalo's amazement. 'We must do our best to frighten off the poachers. That's the only way we might stop them from setting traps and poisoning our water. We'll have to be even more vigilant.'

'You could all come and hide in the forest where we sometimes go,' suggested Baboon's mate. 'There is so much cover in there that I'm sure you could hide from the poachers.'

'It is an idea,' said Stella slowly. 'It would be difficult for the poachers to find us in the forest, and I believe there are little streams in there to drink from.'

'The forest is a long way off, though,' said Baboon, 'and I'm not sure it's big enough for all of you.'

'The buffaloes couldn't live in the forest,' said Buffalo, dismissing the idea from his perspective. 'We need to eat grass from the plains.'

'And we need to eat the buffaloes,' agreed Lioness naughtily, 'The buffaloes certainly mustn't be allowed to move away.'

'It's really the elephants, the rhinos, and perhaps the big cats that need to hide, though,' pointed out Martial Eagle. 'The rest of us don't seem to be targeted so specifically.'

'Yes, and if the hunted species disappeared, perhaps the poachers would stop poisoning the water, and everyone would be a lot safer,' Zebra could not stop himself from saying.

Stella looked around at the elephant herd, taking in Dent's little face as well. Then she looked at Cheetah, who shrank back, not wanting to be in the limelight.

'So, perhaps we shall have to go into hiding,' she said sadly. 'We are endangering the lives of our friends, and none of us want to do that.'

Stella looked at each animal in turn, a serious expression on her face. 'I'm so sorry for what happened today,' she said. 'It is all the fault of us hunted species, I know.'

All of the animals—except for Zebra—answered at once in a chorus of voices to deny Stella's words.

'No, it's not your fault!'

'You can't help the way the poachers go on!'

'You aren't the ones putting poison in the water!'

'Why should you have to go into hiding and lose your freedom?'

The elephants and Dent looked relieved, and Cheetah dared to raise his head, having buried it in his paws. Bright saw that Stella had tears in her eyes and on her cheeks.

The elephant leader smiled gratefully and waited until silence fell again. 'Thank you all,' she said simply.

'What are we going to do, then?' asked Cheetah, trembling in his bravery at speaking in front of so many animals.

There was silence again. Nobody wanted to admit it, but it seemed as if there was nothing any of them could do.

Suddenly, there came a familiar voice out of the darkness. 'I know what we can do!'

CHAPTER 17

The Animals are Tracked

'WHO SAID THAT?' DEMANDED Buffalo.

'It sounded like . . . no, it can't be true. I must have imagined it,' said Stella, looking all around.

'No, you're right,' Bright said, turning to her mother. 'It sounded like Leopard.'

'It is Leopard!' shouted Dent. 'I can smell her!'

The animals all turned to look as three figures bounded towards the group. Leopard appeared out of the darkness with her cubs close at her heels.

'We're back!' she cried. 'I hope you weren't too worried about us!'

Leopard leapt into the middle of the ring of animals and sat down, the cubs flinging themselves at her sides. She looked plump, her fur was beautifully clean and healthy, and she had a vibrancy about her the others had never seen before. The cubs had grown considerably, even though they had only been gone for a short period of time, and it was plain that they, too, had been well-fed.

'Welcome back!' everyone said together, and Leopard felt enormously happy. She had wondered if the others would have noticed their disappearance.

'What happened to you?' asked Giraffe, looking at the three cats in amazement.

'Yes, perhaps you could tell us so we could all do the same,' said Puff Adder with a leer. 'I've never seen such a fat leopard in all my life.'

'There's no need to be rude, Puff Adder,' said Leopard with a laugh. 'It's a long story, one I shall tell you all later. The important thing is that we have two guests at the meeting here tonight.'

The cat nodded her head towards the top of the slope. The animals looked expectantly but saw no one.

'I smell humans,' said Baboon suddenly.

'And something else, too,' added Dent, sniffing the air.

'Humans?' asked Stella in alarm. 'Leopard, we may have to meet your guests some other time. If there are humans around, we must leave at once.'

'Relax!' said Leopard, who was most unusually grinning from ear to ear. 'The human is one of my guests. He is known as the ranger of this area—the humans call it the National Park—and he rescued me from a poacher's trap. He's come to find out how he can better help us in our fight against the poachers.'

There was a short silence followed by mixed reactions from the listening animals.

'Humans are dangerous. We need to charge at him immediately!' exploded Buffalo.

'Humans can't speak our language,' said Lioness. 'How would we communicate?'

'How could we trust any human?' added Zebra, the loss of his family members still uppermost in his mind.

Stella frowned, wondering if Leopard was quite herself. Perhaps it was the shock of being captured.

'How do you think this human can help us, Leopard?' Stella asked gently.

'He's an animal lover who works in the National Park,' explained Leopard. 'It's his job to protect us from the poachers.'

'Well, he's not doing a very good job of it,' said Zebra.

'Let me finish,' pleaded Leopard. 'I know it sounds risky, but I promise you we can trust this man. I've spent all my time away in his house, receiving food and water from him every day. He's also treated my injured leg, and it's completely better now. He can't understand our language himself, but we can communicate with him through his chimpanzee, Alfie. Don't worry – the ranger will stay well away from us all while Alfie comes to talk to us. Alfie will then communicate with the ranger through sign language.'

Stella looked worried. Some of the other animals laughed in disbelief.

'Sorry, did you say we can communicate via his chimpanzee?' asked Buffalo. He shook his head in a rude gesture. Leopard had clearly gone mad. 'What a load of rubbish.'

Even Stella looked doubtful. 'This chimpanzee can talk to humans?' she questioned.

Leopard nodded excitedly. 'Yes, by making signs to the ranger with his hands. If you give me the go-ahead, I'll ask Alfie to come down to join us. Alfie thought it best if I told you about them both before he came too near, so you wouldn't be frightened of him either. Is everyone happy if I go get him?'

Leopard looked around and was disappointed to see how uncertain many of the animals looked. Zebra seemed to be on the point of galloping off, the ostriches were whispering in alarm to each other, and Cheetah had shrunk back even farther behind the group. Dent sat in silence with a peculiar expression on his face as he thought about the prospect of meeting with a member of the species who had killed his mother.

Stella noticed how unhappy many of the others looked, and she thought for a moment. After a while, to Leopard's relief, she said, 'Yes. Go and get your chimpanzee, Leopard. We are in a desperate situation, and if somebody is offering to help us, we cannot afford to turn that offer down.'

Leopard prepared to run back up the slope when a thought suddenly occurred to Bright. 'How did you find us here tonight, Leopard?' she asked.

Leopard stopped in her tracks. 'It was very clever,' she told her. 'The ranger has a tracking device that enables him to find Dent, and also picks up a signal from one of the elephants. We simply followed the signals on his machine until we came near you. Then, my cubs and I left the ranger and Alfie in the van so they wouldn't frighten you, and we came to find you on foot. It was lucky you all happened to be together tonight, I must say.'

Dent looked horrified. Every elephant wondered with some alarm who was the member of the herd being tracked.

'How does this device enable the ranger to find me?' asked Dent.

'At some stage during your life, probably when you were born, you were made to go to sleep and a little metal thing was inserted into your body somewhere,' explained Leopard, trying to remember exactly what Alfie had told her. 'Now the ranger can pick up signals from it on his machine. It means he can keep an eye on you and monitor your movements.'

'But I don't want my movements monitored by humans!' said Dent.

'It's only so the ranger can check in on you from time to time, Dent,' Leopard told him. 'It doesn't put you in any danger.'

Leopard and her cubs bounded off quickly into the darkness and were soon lost from sight. They left behind a bemused group of animals who stared at each other, not quite knowing what to think.

'Suppose the poachers got hold of that tracking device,' said Dent, looking most unhappy. 'They could find me easily then.'

'I feel like my life isn't my own now,' said Mabel in dismay. 'There could be humans watching everything I'm doing. It's like we're some kind of experiment.'

Stella changed the subject quickly. 'If anyone wants to leave before this human and the chimpanzee arrive, please do,' she said, addressing all of the animals. 'I don't want any of you to feel uncomfortable.'

'We're all in this together,' said Buffalo. 'The poachers might hunt mainly elephants and rhinos, but we're all affected by what happens to you.'

There was a chorus of agreement from the animals, except for Zebra, who looked anxious.

The animals fell silent and looked expectantly in the direction the leopards had gone. Then they waited.

CHAPTER 18

Wildlife Quiz!

WITHIN A FEW MINUTES, ALFIE and the ranger plunged through the darkness into sight, together with the three leopards. The moon shone brightly now, and the animals and the ranger could see each other clearly. Alfie leapt along in front of the group, eager to talk to the animals, and the leopards had to hurry to keep up with him. Meanwhile, the ranger stayed well back, stopping several metres away from the group of animals. He sat down slowly, his body language making it clear he wouldn't come any closer. Somehow, the watching animals could tell he meant them no harm, and they relaxed a little.

Alfie found it difficult to hide his delight when he saw the collection of animals in front of him. He had never witnessed a gathering such as this, even in his days in the wild. The animals met his gaze with eyes of different shapes and colours, and the chimp remembered what it was like to live among other species.

Alfie bounced merrily up to the group, stopping in front of the animals. 'Greetings!' he said brightly, waving his hands in the air to get their full attention. He swooped his right hand from above his head down across his body and gave an exaggerated bow. Alfie loved performing in front of an audience, although he didn't often get the chance. Once he knew everyone was watching, Alfie did a little backflip, and the older elephants gasped in awe. For the next few minutes, the animals completely forgot about their problems.

'My name is Alfie,' the chimp said as the animals listened, 'and I'm tonight's host of the popular television show, "Wildlife Quiz". Now, it's time for the first question to contestant number one.' He jumped a quarter turn, so he was facing the elephant herd.

'Welcome to the show,' began Alfie, pretending to be like a quiz show host he had seen on the ranger's television. 'I hope you're enjoying yourselves tonight. First question—listen carefully, contestants. I can only accept your first answer.

'Right, question one for contestant number one,' Alfie continued as the animals looked around uncomfortably, hoping it wouldn't be directed at them. Meanwhile, Leopard watched with a huge grin across her face. She now knew Alfie very well, and she realised he was trying to distract the animals and lighten the atmosphere a little.

Alfie pretended to look at a card in his hand and then addressed Stella. 'Contestant number one,' he said to her, 'your question is, what is the largest animal in the world? Take your time, contestant number one. You have twenty seconds on the clock.'

'What is a clock?' wondered Stella as she thought. She faced the chimp and said carefully, 'I believe the answer is the elephant.'

'That's right,' cried Alfie, clapping his hands. Stella looked pleased and the other elephants nodded in agreement. They knew they were the biggest animals on the plains in overall size, although the giraffes were a little taller. 'Just one moment, please,' said Alfie suddenly. He held his hand up to his ear, pretending to listen through an earpiece. 'I'm just getting information through that your answer is incorrect, contestant number one.

'The world's largest animal is, in fact, the blue whale! The elephant is the world's largest *land* animal. Bad luck, contestant number one. Your answer was good, but not quite right.'

Stella smiled in a dignified way and nodded her head at Alfie. 'It's always interesting to learn something new,' she said pleasantly. Privately, she wondered what the chimp was talking about. She had never heard of an animal called the blue whale. Stella thought it must live in a different area, or she would have seen it in the waterhole.

'I knew the answer to that,' whispered Buffalo to Cheetah, quite untruthfully, as Alfie was beginning his second question.

Unfortunately for Buffalo, Alfie heard his comment, and he jumped around to face him. 'Ah, we clearly have an expert in mammalogy among us,' he cried. 'Contestant number two this evening is Monsieur Le Buffle!' the chimp said, putting on his best French accent.

Buffalo looked at him in dismay and wished he hadn't said anything. What on earth was the chimpanzee talking about?

'Question two, then, to Monsieur,' Alfie continued with a grin. 'This will test your knowledge of Latin, which I'm sure is quite extensive in such a clever animal: how is the *Syncerus caffer caffer* better known?'

Alfie watched as Buffalo squirmed, trying to think of what the answer might be. The long name was unfamiliar to him, and he had never heard of Latin, anyway. He realised that everyone was waiting for his answer and wished again that he had kept his mouth shut.

The other animals watched his discomfort with some amusement. Although they would never have criticised him openly, they knew Buffalo could be a little opinionated sometimes.

Alfie began to imitate a very loud clock. 'Time's ticking away!' he shouted as a warning. 'I'm afraid I'm going to have to hurry you.'

The chimp made a hooting sound and held up his arms for silence. 'I need an answer now, please, contestant number two.'

Buffalo cringed. Feeling his cheeks burn, he said in almost a whisper, 'I don't know.'

'He doesn't know!' said Alfie, pretending to seem surprised. 'How strange that you should know all about the other animals, but you know nothing about yourself. The *Syncerus caffer caffer* is, of course, better known as the cape buffalo, of which you are one.

'Let's have a round of applause for contestant two here, who has just learned his own name. Hooray!'

The animals burst out laughing. The herd animals stamped their hooves in amusement and the others guffawed. Even Stella permitted herself a little chuckle, although Buffalo looked annoyed.

Alfie saw his irritation and realised he should move on. He looked around for his next contestant and caught sight of Cheetah, who was trying to hide behind Zebra and Antelope.

'Please, don't ask me anything,' Cheetah said as Alfie's eyes met his own. 'I won't know the answer. I know I won't.' He said this timidly, and Alfie knew it was time to stop. The chimp didn't want to embarrass the animals, but he wanted to help them forget their worries, even if just for a moment.

'The quiz is over!' he shouted, much to Cheetah's relief. 'You have all been saved by your friend Cheetah here, who had the courage to be honest. Some of us could learn from that, I think,' he added, winking at Buffalo.

'I shall, however, tell you a fascinating fact about Cheetah as he isn't getting a question,' Alfie continued. 'Did you know the cheetah is the only big cat unable to retract its claws?' Alfie stopped and smiled. 'The cheetah just can't do it, which makes walking silently on a stony path a lot more difficult.'

The other animals looked at Cheetah, and Dent and Leader giggled. Cheetah didn't know what to say. He had never noticed that he couldn't pull his claws in, and he certainly hadn't realised that other cats could. He looked down at his paws in dismay and decided he didn't like the outspoken chimpanzee as he was too confident. Cheetah began to wish Leopard had never met Alfie and he was not alone. Buffalo stood there with a scowl on his face, looking to be on the point of galloping off.

Alfie clapped his hands together to gain his audience's attention again before speaking. 'Friends, forgive me,' he said. 'It's so exciting for me to be here with you. I hope you don't mind my teasing you a little. Of course, the real reason I am here is that I want to help you. Leopard has told me about the problems you have recently had with the poachers, and I think it's time to try to stop the poaching forever.'

The animals looked back at Alfie and remembered why they were there. Even Buffalo looked at the chimp, although grudgingly.

'There is something Leopard doesn't know,' broke in Zebra, his eyes brimming with tears. 'Our waterhole has been poisoned by poachers. Three members of my family died there this morning.'

Alfie felt himself grow breathless. This was even more awful than he had imagined. The ranger had not told him about waterholes being poisoned before. The poachers were trying something new, something worse! He looked at poor Zebra and wondered what best to say.

'What are we to do, Mr Alfie?' asked Stella. 'What if the poachers poison all of the waterholes? What would we do? We have to drink!'

'It's not only the hunted species who are affected,' added Baboon. 'Baboons need to drink, too.'

'And so do antelopes!'

'And giraffes!'

'Lions, as well!'

The eyes of the animals were fixed on Alfie as he thought. He was just on the point of speaking when there came an unexpected interruption.

CHAPTER 19

A New Plan

ATWO-LEGGED FIGURE CAME RUNNING towards the group from out of the shadows. Stella frowned as she tried to identify the creature, and then the long, spindly legs and dark crest gave away her identity. 'Of course, it's the secretary bird,' she said. Stella couldn't think of a time when the bird hadn't arrived late.

The secretary bird raced up to the group, almost bursting with the information she had to tell them, but she stopped suddenly in alarm. 'There's a human over there!' she said, looking horrified. 'Haven't you seen?'

'It's okay,' said Stella. 'We know he is there. Leopard has vouched for him, and the chimpanzee, Mr Alfie, is here to speak with us on his behalf.'

'Good evening,' said Alfie in his deep voice.

The secretary bird jumped at the unfamiliar voice. She noticed the chimp for the first time and nearly forgot the information she was bringing. 'Who are you?' she asked in surprise.

'My name is Alfie,' said the chimp. 'Weren't you supposed to be taking the minutes of this meeting?' he added mischievously.

'Do you mean me?' asked the secretary bird, wondering what he was talking about.

'Well, isn't that what secretaries are for?' asked Alfie.

The bird had no idea what he meant. 'I'm not a secretary. I'm a secretary bird,' she explained, hoping it was a good answer.

'That's lucky, especially if you are always this late,' said Alfie with a straight face.

'I'm not normally late,' answered the secretary bird. 'I just had a lot of things to do before the meeting.' She gave a nervous laugh. 'You know, children to feed, things to arrange . . .'

Puff Adder grinned, knowing the bird didn't have any children. He was about to say so when the secretary bird saw him and added defensively, 'I'm helping to look after my sister's fledglings.'

Alfie smiled at the secretary bird, who felt herself blush a little under his gaze before remembering what she had to tell them.

'Don't distract me, everyone!' she chirped in her high-pitched voice. 'I've got something very important to tell you: I think the other waterhole has been poisoned! I just saw two men pouring liquids into it before driving away in their van.'

The animals gasped, and Stella felt her heart sink. It was the news they had dreaded. The animals fell silent, and they all turned to Alfie, expectation in their eyes.

'Well then, cousin,' said Baboon, 'what do you suggest we do?'

'There's nothing you can do,' said the chimp thoughtfully. 'Only the ranger can get the water cleaned so it is safe to drink again. I shall tell him what has happened, and I'm sure he will be able to arrange to have the poison neutralised. Nobody must drink from any of the waterholes until I've given you the all-clear, though. That's very important. If necessary, we'll arrange to bring you fresh water until the waterholes are safe.'

'That might solve the immediate problem,' lisped Puff Adder, 'but what's to stop the poachers from returning to poison the water again?'

'Yes, and that won't prevent the poachers from returning with their guns,' remarked Lion.

'The ranger can try to keep watch over the National Park for you,' Alfie said, 'but the problem is the park is so big that he can't be everywhere at once. Really, we need to have more rangers so the poachers will always be spotted.'

The animals looked dismayed. Alfie saw their downcast faces and knew what they were thinking. They were all independent, wild animals who hated to depend on somebody else for their survival. Having to rely on one set of humans to protect them from another set of humans seemed a dreadful situation. Stella looked especially glum, as she could usually think of solutions to the problems the animals faced. It went against everything she stood for to have to ask humans for help.

'Well, there's nothing we animals can do about that, is there?' said Baboon. 'Surely, it's up to the humans to engage more rangers.'

'I'm not so sure,' said Alfie. His face suddenly lit up as he thought of something. 'Friends, are you prepared to try another tactic? It may not immediately appeal to you, but it might be just what is needed to stop the poaching once and for all.'

The animals listened with interest, except Buffalo, who muttered something about charging at all humans.

'Go on,' prompted Stella.

'I think the best way to help beat the poachers is to have more rangers,' said Alfie. 'We need to tell the humans in the world what is really going on in the National Park, so they can pay for more rangers to do this important job. The ranger says there are many people who care about animals like yourselves, who would be most unhappy if they knew about the poaching.

'Animals of the savanna, we need to stand up and tell the humans what is really happening. Otherwise, the humans won't know, and they can't help.'

'And, pray tell, how exactly are we supposed to do that?' asked Puff Adder. 'Do we visit local towns and speak to the humans directly? Not that any of them would understand us, of course.'

'I don't think anyone would listen to me,' Lion said with a smirk. 'I have a feeling I'd find myself at the wrong end of a gun.'

'I am trying to think of ways to help you,' said Alfie. 'Of course, I didn't mean for you to go into local towns. I know you can't talk to humans, but your big advantage is that I can. I can talk to the ranger in sign language, and he can relay your message to the other humans. That way, we can tell the human world what's really happening. Then, the humans who care about you can help by paying for more rangers to protect you.'

The chimp looked excitedly around at the animals' faces and was pleased to see some hope flicker in their eyes. The herd animals—Zebra, Antelope, and Wildebeest—looked a little happier. The older elephants nodded and whispered amongst themselves. Buffalo looked roused and ready for action. Even Cheetah looked interested in what he was saying.

'And with whom are we supposed to speak?' asked Puff Adder, who still thought Alfie was being ridiculous. 'Surely, there are a lot of humans in the world, and we can't possibly talk to all of them.'

'What about speaking to a human leader?' suggested Stella. 'Do they have a leader like many of our species do? Mr Alfie could help us communicate to their leader via the ranger.'

'That's a very good idea,' said Alfie, nodding at her and smiling. 'I can see why you are such a respected leader yourself.'

Stella blushed, and Buffalo couldn't stop himself from scowling. He thought he was just as good a leader as the elephant, but somehow, she was always the one to get the praise. Puff Adder noticed his annoyance, and he smiled a little maliciously.

'What instructions should I give the troops?' piped up the high-pitched voice of the commander-in-chief.

Alfie looked surprised, but then he remembered what Leopard had told him about the organised nature of the meerkat clan.

'Don't worry, ma'am!' he said, jumping to attention and saluting the little animal. 'We are just about to draw up our battle plan.'

'Good,' broke in Lion, 'because I, for one, am extremely bored of this meeting, and I'm also getting hungry.'

The herd animals shuffled backwards ever so slightly, and Lioness gave her mate a warning glance.

'I think we should thank Alfie for offering to help us,' said Leopard hastily, worried Lion might start to be rude. 'After all, without him, we would be in real trouble. Everyone, please join me in saying thank you.'

The animals answered with their curious mixture of voices, some high and shrill, others deep and commanding. The herd animals pounded the ground with their hooves, and the baboons hooted their support. Martial Eagle beat his wings against the air, creating a powerful current, and the ostriches sprinted around the little group. Dent and Leader did a little dance of thanks. Even Cheetah purred, although he hadn't forgotten the chimpanzee's remark about his claws. The secretary bird was extremely noisy, and she shrieked loudly about how glad she was that Alfie was going to help them. She was the last one to fall quiet. She sat gazing starry-eyed at the chimp, which some of the others noticed.

Alfie was quietly delighted at the applause, and he bounded into a little tumbling routine inside the circle of animals. When he finished, he bowed and nodded as they cheered. He felt so energetic that he thought he could have run a marathon.

Silence eventually fell again, and Alfie continued. 'Gather round and come closer, just in case anyone's listening,' he instructed, making a shiver run down Leader's spine. 'Here's what we're going to do: we are going to take our problems to a local leader who lives in the park. He is a wealthy businessman and I believe he has the power to influence employing more rangers, to help tackle the poaching once and for all. Maybe he doesn't know what is happening, or he would have helped. For the first time, we animals will have the chance to tell the humans what we need through our own mouths.'

Alfie stopped. He looked around at the different faces watching him from the shadows. 'Together, we will beat the poachers!' he said with determination.

'Together, we will beat the poachers!' echoed the animals. An almost magical energy darted between them as the many different creatures spoke with one united voice.

CHAPTER 20

Two New White Rhinos

OVER THE NEXT FEW days, the animals saw a great deal of Alfie and the ranger. As promised, Alfie told the ranger about the poisoned waterholes. The ranger was as horrified as Alfie to hear what the poachers had done. He wasted no time, summoning help from chemical experts to deal with the problem straight away.

The morning after the meeting, Martial Eagle and the meerkat on lookout duty both reported seeing Alfie and the ranger with two other humans at the waterholes. 'They had all kinds of equipment with them,' Martial Eagle told Stella and Bright. 'Long things, round things, big containers with liquid in them. It looked like all the humans were wearing clothing on their hands, too, so whatever was in the water must have been dangerous.'

'If only the zebras hadn't drunk the water.' Stella sighed. She still blamed herself for the animals' sad deaths. She felt as if she should have trusted her instincts and told everyone to avoid the water that morning. 'And poor Crocodile, too.'

A short time later, Meerkat number 23 arrived at where the elephant herd was grazing. 'Mr Alfie said the water in both waterholes should be safe to drink now,' he squeaked to Stella with satisfaction. It was always nice to deliver good news.

The elephant smiled and thanked him. She called out the message to the rest of the herd. The older elephants looked delighted, and Leader and Dent cried, 'Hooray!' in unison. Although neither had been fond of the water at first, both loved to play and splash around in it now.

'Can we go to the waterhole now, Mum?' Leader asked eagerly.

Stella nodded. 'Be careful, though,' she warned. 'You never know when the poachers might arrive.'

The elephant leader watched with pleasure as her son and Dent, whom she had come to think of as a son, raced off together. They kicked up the earth behind them as they ran and were soon lost to her view in a cloud of dust.

Stella turned to look at the rest of the herd, who were feeding in the grass and felt happy for the first time in several days. She plodded slowly across to where her daughter was pulling at a small bush with her trunk. 'It looks as if the ranger really does want to help us,' Stella said, laughing as Bright tugged determinedly.

'This one's a tough one.' Her daughter panted and she let the branch drop for a moment's rest. 'Yes, indeed,' she said. 'He will be very useful to have on our side, especially if we can tell him what we need through Alfie.'

'It must be so interesting for Alfie to be able to communicate with humans as well as animals,' commented Stella, gazing into the distance. 'He must understand both worlds, whereas we can never truly comprehend the way humans behave.'

Leopard called across to the two elephants as she and her cubs wandered past in the grass. 'Did I hear you talking about Alfie?' she asked.

The elephants nodded, and Leopard smiled as she stepped towards them. 'He's quite a character, isn't he?' she said. 'He can do all kinds of clever things like play instruments that make musical sounds, and human games with wooden pieces. He can make pictures, too, of the savanna with lots of different animals. Of course, he used to live in the wild himself until he was captured.'

'Who captured him?' asked Stella in surprise. She had assumed the chimp had been born in captivity.

Leopard explained Alfie's story to the two elephants, and Bright nodded. 'That might be partly why he's so keen to help us,' she said. 'He wants to avenge the members of his family who were taken away and never seen again.'

'I think you may be right,' said Leopard, 'and he's absolutely convinced we can beat the poachers if we work together with the ranger.'

'He's fun, too,' said Stella, remembering how Alfie had teased Buffalo. 'He makes me laugh.'

'Me too,' said Leopard with a grin, 'and the cubs adore him.'

She looked round to where her cubs were tumbling over each other in the grass, each of them trying to knock the other to the ground and be the winner. They were getting stronger every day, and Leopard was immensely proud of them.

'I must go,' she told Stella and Bright. 'I promised the cubs I would continue teaching them to hunt this morning. I shall see you both later.'

Leopard turned to stalk away when she suddenly remembered something and stopped. 'By the way, you might like to tell Dent that two other white rhinos have been spotted in the area. Apparently, it's a mother and her calf. I haven't met them myself, but Martial Eagle had a conversation with them this morning.'

Stella looked delighted. 'Dent will be overjoyed!' she said. 'Thank you for letting us know, Leopard.'

'My pleasure,' said the cat, and she bounded off to jump on her cubs in a mock fight.

'Happy hunting!' Bright called after her.

The elephants looked at each other with smiles across their faces. 'It would be so nice for Dent if he could meet some of his own kind,' said Stella, swinging her trunk backwards and forwards in the way she did when she felt happy.

'We must ask Martial Eagle and the meerkats to look out for the rhinos again,' said Bright, 'although I expect Dent will soon pick up their scents, and they will find each other.'

'Look out—the buffaloes are coming over the horizon,' said Stella. 'I don't want to see Buffalo again this morning. He hasn't stopped complaining about the way Alfie "victimised" him yesterday.'

'Everyone else thought it was funny,' said Bright with a mischievous smile, 'but I agree with you. Let's gather the herd and move on before they get here.'

CHAPTER 21

Two Animals Feel Cross

THE ELEPHANTS HURRIED AWAY in the other direction, but they need not have worried as Buffalo had found another listener to whom he could express his annoyance. An unfortunate meerkat was on lookout duty in the area and was strictly forbidden by the commander-in-chief from moving from the spot. The meerkat had no option but to listen to the enormous animal towering above him until Buffalo decided to move away.

'I mean, who ever heard of Latin?' said Buffalo, shaking his head. 'I'm very sure no one else would know the name of their species in another language, but he had to pick on me, singling me out in front of everyone. It's very unfair, really it is.'

'Yes, Mr Buffalo,' said the meerkat, feeling he was expected to say something in agreement, but Buffalo didn't care whether the little animal said anything or not, and he opened his mouth to begin again.

Out of the corner of his eye, the meerkat saw that the rest of the buffalo herd had begun to graze. They knew their leader and realised they wouldn't be moving on for some time. The meerkat wondered how long it would be before he was relieved by the arrival of the next lookout.

'Everyone knows I'm not a boastful creature,' continued Buffalo, to the meerkat's slight doubt, 'but that chimpanzee treated me as if I were a know-it-all. He's got me all wrong, you know. Well, I'm sure I don't need to tell you that. I'm not the kind of animal who needs to talk about himself all the time or—'

The meerkat had had enough. He decided it was better to risk the commander-in-chief's wrath than endure another lengthy spell with the complaining Buffalo. 'I'm dreadfully sorry, sir,' he said politely, 'but my schedule says I have to move on to another lookout now.' The meerkat blushed at his little lie, and Buffalo looked down at him with disappointment.

He tried to make Buffalo feel better: 'Oh, look—there are the ostriches. I'm sure they'd be interested in hearing what you have to say, but I must be off. Goodbye!'

The meerkat scampered away, hoping the commander-in-chief wouldn't find out he had moved, and Buffalo turned to talk to the ostriches. He liked the ostriches. In his opinion, they were simple creatures who would listen to anyone without interrupting too much.

Unfortunately, the ostriches took off and sprinted away before Buffalo could even get close. He realised they were already too far away for a conversation with him.

The big animal felt disgruntled, and he looked across the plains for somebody else to speak to. In the distance, he saw the zebra herd but even Buffalo was sensitive enough to know that Zebra had more important things on his mind. Farther across to the right, he saw the backs of the elephants as they moved away from him and towards the sun. For a moment, he thought about catching up with them, but they seemed to be in something of a hurry, so he dismissed the idea.

Something flashed in the grass, catching his eye, and Buffalo thought he saw Puff Adder's gliding movement. However, the snake had seen him first, and when Buffalo called out to him, Puff Adder sat silently in a deep thicket waiting for Buffalo to go away. He had no time for Buffalo at the best of times, and he certainly wasn't going to listen to a monologue of hurt pride. Besides, the snake was on a mission of his own and didn't want to be interrupted.

Puff Adder flicked his tongue from his mouth, sampling the smells around him while waiting for Buffalo to move on. The scent of a meerkat was quite strong, and the snake knew he should be in the right area. He had managed to overhear the commander-in-chief's secret schedule for the day . . . now, where was the creature?

Puff Adder felt very cross with the meerkats. For some time now, the commander-in-chief had been training up a group of youngsters, and Puff Adder knew what that meant. He had had no peace for days now. The snake would find himself a comfortable place to bask in the sun and doze off for a while, only for a great hullabaloo to break out with a group of meerkats surrounding him, making their terrible war cries. Then, once they had his attention, the attack would begin. Meerkats would dart in at him from one side and then the next and give him a little nip with their pointed teeth. It didn't really hurt, but the snake would grow more and more exasperated as they were too quick for him to catch. After a while, he would begin to feel silly. The meerkats were tiny creatures, and he was a venomous snake. They shouldn't be able to annoy him the way they did.

The meerkats always managed to find him, no matter where he tried to hide. Puff Adder was beginning to realise they must be monitoring his movements very closely. Perhaps there was even a lookout specially engaged to keep the commander informed of his whereabouts.

Puff Adder looked around him and put out his tongue to sample the air again. He had glided away from the meerkats that morning during the daily changing of the meerkat guard and felt confident he'd given them the slip for a while. Now he planned to sneak up on one of the wretched creatures and give it the shock of its life. Perhaps that would stop them from bothering him.

Buffalo had moved on in the hope of finding a listener elsewhere, so Puff Adder began to make his way through the grass in the direction he thought the meerkat might have taken. The scent was still present, and he knew the meerkat was not far away. Probably that stupid buffalo had scared it off. As he moved, the scent got stronger still, and the snake knew he was getting close. He froze upon hearing voices ahead. He recognised Giraffe's soft tones and strained to hear the other voice. It sounded as if it might be the meerkat, but he wasn't sure.

The snake moved in a little closer, causing the grass to rustle ever so slightly, and Giraffe heard the noise.

'Oh, look—it's Puff Adder!' he exclaimed in a friendly way. Giraffe was so tall that he could look down into the grass with almost a bird's eye view, and it was easy for him to pick out the snake.

'Is it?' gasped the meerkat in alarm. 'I must go and tell the commander-in-chief at once. Goodbye, Mr Giraffe!' He saluted and raced off to report that the snake had been sighted, leaving an irate Puff Adder to hold a stiff conversation with his detector.

CHAPTER 22

Wanda and Felicity

MEANWHILE, LEADER AND DENT made their way down to the familiar waterhole, the place where they had first become friends. The young animals were in high spirits, and they head-butted each other's sides playfully as they ran.

'We're going to be famous!' shouted Dent.

'Yes! Everyone will know about our fight against the poachers,' Leader yelled back.

'The humans will be more interested in me because my mother was killed by the poachers,' Dent told his friend a little boastfully.

'No, they won't,' replied Leader at once. 'They'll be just as interested in me. My grandfather was incredibly famous. Even the humans must have heard of him.'

'Yes, but I might be the only white rhino left in the savanna now,' said Dent, slowing his pace to look meaningfully at Leader. 'That makes me very important.'

The two friends stopped running to continue the argument. Leader tried to think of another reason why he was just as important as Dent. He looked over the rhino's shoulder towards the waterhole, and a grin spread across his face.

'So, if you weren't the only white rhino in the savanna, that would mean I was just as important as you, and perhaps even more important?' he asked.

Dent thought for a moment and then nodded. 'Yes, I suppose it would,' he said, 'but I think I am the only white rhino, so that's not a good argument.'

'Ha!' said Leader triumphantly. 'No, you're not! Take a look over there.'

Dent swung round to face the waterhole, but his eyesight wasn't good enough for him to pick anything out. However, his powerful nose picked up the scent. 'I don't believe it,' he said excitedly. 'There must be white rhinos in the area. I can smell them!'

'And I can see them,' said Leader, laughing at his friend's delight. 'Shall we go and introduce ourselves?'

Dent didn't need to be asked twice. He raced off in front of Leader towards the waterhole, following the rhinos' scents. Leader hurried after him, but Dent ran so fast that the elephant couldn't keep up.

At last, Dent made out the two shapes with his eyes, and he slowed to a walk to approach them. He felt a little wary as there was no guarantee the rhinos would be friendly.

An adult female rhino stood at the edge of the waterhole with just her feet cooling in the water. She was huge and had two enormous horns that had protected her on many occasions, but Dent hardly noticed her. At her side was a female, whom Dent judged to be perhaps a little younger than him. She was quite small, and she had the most beautiful, soft, grey skin. Her ears flicked cautiously as Dent approached, but she gave him a shy smile, and Dent felt his heart jump for joy.

'Good morning,' said the big female in a deep voice. 'I was beginning to think we were the only white rhinos left in this land. I haven't seen another rhino for over a season now. We've travelled a long distance to look for others of our own kind. I'm very pleased to meet you.'

The female backed out of the water and moved slowly towards Dent. She bent her head down and rubbed his nose with hers by way of a greeting. 'I'm Wanda, and this is—'

'I'm Felicity,' said her daughter, forgetting her shyness. 'Pleased to meet you.' She stepped in front of her mother and greeted Dent in the same way. 'What is your name?' she asked.

'I'm Dent,' the rhino began. He stopped when Felicity giggled.

'I think I know why you're called that,' she said, and Dent laughed along with her.

'I hope it will straighten out as I get older,' he admitted. 'This is Leader,' he added, remembering his friend who was standing a little way away, not wanting to interrupt. The elephant trotted forward and was delighted to be greeted in the same friendly way.

'Are you with a herd?' asked Wanda. 'We were hoping to join up with another group of rhinos so we might be safe.'

Dent nodded. 'I am with a herd, although not the type you mean,' he replied. 'I live with the elephants now. My mother and I were together, but she was killed by poachers.'

'So, you're an orphan,' said Felicity with a deeply sympathetic look. 'You poor thing. It must have been terrible for you.'

Dent found there was a lump in his throat. He tried to speak, but he couldn't, so Leader spoke for him instead. 'Yes, it was dreadful,' he said, 'but he's one of our family now, and we all think of him as another elephant.'

'But you're not an elephant, are you, Dent?' said Wanda.

'It must be quite strange living with animals of another species,' exclaimed Felicity. 'I can't imagine it.'

'Yes, it can be rather difficult sometimes,' said Dent, anxious to agree with his new friends. He forgot that Leader was standing next to him.

'Oh, well,' snorted the elephant, 'if that's how you feel, I trust you won't be staying with us anymore. Now that you've found other rhinos, I suppose we are no longer needed.'

Leader stomped off furiously, blowing hot tears from his cheeks as he walked. After everything the elephant herd had done for Dent! The little elephant felt hurt and indignant. He plunged through the grass away from the waterhole without looking back. He thought he heard Dent calling after him, but he didn't care.

Let him call, he thought. *It's for him to come after me.*

There was a group of large fever trees to one side of the waterhole, and it was towards these that Leader walked. At his angry pace, he soon reached the trees and darted inside their cover to cool off a little. There, he knew he was hidden from view. The elephant risked a cautious peep out of the trees to look at the rhinos, which only served to make him feel more cross.

He could see the trio standing close together, and the sound of happy voices and laughter reached his ears. Dent appeared not to have even noticed that he had gone.

'Well, that's it!' said Leader, preparing to storm out of the trees and back to the herd, but something made him stop. He paused and listened carefully – was that the sound of a human voice?

A minute passed, but the elephant didn't hear the noise again. He waited a little while and then poked his head out of the trees. There was no sign of any humans, yet Leader was sure he had heard something.

The elephant drew back, feeling a bit agitated. What should he do – wait until he could hear the noise again or hope they had gone? Perhaps they were creeping up on him from outside the trees … he listened again for any sound that might give the humans away but still heard nothing. Frustrated, he decided to risk taking another look.

Leader peered out of the trees and then he heard the voice again. It was no more than a whisper, but he was sure it was from a human. The elephant looked to his right and then he saw the van and the two men standing next to it. Both men were clutching guns to their chests and staring in the direction of the rhinos.

CHAPTER 23

A Young Hero

THE MEN WITH GUNS were a little way away from Leader, but quite close to where Dent, Wanda, and Felicity were standing. However, there were bushes between the men and the rhinos, and Leader realised the rhinos probably couldn't see the men. The men were also downwind of the rhinos, so it was unlikely the rhinos would smell them.

Leader panicked. He felt sure the men were poachers, and the rhinos were in terrible danger. He had to do something and fast!

Hardly caring about himself, Leader charged out of the trees, heading away from the men. He knew he wasn't a target for the poachers as he was still too young to have any tusks. He had to find someone else who could help, or the rhinos might be killed ... even Dent! Leader tried not to think about it as he ran across the plains.

Unfortunately, there wasn't a soul in sight. The elephant stopped to look up into the sky, hoping to see Martial Eagle or perhaps the secretary bird, but it was the hottest time of day, and the birds were taking shade. He scanned the horizon again, looking for a giraffe, a zebra, a lion–anyone who could decide better than him what to do. He saw the buffalo herd in the distance, but they were too far away, and he needed help now.

Leader tried to remember where the herd had been when he had left them, but they appeared to have moved on. He felt helpless. His best friend was in danger of being shot, and there seemed to be nothing he could do about it.

That was when Leader had an enormous and sudden piece of luck: he caught sight of Alfie bounding along not too far away, and just behind the chimp was the ranger. Leader raised his trunk and shrieked at Alfie, who heard and turned to look at him.

'Alfie, come quickly–there are poachers near the waterhole!' the elephant screamed. 'Dent is down there with two other rhinos. The poachers will shoot them if you don't do something.'

Alfie hurried over to the ranger. He gabbled off a series of hand signs and pointed towards the waterhole several times, and the ranger and Alfie raced off in the direction from which Leader had come. Meanwhile, the elephant stood there in shock, thankful he had done all he could. It was up to the ranger now.

'What's going on?' called a voice from above him. Leader looked up to see Martial Eagle whirling around his head and wished he had been there sooner. The bird could have taken the message to Alfie and the ranger more quickly than he had done.

'The poachers are back!' Leader shouted up to him. 'Alfie and the ranger have gone down to try to save the rhinos.'

Martial Eagle flew off to see if he could help, leaving Leader to watch from afar. From his position, Leader could see everyone now: the poachers, Alfie and the ranger, and the rhinos, who were still quite oblivious to the danger they were in. Leader saw Alfie and the ranger hurry into the trees where he himself had been. The poachers didn't seem to have spotted them yet.

The poachers appeared to be preparing for the kill. One of them raised his gun to his shoulder, and Leader hardly dared to breathe. There was an awful pause as he waited for the shot to come. Perhaps the ranger was too far away to do anything.

The gun exploded, and Leader closed his eyes, a severe sick feeling sweeping through his stomach. He stared into the trees, unable to bring himself to look at the rhinos, feeling sure that one of them would now be lying on the ground.

Another shot rang out across the plains. This time, Leader had to look to see what had happened. To his joy, he saw the three rhinos galloping away from the waterhole, apparently completely unharmed. He swung his eyes across to where the poachers had been and glimpsed the men jumping into the van. They drove off like madmen with great clouds of dust rocketing out behind them.

There came another shot and the sound of a bullet bouncing off metal, and Leader realised it must have been the ranger pulling the trigger.

Meanwhile, the rhinos were a considerable distance away and quite safe. Leader felt like dancing for joy. They were alive, and it was all thanks to him, Alfie, and the ranger.

The poachers were soon no more than a tiny speck zooming away into the distance. Alfie and the ranger emerged from the trees, and the chimp came charging towards Leader with a gleeful skip in his step. Martial Eagle flew back down like an arrow and perched on the ground in front of him.

'That got rid of them!' Alfie shouted. 'It was a shame we weren't in our van, or the ranger could have chased them and tried to catch them. Still, what matters most is that the rhinos weren't hurt in any way. Well done! I think you're a bit of a hero!'

Alfie patted Leader on his side. His words made the little elephant think of his grandfather.

'You don't know how much that means,' Leader said. 'My grandfather's name was Hero.'

The ranger walked towards the animals and stopped a careful distance away, not wanting to frighten Leader. He said something quickly to Alfie in the human tongue, and Alfie answered him with his hand signs as Leader watched in awe. He thought it was wonderful the way the chimpanzee could communicate with humans, and he wished he could do the same.

'What did he say?' the elephant couldn't stop himself from asking.

'He says we have to go back to our van to see if we can catch up with the men,' Alfie explained. 'There's a danger they might try to shoot another animal. If we catch them, the ranger can arrest them. I'm sorry, but we must go now.'

Alfie turned to Martial Eagle and said, 'I think the others should know what a brave thing Leader did today. He was very courageous to run out to find help, risking being shot at himself.'

Leader was thrilled at the praise from the clever chimpanzee. He tried, without much success, to look modest.

Martial Eagle smiled and nodded. 'I'll make sure everyone knows,' he promised.

Alfie waved a farewell and hurried to catch up with the ranger, but then the chimp turned around again and called out, 'I forgot to mention—the meeting with the human leader will be in two days' time. We'll meet in the ridged valley when the sun is at its highest point in the sky. Make sure you pass the message on—we need everyone to be there.'

Martial Eagle and Leader nodded together, and they watched Alfie sprint off through the termite mounds after the ranger.

Leader looked across the plains, trying to see where the rhinos had gone, but there was no sign of them. He suspected they had hidden in a large patch of scrubland not far from the waterhole, and he felt a little disappointed. None of them would even know that he had been the one to save their lives.

Martial Eagle sensed what he was thinking. 'I'll make sure they know what happened, don't worry,' he said kindly, and Leader beamed.

'Thank you, Mr Eagle,' he said. 'Now, I must get back to the herd, or my mother will be worried. Do you know which direction they are in?'

The bird pointed east with his wing. His eyesight was good enough to make out the herd from where he and Leader were standing.

'Thank you,' Leader said again. 'I'd better go.' The elephant's face looked a little sad. 'If you see Dent, please tell him where we are,' he added. 'Maybe he will still want to find us.'

✦✦✦✦✦

The elephants were beside themselves with pride when Leader told them what he had done. The older members of the family insisted on coming up to their little nephew and embracing him with their trunks in a vice-like grip so tight that he could hardly breathe. Leader eventually disentangled himself after several minutes of near strangulation, feeling that he'd really had enough.

'What a little hero you are!' cried Mabel, tickling him under the chin with her trunk.

'Auntie's so proud of you!' crowed Ethel in turn.

'We all knew you were going to be somebody very special,' said Maud. Leader looked at her in disbelief. As far as he could remember, the only thing Maud had ever said about him was that he was a proper little nuisance with no manners.

The little elephant edged away from his aunts and went to where his mother and Bright were standing.

'Well done, Leader. Those rhinos have a great deal to thank you for,' said Bright with a big smile when she got near the hero of the hour.

'Thank you, sister,' he said, feeling a little shiver run down his back, but the praise that meant the most to him was from his mother.

'That was an act worthy of your grandfather,' Stella said quietly. 'I'm very proud of you, Leader.' She nuzzled Leader with her trunk, and he felt as if he might burst with pride.

'Is Dent going to come back to live with us?' asked Bright. 'I must say that I think of him like a little brother.'

Leader's happy face fell. 'I don't know,' he said. 'The last thing I heard him say was that he found it difficult living with us. He seemed to be much more interested in the other rhinos than me.'

'You have to remember that he hasn't seen another rhino since he lost his mum,' Stella reminded him gently. 'He will be over the moon at the moment, but he won't forget a good friend like you. He'll be back. You'll see.'

'Maybe, but he'll have that girl with him,' said Leader, making his mother laugh at the disgust in his voice.

'Well, she can be a friend, too,' she told him. 'There's nothing wrong with girls.'

'No, there isn't,' chorused the rest of the herd.

Leader realised he was rather outnumbered. He opened his mouth to reply but wisely decided to say no more.

CHAPTER 24

Where Is Cheetah?

OVER THE NEXT FEW days, Leopard noticed that Cheetah seemed to be missing. She kept her eye out for him and asked the animals she came across if anyone had seen him, but nobody had. Leopard grew increasingly concerned, and on the morning of the meeting, she realised it was time to go and look for him properly. She went from one animal to the next, enquiring about the cat.

'No, I haven't seen Cheetah for days,' said Lioness, shaking her head, 'not since the meeting with the chimpanzee, in fact. Where could he possibly be?

'Lion, have you seen Cheetah recently?' Lion pretended to think. He had spent most of the previous few days asleep, so he was quite certain he hadn't seen Cheetah, but he loved that the other animals were waiting for him to speak. 'No, I don't believe I have,' he said at length, and Leopard looked disappointed.

'I was hoping one of you might have seen him when out hunting,' she said. 'I've been too busy with the cubs to look for him, but I'm beginning to get worried. He might have been hurt or captured by poachers, and no one would know. Stella hasn't seen him. The meerkats haven't seen him. Not even Martial Eagle has set eyes on him for a few days now.'

'Lion, you should go and see if you can find him,' Lioness said to her mate. 'He might be lying injured somewhere with nobody to help him.'

Lion attempted to look apologetic. 'I'd love to help,' he said, 'but my leg's still rather stiff from all that hunting we did yesterday. I'm not sure I'm up to walking very far.'

Lioness glanced at him. 'He came with me for a short spell,' she explained to an amused Leopard, 'and then he got so angry when he couldn't catch anything that he went away in a sulk.'

'I hurt my leg,' Lion protested in a pitiful voice. His mate rolled her eyes at Leopard.

'He's wounded beyond repair, you know,' she said. 'Well, the lionesses have agreed: we're not going to do all the hunting any longer, so he'll have to start pulling his weight if he wants to eat. I feel quite confident his leg will get better if he's threatened with starvation.'

'Oh, you are cruel,' whined Lion. He made a great show of struggling to his feet and limping away, and Leopard didn't know whether to feel sorry for him or laugh. The supposed king of the savanna was having a hard time with his mate.

'Well, I must move on to see if I can find Cheetah,' Leopard told Lioness. 'I've been to all the places where he can usually be found, but there's no sign of him anywhere.'

'Sorry we couldn't help,' said Lioness, and Leopard set out to find someone else who might have seen Cheetah.

She picked up her paws and sprinted across the grass with the wind brushing gently over her face and head. The ground shot past beneath her, and within a few minutes, she was a long way away from the lion pride. She had left her cubs with the elephant herd for babysitting, which meant she was free to run fast for the first time in ages, and she realised how much she was enjoying it.

Leopard wondered if Cheetah might be deliberately hiding away somewhere. She went over her secret haunts in her mind, trying to imagine where she would go if she were hiding. There was the wide-branched tree on the edge of the valley, but she doubted Cheetah would go there because her scent would be very strong. She had already checked the group of bushes surrounded by the termite mounds, and there wasn't the faintest scent of Cheetah. Leopard stopped running and bit her lip in frustration.

'I can't think of anywhere else,' she said aloud.

Just ahead of her, Leopard saw the baboon troop scattered across the rocky hills. She realised that she hadn't asked any of the baboons, and she bounded towards them with a bit of hope in her step.

The troop looked up with hostility when they saw Leopard approach, and she stopped in her tracks. Although she didn't know it, she was interrupting another challenge to Baboon's leadership.

Poor Baboon always had to watch out for new alliances being formed within his troop and for ambitious animals who thought they could do a better job of leading the troop than him. Now, yet another of his sons had challenged him to a fight. Baboon didn't want to fight his son, mainly because he was his son, but secretly, he also feared losing. His son was much smaller, but he was strong for his size and quicker on his feet than Baboon, who realised he had to act like the wise statesman who knew better than to fight.

'I believe you're afraid you'll lose,' shouted his son. 'That's why you won't fight me, isn't it? Come on—admit it!'

The eyes of all the watching baboons turned towards Baboon, and there was an expectant hush. What would their leader say now?

Baboon refused to let himself be goaded. Pretending to look sad, he shook his head for a long time while his son looked at him.

'It's my duty to protect you from yourself,' Baboon explained to his son. 'I don't want to injure you in a fight, but I would have to if you chose to fight me. You are so young and lacking in strength compared to me that you could only lose. Wait until you are older, my son. Then I might be ready to move aside for you.'

'You said that last season,' exclaimed the young animal angrily. 'No, I want to fight you now.' He tried to sound fierce, but Baboon detected a waver in his voice for the first time, and he knew he had won.

The old leader lifted himself calmly to his feet and walked on all fours to where his son was standing. He drew himself up to his impressive full height so he would tower over his son and stared into the younger animal's orange eyes.

'Why don't you go back to your friends?' he suggested in a soft voice. 'After all, you wouldn't want them to see you lose horribly. Think how embarrassed you would be. If you go back to them now, we'll say no more about your behaviour.'

The young baboon felt his anger rise again at his father's words—he always treated him like a child! However, he suddenly felt afraid to fight him. He hesitated for a moment, wondering if he would look silly to step down now. Baboon knew what was going through his son's mind, and he gave him an encouraging smile.

'If you let me, I can help you prepare to be a fine leader yourself one day,' he said.

His son caved in and bowed his head in submission. 'Okay,' he said meekly, 'you win.'

Baboon's allies cheered and jumped up and down, whilst the animals supporting Baboon's son in his leadership bid suddenly felt anxious. They hoped they wouldn't be in trouble with their leader.

Meanwhile, Leopard decided it was a good time to interrupt. She stepped forward, half-afraid that Baboon wouldn't want to speak to her, but Baboon was delighted at the excuse to leave the troop for a moment.

'Sorry to interrupt, but have you seen Cheetah by any chance, Baboon?' Leopard asked politely.

'Yes, I did see Cheetah a couple of days ago, the morning after the meeting with Alfie,' Baboon replied. 'He was wandering around in the group of trees just over there. He looked rather miserable, I thought.'

Baboon nodded towards a small group of baobabs, and Leopard felt her hopes rise. Perhaps Cheetah hadn't met with poachers after all.

'Thank you, Baboon,' she said gratefully. 'I'll see if I can find him. I've been worried as it's not like Cheetah to disappear. I know he's very quiet, but he's usually around somewhere across the plains.'

Leopard hurried away towards the trees, leaving Baboon to go back to his family. She sprinted over the rough ground, dodged around the termite mounds, and in no time, she reached the trees, where she came to a halt.

Leopard sniffed the air and thought she could detect Cheetah's scent, but it wasn't strong enough for her to know if he was still there. At least she was certain he had, indeed, been there quite recently.

The scent seemed to grow stronger to her right, so she turned and followed her nose into the trees, growing more confident that she would find Cheetah. Her powerful sense of smell guided her towards a particularly large baobab tree with huge branches spreading out from a sturdy bough. As she circled its trunk, Leopard found that it had split in one place to create an opening just large enough for a medium-sized animal to squeeze through. She guessed it led to a hollow inside the tree trunk, and she peered through the opening, but it was dark inside, and she could see nothing.

Nevertheless, Cheetah's scent was strong, and she knew he must be in there.

'Cheetah,' she shouted, her nose pointed into the gap, 'come out now! What are you doing hiding in there?'

There came a faint moan from inside the tree. 'No, I don't want to come out.' If Leopard hadn't been certain it was Cheetah, she wouldn't have recognised his voice as it sounded strange echoing from inside the tree.

'But we need you to come to the meeting with the human leader,' said Leopard. 'It's important that you're there because cheetahs are one of the species threatened by poaching. We have to have a cheetah there as well as a leopard.'

'Well, find another cheetah somewhere,' the voice told her. 'I'm not going anywhere near that chimpanzee.'

'Is that why you don't want to come?' asked Leopard, surprised. 'Because you don't like Alfie?'

Cheetah's eerie tones floated out to her again. 'He's so rude. I'm really embarrassed that I'm the only member of the cat family who can't retract their claws, and now everyone knows about it.'

'Oh, don't worry about that..,' Leopard began, but Cheetah interrupted.

'I've been sitting inside this tree for two days practising, and I still can't do it,' his voice said mournfully. 'I'm a complete failure, and everyone knows it.'

It was all Leopard could do not to laugh, but she knew it would offend the very sensitive Cheetah. She thought for a moment, wondering how she might persuade him to come with her. Alfie was keen for all of the animals to be at the meeting with the human leader.

'Cheetah,' she said, 'I'll ask Alfie to apologise to you if you come to the meeting. We'll all miss you if you aren't there.'

'Nobody would even notice,' replied Cheetah's voice at once. 'I'm always too nervous to say anything in front of all those other animals. Don't try to tell me you would miss me.'

'Well, I would,' said Leopard. 'You don't have to be loud and confident to be important. You've got lots of excellent qualities, Cheetah: you're trustworthy, kind, caring and sensitive, and you're my friend.'

'Yes, and I'm also boring, lonely and stupid,' said the voice.

Leopard felt sad. She had never heard Cheetah be so open before, and she hadn't realised he was lonely.

Leopard had an idea. 'You might like to know that a female cheetah has been spotted in the area,' she told Cheetah, completely untruthfully. 'I expect you'd like to meet her, wouldn't you?'

There was a long silence as Cheetah thought about this piece of information. 'Is that true?' he asked, and Leopard thought she detected some interest in his voice.

'Absolutely,' she lied again, feeling rather guilty, 'but you'll never meet her unless you come out of that tree. Martial Eagle said he'll try to find her and tell her about the meeting, so you might meet her there.'

Leopard couldn't see Cheetah, so it was difficult to know how he was reacting. There was another silence, during which Leopard tried to contain herself. She wanted to drag Cheetah out of the tree and tell him not to be so silly, but she knew that wasn't the right thing to do.

'Gosh, a female cheetah,' said Cheetah's voice at last. This time, there was no doubting the excitement in his voice. 'Wait a moment, Leopard. I'm coming out!'

Leopard grinned and stretched her front paws up against the tree in victory. *Now we've got to find a female cheetah somewhere,* she thought. *He'll be so upset with me if he realises he's been tricked.*

Cheetah's head emerged from the middle of the tree, and he screwed up his eyes at the sudden bright light after having spent two days in darkness. He pushed on the edge of the hollow with his front paws and jumped out of the tree, landing softly on the ground beside Leopard. 'Where was the female cheetah seen?' he asked, looking more enthusiastic than Leopard had seen in a long time.

'I couldn't tell you myself,' said Leopard, pretending to focus on scratching her ear. 'You'll have to ask Martial Eagle.'

Leopard turned away from Cheetah to lead their way out of the trees and cringed. She would have to speak to Martial Eagle and fast.

'Right. Shall we head off to the valley, then?' said Leopard. 'By the time we get there it will be the middle of the day.'

'Yes, let's go!' said Cheetah, doing a little skip. 'I do hope the female cheetah is there.'

Leopard felt her stomach twist inside her. 'Well, you never know,' she said as brightly as she could.

CHAPTER 25

Wanda Is Very Rude

MEANWHILE, DENT HAD FINALLY set out to find the elephant herd and introduce his new friends to them.

He had spent the past two days in great happiness, telling Wanda and Felicity about his life and listening to their stories. When they had grown tired of talking, Dent and Felicity had galloped off to play together, and Dent felt exhilarated to be with another rhino again. Although Felicity was a little younger than he, she was clever and funny, and the pair often ended up helpless with laughter. Dent felt as if he had known Felicity for a long time, and he quickly became attached to her. Wanda didn't fail to notice how he hung on every word her daughter said.

Dent first introduced Wanda and Felicity to Stella and Bright, who were grazing at the edge of the herd. The two new rhinos were rather alarmed to see Leopard's cubs mingling with the elephant herd and Mabel and Ethel being run off their feet trying to keep up with the cubs, who were eager to play.

'Ooh, you're a naughty little thing!' squealed Mabel when one of the cubs dug her claws into Mabel's trunk and hung on as she swung it around. 'That hurts! Get off my trunk at once!'

'Stop pulling my tail!' cried Ethel when the other cub jumped up and nipped her tail with his razor-sharp teeth.

'I don't know how long I can cope with this!' gasped Mabel, still trying to shake the cub off her trunk. She looked down her nose at her. 'You think this is funny, don't you!'

'What are they doing here?' was the first thing Wanda said to Stella. 'Why are you letting them annoy members of your herd? Surely, you don't have leopards in the herd as well as rhinos?'

Stella laughed whole-heartedly. 'No, they don't belong to us,' she said. 'They are the cubs of a very good friend who needed a babysitter for the morning. As for their annoying members of the herd, don't you believe it—Mabel and Ethel are loving every moment of this. It reminds them of their own children.'

'Except their own children didn't have vicious little claws and carnivorous teeth, I don't suppose,' said Wanda curtly.

Stella was taken aback by the tone in her voice. 'I'm glad Dent has met up with some other rhinos,' she said kindly. 'I know he's happy living with my herd, but it's lovely for him to have members of his own species for company.'

'Yes. I really don't think it's right for him to be spending all his time with a herd of elephants,' said Wanda. 'It's not natural, and it must be very difficult for him and you.'

What an interfering animal, thought Stella uneasily. She didn't like the direction the conversation was heading.

'Of course, he was completely alone when we took him in,' said Bright with a welcoming smile but a warning note in her voice, 'and we didn't force him to join us. He chose to become a member of the herd.'

'I think he enjoys being with us,' said Stella, looking worried. She wondered if she had missed that Dent was unhappy.

The three animals looked over to where Dent and Leader were greeting each other in delight while Felicity looked on. The rhino rubbed his nose against the elephant's grey cheek whilst Leader curled his trunk over Dent's back and gave him a friendly squeeze.

'I'm so glad you came back,' Leader told his friend when they pulled apart. 'I've missed you so much these past two days.'

'I've missed you, too,' said Dent, and Leader saw he had tears in his eyes. 'I'm sorry. I just got so excited about meeting other rhinos. This is Felicity, by the way.'

The young rhino stepped forward a little shyly but with a friendly smile, and Leader took to her at once.

'Pleased to meet you again,' they said simultaneously. They both giggled. Dent joined in, and the three of them laughed merrily. Soon they were scampering across the grass in a game of chase.

'He looks happy to me,' said Bright.

'Wanda, would you like to join us at our meeting today?' she continued. 'I expect Dent has told you about our problems with the poachers, and about the ranger who has offered to help us.'

The rhino grimaced. 'Yes, he did,' she said. 'I must say, I do find it most peculiar the way the species in your group come together and treat each other as if they are the best of friends. I'm not sure we want to be involved in those kinds of goings-on. I was always brought up with the idea that lions and leopards are dangerous creatures and to keep well away from them, especially a young rhino like Felicity.'

'This is very different,' said Stella. 'We have all been friends ever since my father brought the animals from this area together to unite against common dangers. Everyone in the group has taken a vow not to hunt or threaten other members during group meetings, and I assure you that no one would dream of breaking that vow.'

'What about this ranger?' asked Wanda, looking doubtful. 'I can just about understand an alliance between different species against the common enemy of man, but then you tell me you are relying on this human for help. I think you're mad to trust him. I know he says he's on your side and against the poachers, but suppose it's all a trick? He could gather you all together and shoot the elephants and the rhinos and any other animals he wanted, and you wouldn't be able to do a thing to stop him.'

'I think it's time Wanda knew why she's still alive,' said Bright with a little nod of her head.

'I do know,' replied the rhino. 'I was very lucky. We were all very lucky that the poachers were bad shots.'

'The poachers never had the chance to shoot their guns,' Stella told her, 'and the reason they didn't have the chance was that our ranger frightened them off by shooting in their direction.'

'If it hadn't been for the ranger, you would almost certainly be dead now,' Bright added, 'so I think you owe the ranger a little bit of trust.'

The two elephants looked at Wanda, who realised she had been cornered. 'Well, I didn't even know the ranger was there,' she said. 'How was I to know he saved us from the poachers?'

'You couldn't,' agreed Stella, 'but now that you know, perhaps you ought to support him at the meeting today. Alfie says it's important that there are as many different species there as possible, especially the hunted species like ourselves. I expect the human leader will be amazed if hundreds of animals come together as one big group.'

'We ought to be going soon,' Bright reminded her mother. 'The sun isn't far from being at its highest point in the sky, and we are a long way from the valley.'

Bright turned to face Wanda. 'So, make up your mind please,' she said, 'are you coming with us or not?'

The rhino recognised the impatience in Bright's voice. She nodded reluctantly and looked around for Felicity, who was still happily engaged in the game with Leader and Dent. 'Yes, we'll come,' she said, 'although I won't pretend that I feel comfortable about it.'

'Good,' said Stella. She smiled, although privately, she didn't really mind whether the rhino came or not. The conversation between them had proven rather difficult.

The elephant leader called to the rest of the herd and told them they should get ready to leave. 'Leader ... Dent,' she cried, 'don't get left behind! It's time for us to go to the meeting.'

Just then, Leopard and Cheetah bounded up to the group. Stella and Bright exclaimed in delight when they saw Cheetah. 'Where were you?' Stella asked, but Leopard shook her head and frowned.

'Ah well, it doesn't really matter where he was,' said Bright, seeing Leopard's warning. 'All that matters is he's back now.'

Cheetah hardly heard what they were saying. 'Have you seen the female cheetah?' he asked with great excitement.

Both elephants looked at Leopard.

'Er ... the female cheetah?' said Stella slowly, 'I'm not sure — have we seen her, Bright?'

'I don't think so,' said Bright equally slowly, before realising what Leopard must have told Cheetah. 'Well, I haven't seen her, but some of the other animals have. She's charming, apparently.'

Stella saw what was going on, and she, too, jumped in to rescue Leopard. 'I think somebody may have mentioned she was planning to move on, though,' she said. 'It's a shame she didn't get to meet our Cheetah.'

'She might still be around today, though,' interjected Leopard. 'Isn't that what Martial Eagle said?'

'Yes!' said Bright and Stella together, a little too quickly.

Cheetah looked at them suspiciously, but their kind smiles persuaded him they wouldn't lie to him.

'Allow me to introduce you to Wanda,' said Bright, seeing an opportunity. 'She and her daughter, Felicity, are new to the area, and we'll hopefully be seeing a lot of them from now on.'

'Hello,' said Cheetah timidly, backing away in alarm when Wanda bent down to sniff at him.

'Well, you're a cowardly cheetah if ever I saw one,' remarked the rhino, making Leopard and the elephants gasp at her rudeness.

Cheetah looked at her in amazement and couldn't think what to say.

Leopard was quicker thinking. 'Don't bother introducing *me*,' she said to the elephants, keeping her back facing Wanda. She winked at Stella and Bright, who had to stop themselves from bursting out laughing. 'I don't need a character analysis, thank you.'

Leopard marched off to pick up her cubs. 'I'll see you at the meeting,' she called without looking back.

'Well, how rude!' exclaimed Wanda. 'Is she always as unfriendly as that?'

For a moment, Cheetah forgot his shyness. 'Leopard's very nice,' he said. 'She's not unfriendly at all.'

'Shall we move on to the meeting, then?' said Bright, foreseeing trouble. Cheetah was timid, but he was loyal to his friends, and the elephant could see he was upset.

'Yes, let's go,' agreed Stella, and she called to Leader and Dent again before setting off in the direction of the valley.

Bright hurried up to her side, leaving Wanda to walk amongst the older elephants. Mabel crooned about how lovely the little leopard cubs were, and Wanda found herself unable to get a word in. Cheetah slunk along at the back, keeping as far away from the big rhinoceros as he could. His thoughts soon drifted back to the prospect of meeting the female cheetah, and he forgot about Wanda.

'Isn't she awful?' Bright whispered to Stella.

'I've never met such a rude animal,' agreed Stella, 'and she had the nerve to call Leopard rude! Leopard doesn't go around addressing other animals as cowardly.'

'Maybe we should persuade her that this area is too dangerous for older rhinos,' said Bright with a grin, 'and that she'd be much better off moving on.'

'We shouldn't be too unkind,' Stella told her, feeling guilty. 'Perhaps she just comes across badly. She might be very nice underneath.'

Bright snorted. 'Well, in that case, she hides it well,' she said. 'You are always too ready to see the best in animals, Mum. Mark my words: Wanda is going to be trouble.'

CHAPTER 26

Getting Ready to Meet the Human Leader

THE ELEPHANTS REACHED THE edge of the ridged valley and stopped at the top of the slope. They were amazed to look down and see several hundred animals gathered there. The animals seemed to be assembled neatly in their species groups. All of the zebras were in one line, and next to them were the buffaloes, then came the antelopes, then the wildebeests, and then a much smaller group of giraffes. The lion pride was next in line. Leopard and her cubs were sitting next to them. Next came the ostriches and the baboons, and Stella could just make out Martial Eagle's diminutive figure perched on Giraffe's back. To her surprise, even the secretary bird had arrived before them and was busy preening next to Giraffe.

The herd plodded down the slope, with Cheetah trying to hide at the back. As they got closer, Stella heard the familiar voice of the commander-in-chief's deputy issuing orders to the other animals.

The deputy commander stood at the front. Now, Stella could see there was also a meerkat at the head of each animal group, positioned as if to manage it. Behind each meerkat was the leader of the species, the leader's mate, and then the rest of the group, assembled neatly behind them. Even Puff Adder had his own little place in the line-up.

The deputy commander saw the elephants coming, and he scuttled over to them. 'You are all late!' he shouted, although his small voice came out as a high-pitched squeak. 'None of you would last a day in one of my brigades. I am acting on behalf of the commander-in-chief today, and Alfie has asked me to get the animals in order, ready for when the human leader arrives. We need to impress him with how organised we are, so get into formation at once, please. Quick march!'

The elephants hurried to line up next to the zebras, and Cheetah tried to go with them, but the unfortunate cat didn't get that far.

'Not you,' yelled the deputy commander. 'You are not an elephant. Start another line.

'And you — make a line for the rhinos,' he continued, looking at Wanda. 'I presume you are the leader?'

Dent and Felicity obediently went to stand in line. Dent had told Felicity about the meerkats, and they were both a little scared of being told off. However, Wanda stood obstinately still with the elephants, waiting for the deputy commander to challenge her. She wasn't going to take any notice of what a meerkat said.

'Are you deaf?' shouted the deputy commander, seeing that Wanda hadn't made any attempt to move. 'I know rhinos are almost blind, but you seem to be deaf as well. Line up at once, please!'

'No, I won't, you silly creature,' said Wanda. 'I don't take orders from animals smaller than myself.'

There was an audible gasp from the other meerkats, who would never have dared to question anything the deputy commander said.

'Would you please get into line?' the deputy commander said again, with a steely edge to his voice.

'No,' said Wanda, 'I won't.'

'Alfie has asked me to get everyone ready for when the humans arrive,' said the deputy commander, trying again. 'For the last time, would you please cooperate?'

Wanda looked away as if she hadn't heard a word. She gazed into the distance, and to the deputy commander's annoyance, even started to hum a tune to herself.

'Right, meerkats!' he shouted. 'Code Fang, please!' The deputy commander traced a large circle with his arms, and dozens of meerkats rushed forwards at once. The other animals watched to see what Code Fang would turn out to be.

The meerkats hurried over to where Wanda was standing and divided into four neat groups, with one group at each of the rhino's legs. They waited for the deputy commander to give them the signal whilst Wanda looked down at them, irritated.

'Go away!' she said, kicking out with her front foot. One of the meerkats was unfortunate enough to catch the edge of her hoof and was catapulted high into the air, landing some distance away from where he had been.

'GO,' shouted the deputy commander, and the meerkats darted in to nip at Wanda's ankles. They didn't bite hard, but it felt like several pins plunging into all four of her legs at once.

Wanda shrieked, as much in annoyance as in pain, 'Get them off me! Get them off!' The rest of the animals couldn't help but laugh as they watched the huge rhino jumping from one foot to another, squealing and shaking her legs in her attempt to free herself.

'All right—you win!' Wanda cried in the end. 'Anything to get rid of these little vipers.'

'I object to that description,' came Puff Adder's voice from somewhere.

'Stop,' shouted the deputy commander, and the meerkats dropped from Wanda's ankles and moved back into formation to await their next instructions.

'Now, please get into line,' ordered the deputy commander again, looking hard at the rhino. Wanda hesitated for just a moment, but she didn't dare to disobey again. She stepped slowly and deliberately to where Dent and Felicity were standing and settled at the head of their little row.

'Good,' said the deputy commander with satisfaction. 'Meerkats! Attention! March!'

The meerkats marched beautifully in time back to their stations whilst the deputy commander watched with pride.

'Good,' he said again. 'Well done, everyone. Now, we are all ready and in perfect order.'

'Thank you for your help in organising us, Deputy Commander,' said Stella nicely. 'Your troops do you credit.'

Stella looked across at Wanda as she sulked and at poor Felicity, who looked embarrassed. The elephant tried not to smile. It didn't hurt the older rhino to learn that other species were just as important as she was.

'There's Alfie!' said Giraffe suddenly, and sure enough, the chimp came tumbling down the slope on all fours, as fast as his legs would carry him.

'Oh, good,' said Buffalo sarcastically. He hadn't forgotten the way Alfie had teased him at the previous meeting. Meanwhile, Cheetah backed away even farther behind the giraffes.

'They're coming!' Alfie shouted. 'The ranger's on his way now, along with the human leader. Don't worry—everything's going to be fine.'

Alfie took up his position in front of the animals and beamed at them with excitement. The chimp did a quick somersault on the spot and clapped his hands whilst the secretary bird watched in awe.

'Hello, everyone,' he called. 'It is excellent to see you. And well done in lining everyone up so well, Deputy Commander.

'Dear friends, I know that when you see the human leader, your instinct will be to run away, but I promise you have nothing to fear,' said Alfie. 'You really can trust this man. He is an important businessman and local leader. He won't hurt you. Are you all ready with your stories?'

'I do hope he's right,' said Zebra, feeling uneasy. He was not sure he would ever trust humans again after the deaths of his family members.

'Oh, and welcome to our two new rhinos,' said Alfie when his eye caught Wanda and Felicity at the end of the assembly. 'Hello. I'm delighted to meet you. I'm Alfie.'

Felicity smiled and said hello, but Wanda just ignored him. 'Mum, say hello,' said Felicity in dismay, but her mother remained silent.

Alfie looked surprised. He turned to face the wider group of animals. 'Is everyone ready to meet the leader?' he asked a little anxiously.

'Yes!' cried the animals together, and Alfie felt relieved. He scrambled back up the slope and waved.

There came the sound of an engine being started. Soon a van drove over the brow of the hill and slowly descended the slope. The animals saw there were three men inside the van. As the vehicle came closer, the leaders of the various species recognised one of the men as the ranger.

Meanwhile, Alfie raced down the slope behind the van and arrived, breathless with excitement.

The animals watched as the van came to a halt. They waited nervously for the human leader to get out of his van. This was the man who would help them to solve their problems and ensure the savanna was free from poaching. The animals knew the meeting needed to go well.

CHAPTER 27

The Leader, Mr Rich

STELA LOOKED AT THE three men, feeling her heart pound. She, too, was hopeful to meet the human leader and ready to tell him her father's story. She thought that even a human would be touched by the bravery her father had shown. The elephant scanned the faces of the other animals. Buffalo, who normally only wanted to charge at humans, was looking at the van with keen interest, whilst Zebra seemed on high alert.

Stella watched as the ranger jumped out of the van and went to open the back door for the other two men. Suddenly, she felt most uncomfortable.

What's the matter with me? she wondered. The elephant knew she could trust Alfie, and she knew that Alfie trusted the ranger, so there was no reason to feel uneasy, yet she felt really agitated.

Bright sensed her mother's discomfort and turned to her. 'What's the matter?' she whispered. 'Aren't you feeling well?'

Stella shook her head. 'I don't know,' she started to say, but she stopped when a second man stepped slowly out of the van. He was dressed neatly in a safari-style shirt, cream trousers, and large sunglasses. He carried an enormous gun across his back, and a shudder went through the animals at the sight of it.

'That's the leader's bodyguard,' hissed Alfie to the watching animals. 'He's here to protect the leader.'

'From us?' asked Ostrich in surprise.

Alfie nodded. 'Yes, exactly,' he said. 'You don't realise how frightened humans are of wild animals. They trust you even less than you trust them.'

'Hmm,' muttered Buffalo under his breath.

There was a hush as the animals waited for the leader to emerge from the van. His bodyguard held open the door, and the ranger brought his hand to the side of his head in a salute. The other humans obviously considered the leader an important man.

The leader stepped out of the vehicle and looked around. To the deputy commander's dismay, the animals immediately forgot their neat little groups and moved around to get a better view of the leader. The smaller animals found their view blocked by the taller species and had to push to the front to see anything.

A disgruntled Puff Adder found himself looking at hundreds of sets of feet and wondered why he had bothered to come at all.

The leader wore big sunglasses and a wide-brimmed hat to protect him from the sun, which was now shining down fiercely. He noticed the huge group of animals move towards him and clung to the side of the van door in alarm.

'Move back! Move back!' shouted Alfie. The leader was clearly afraid.

The animals shuffled obediently back a few paces, the ones in front accidentally stepping on those behind them, and the leader let go of his grip on the door. The ranger walked away from the van and stood next to Alfie, no more than a few metres away from the animals. He beckoned for the other two men to follow him, which they did but reluctantly so, with the bodyguard in front and the leader keeping close behind him.

'He doesn't seem much like a leader to me,' remarked Lion. 'He looks like a bit of a coward.'

'I agree,' said Lioness in surprise. 'I expected him to be bigger than that, too.'

'You must realise how daunting this is for the men,' Alfie reminded the animals. 'They have never been in a situation with hundreds of wild animals in front of them before. If you chose to charge at them, they would not have a chance. They are having to be as trusting as you are.'

'Charging at them sounds like a good idea to me,' growled Buffalo.

The two men stood next to the ranger and faced the sea of animals standing in front of them. There was another silence as the humans and animals surveyed each other. The ranger kept shaking his head and smiling as if unable to believe the animals had all come together for this purpose, and he felt determined not to let them down.

The animals peered at the men, trying to size up the human leader. From his posture, he appeared to be middle-aged, and his belly was slightly round. His sunglasses hid his eyes, which made it difficult to understand much about his character, but he had a large moustache on top of what Stella thought looked like quite a cruel mouth. He, too, carried a gun, and the way he held it made it clear he knew how to use it.

It was also obvious to the animals that the leader's bodyguard was afraid of his boss, as the bodyguard nodded repeatedly and with some nervousness whenever the leader said anything. The ranger bowed a few times to the leader, and Alfie could tell he was anxious to please him.

'Would you introduce the animals to Mr Rich, please, Alfie?' said the ranger brightly, but the chimp detected tension in his voice. 'If I call out one species at a time, you can tell them who I'm calling and ask them to bow.'

Alfie was amazed. He couldn't believe what the ranger was asking him to do. 'They won't want to do that,' he signed back. 'Mr Rich may be a human leader, but he isn't the animals' leader. You can't ask them to bow to him as if he were more important than them.'

'What is he saying?' chorused some of the animals impatiently.

'The ranger wants you to bow to the leader, Mr Rich, by way of greeting,' said Alfie, looking rather puzzled. 'I know you won't want to, but could you all just bow quickly to please him? We do need to get Mr Rich on our side. I'm very sorry about this.'

'I won't be bowing to any humans,' said Puff Adder with a sneer. 'He'll have to accept my sincere apologies, but I'm afraid I can't go any lower.'

'I'm not going to bow either,' said Buffalo, 'not unless it's to charge at him.'

'Would everyone do what Alfie has asked, please?' said Stella, looking worried. 'It won't hurt us to do a small bow. On the count of three—one, two, three.'

Buffalo stood obstinately straight, but the rest of the animals dipped their heads slightly, feeling awkward. The ranger shook his head, and the bodyguard let out a guffaw, which he promptly silenced when Mr Rich turned to look at him. The leader himself showed no reaction at all, and the animals found it impossible to tell what he was thinking as the sunglasses still hid his eyes, and his mouth remained in a straight line.

'I don't like that leader,' whispered Bright to Stella. 'He doesn't look interested in us at all.'

Stella grimaced. 'I agree with you. The strange thing is, I had a bad feeling when I saw him arrive, too. Oh dear, I'm not sure this was such a good idea.'

Meanwhile, the ranger was busy talking to Mr Rich and the bodyguard. He pointed at the animals frequently, sometimes at individual species and sometimes at the group as a whole, although Mr Rich didn't seem to follow his pointing. The animals didn't understand anything that was being said, and they began to feel rather like they were there to be gawped at.

'I know what it must be like to be in a zoo now,' thought Leopard, remembering what Alfie had told her about humans going there to point and stare at the animals.

'The ranger is telling Mr Rich how important it is that we have more rangers in the park,' explained Alfie, realising the animals were looking rather bemused. 'He's making certain the leader understands how desperate the situation is and that there are only a small number of animals left in some species. He's doing his best for you. Mr Rich is a powerful man in the local area.'

'Yes, but it's quite plain the leader isn't listening,' said Puff Adder, voicing what everyone else was thinking but didn't like to say.

'Well, we must make him listen,' said Alfie. 'I think it's time for him to hear some of our stories. Leopard, would you like to be the first?'

CHAPTER 28

The Animals Tell
Their Stories

LEOPARD LOOKED AT THE chimp's worried face, so different from his usual vivacious expression, and she knew she couldn't let him down. 'Of course,' she said, smiling and stepping forward. For the first time, Mr Rich's attention seemed to be captured, and he turned to stare at Leopard as she walked towards the human trio.

'Alfie, tell the leopard to raise her right paw,' said the ranger excitedly, much to the chimp's disappointment. He couldn't believe what the ranger was asking the animals to do just because they were in front of a human leader.

Alfie repeated the request to Leopard apologetically, but she just laughed and did as she was asked.

'I suppose it's also so Mr Rich believes you really can communicate through me,' Alfie said.

Leopard raised her paw again and did a little wave, and the ranger clapped his hands and laughed in delight. The bodyguard also grinned and shook his head, but Mr Rich remained completely unmoved. If anything, the corners of his moustache seemed to turn further downwards.

Leopard told her story succinctly and with great style, and Alfie duly translated it through hand signals to the ranger. Of course, the ranger already knew what had happened to Leopard, but Alfie was keen for the animals to tell their own stories.

The animals saw the ranger use a lot of hand gestures as he translated to Mr Rich, and his face showed how terrible he thought it was that the poachers had set a trap to catch innocent wild animals. It was obvious to all the watching animals that the ranger cared very much, and they watched the leader to see how he would react.

The man still didn't say a word but dismissed Leopard's story with an impatient nod.

Leopard hesitated for a moment, wondering if she would have to answer any questions. Alfie had a brief conversation in sign with the ranger, who spoke to the other men again.

Alfie thanked her and told her that was all she needed to do. The cat was a bit surprised, but she walked back to her cubs without another word.

'Stella, would you tell your story now, please?' asked Alfie.

The great elephant stepped forwards, and the zebras in front of her moved aside to let her through. All eyes followed the famous leader of the elephant herd. Bright noticed that the human leader's attention was captured once again.

Stella settled herself, careful not to get too close to Mr Rich as, in her usual considerate way, she didn't want to frighten him.

'Alfie, ask the elephant to raise her left foot instead of the right one,' said the ranger, winking at the chimp.

Alfie looked at him with dismay. He hesitated for a moment and then sighed. 'Stella, I'm so sorry to ask you,' he said, 'would you mind lifting your left foot? Again, it's so Mr Rich believes we really can communicate with each other. Thank you.'

The elephant leader steadied herself and with the greatest of dignity raised her front foot for a moment before returning to stand on all fours. She looked from one face to the next, taking care to address all three men.

'My father was one of the bravest elephants who has ever lived on these plains,' she began in her clear, deep voice. Alfie translated everything she said to the ranger as the words left her mouth, and the ranger spoke aloud to the human leader and the bodyguard.

'He was the kindest and most generous leader. Everyone who knew him admired and liked him, and he made sure the herd wanted for nothing, even if it meant hardship for himself. He would go without food so our young elephants could eat. He would venture on long journeys alone to find the best areas for us to inhabit, and he risked death to defend our territory, even stretching its boundaries farther back. In all his years, he never hurt a single animal other than in the defence of his herd.'

Stella paused for a moment to collect her thoughts. There was total silence, with every animal listening to what she said. Even the human leader was paying attention, although Bright noticed he seemed to be eyeing her mother's gentle face with a steely gaze.

'My father was murdered, ruthlessly shot by poachers,' cried Stella in distress as the memory of that terrible day came back to her. 'A few bullets from a gun were all it took to end the life of a magnificent leader and wonderful father.

'Did the men pause or feel guilt for the great animal they had killed as his body lay in the dust? No. They couldn't wait to jump on him and saw the tusks from his noble face. So, while the herd was in utter devastation, the poachers carried off their trophies without even a hint of remorse and left my father's body just lying there, dead and butchered.'

The rest of the elephant herd nodded solemnly as she spoke. Mabel burst into tears as she remembered seeing Hero fall.

'We visit his grave every year on the anniversary of his death,' Stella told them, 'but there's nothing we can do to bring him back. Yet all they wanted were his tusks!'

The listening animals were so silent you could have heard a lion roar several miles away. The ranger looked grim. The bodyguard had a sympathetic expression on his face as Alfie translated and the ranger spoke, but the leader's face remained impassive, and Stella realised her story hadn't impressed him at all. The man seemed to stare back at her through his sunglasses, making her feel uncomfortable.

The elephant leader looked hard at the human leader in return. Was there something familiar about him? She tried to think back over the humans she had seen before, but she couldn't quite recall where she'd seen him. His scent seemed familiar, too. Stella wondered if she would recognise his voice.

'Alfie,' she said suddenly to the chimp, 'would you ask Mr Rich what he thinks he could do to help us? I'd like to hear his ideas from his own mouth.'

'Yes, of course,' said Alfie, pleased to be useful. He put the question to the ranger, and the animals listened as the ranger asked Mr Rich, who answered with a few brief words.

Stella stared into the distant plains as the leader spoke for the first time. Now she felt sure the man was familiar. She had also heard his voice before, but where?

'He said he is going to have to think about it,' said Alfie, by way of reply. 'I expect he will have to talk to other local leaders, too, before they can make any decisions.'

So we need a committee to decide whether we should be allowed to go on living, thought Leopard rather bitterly. She glanced at her cubs, who were wandering around at the back of the group and starting to look bored. Leopard knew they would much rather be off playing in the grass.

'Who else would like to tell their stories?' asked Alfie, scanning the group.

A figure trembling between Giraffe's legs caught his eye. 'Cheetah,' he said gently, 'do you think you could tell the leader how difficult it is to find a mate?'

Some of the animals tittered, and Leopard cringed. Cheetah stared at Alfie, unable to believe his ears. First, the chimpanzee was rude to him about not being able to retract his claws, and now he was asking him to tell the whole crowd how unpopular he was.

Alfie realised his mistake. 'By that I mean there are very few other cheetahs around because of all the poaching that has taken place,' he explained.

'There's more cheaters than you think,' called out one of the meerkats cheekily. 'Have you ever played a game with Puff Adder?'

The meerkats shrieked with laughter until the deputy commander told them to stop, whilst Puff Adder had poisonous thoughts about what he would like to do to the meerkats.

Cheetah was slightly mollified by Alfie's explanation, but the prospect of talking in front of all the other animals and the humans made his heart race with anxiety. 'I'm sorry, I'm afraid I can't,' the cat almost whispered. Alfie was about to encourage him when he caught sight of Leopard frowning and shaking her head.

'I'd like to tell my story,' said Zebra suddenly. 'I want this leader to know that all the animals are being affected by the terrible things the poachers do, and not just a few species.'

Alfie nodded. 'Of course,' he said. 'That is exactly why I wanted everyone to come today. Please come forward, Zebra.'

As Zebra moved away from the group to stand in front of the men, Dent stepped in to take his place in the crowd. For the first time, Dent was able to see the leader and his bodyguard. While Zebra told the dreadful tale of what had happened to his daughter and two little nephews, Dent looked in Mr Rich's direction and sniffed for his scent. The rhino stepped closer until he could detect the leader's scent quite well.

A horrified expression came over Dent's face and he fell into a dead faint, collapsing on the ground just in front of the elephants and other rhinos.

CHAPTER 29

Who Is Mr Rich, Really?

LEADER AND FELICITY GASPED and rushed forwards to look after their friend while Stella followed quickly behind them.

There were cries from the other animals: 'What happened?' 'Is he all right?' 'Perhaps it was the heat.'

'Perhaps he was over-excited,' suggested Mabel.

'What by? The fantastic promises of help the leader has been offering us?' asked Puff Adder sarcastically.

Dent felt as if he were swimming in a hot sea that gently lifted him this way and that. He drifted along on the waves, feeling quite helpless and unable to fight the strength of the tide. He could see the clouds above him in an otherwise crystal-clear sky, and they floated past quickly as he was tossed from one wave to the next.

The clouds seemed to form distinctive shapes that he recognised. There was Leader and his new friend Felicity, playing on what must have been rocks. There was the motherly Stella and Bright, both of whom he knew he could always trust. His mind turned slowly further back. There was a mouse he had almost forgotten, and an oxpecker perched on a large figure. It was his beloved mother, and she turned to speak to him, her eyes full of concern, but before she could say anything, there was an explosion, and the form of his mother merged into the cloud that was the ground.

Another shape rushed towards her and bent over while Dent watched in dismay. It was a human man! The man seemed preoccupied with the body of his beautiful mother, and Dent knew he mustn't make a noise in case the man noticed him. For some reason, the man looked up and stared straight at him, and Dent shrank back in terror, knowing he was in danger. He caught the man's scent, glimpsed his blood-stained face, and the dream blurred . . .

Dent jerked his head up from the ground. 'It's the leader! It's the leader!' he shrieked uncontrollably. 'It's Mr Rich, the leader!'

'Calm down, Dent,' he heard Stella's soothing voice say. 'You've had a nightmare. The leader's gone. The ranger's gone. They aren't here now.'

'It's the leader!' cried Dent again. 'It was him! I saw him, and I recognised his scent. I remember!'

The little group standing over him included Stella, Bright, Leader, Felicity, and Alfie, and they all looked very concerned.

Dent tried again, beside himself with frustration. 'I remember now. I've smelt his scent before. It was the leader who did it, I'm certain.'

Stella and Bright looked at each other. 'What do you mean, Dent?' asked Stella gently.

'What did the leader do?' asked Alfie, suddenly realising what the little rhino might be saying.

'It was him!' cried Dent again. 'The leader killed my mother!'

There was a dreadful silence while the animals thought about the implications of Dent's words.

'Are you sure?' asked Bright, horrified.

'I'm absolutely positive,' said Dent. 'I thought I was picking up a familiar scent, but I couldn't be sure as it wasn't very strong, but then Zebra moved, and I went a bit closer, and I smelled him. I know it's him. I remember the scent from my mother's body, and I also remember the voices of the men as they stood over her.'

'I can't believe it,' said Alfie, looking aghast. 'Mr Rich is one of the leaders responsible for engaging new rangers for the park. That's why I thought he was important for us to talk to. He has previously told the ranger there isn't enough money to pay for any more rangers. Maybe he just doesn't want more rangers, or they might discover what he is up to.'

'I thought I recognised him, too,' Stella admitted, 'but I couldn't be certain because it was a long time ago, and I was standing too far away to see him clearly, although I did hear him shout.'

She turned to Bright. 'Do you remember the poacher who shot your grandfather?' she asked.

'I remember seeing three men,' her daughter replied.

'Yes, but the one who actually had the gun,' said Stella, 'don't you remember? The one with the moustache, that distinctive stance.'

'Do you think it was him?' Bright asked with wide eyes.

Stella nodded slowly. 'I couldn't remember where I'd seen him before until I heard what Dent said,' she told her. 'Now I think we've just met with the man responsible for the death of your lovely grandfather.'

The little group stared at each other, the realisation of how awful the situation was sinking in.

'He's just pretending to be concerned for the park animals then,' said Alfie, looking angry.

'All the time, he was probably sizing up the horns and tusks and fur coats he could see,' said Bright. 'I saw him looking at your face with great interest, Mum.'

'The ranger plainly doesn't realise either,' said Stella, 'or surely he would never have asked us to meet this man.'

'No, absolutely not,' said Alfie. 'No, the ranger doesn't know Mr Rich's little secret. I guarantee it.'

'Why don't we tell him?' suggested Leader. 'Then Mr Rich could be taken away.'

All eyes looked at Alfie, who smiled rather sadly. 'I'm afraid I don't think the ranger would believe me,' he said. 'He is a wonderful man, but he is, after all, a human. I'm not sure he would believe the claims of wild animals over someone like Mr Rich. I think the ranger would laugh if I tried to tell him Mr Rich was a poacher. Even supposing he did believe me, I'm not sure he would dare to do anything about it. If he made any accusations against Mr Rich, I suspect the only thing that would happen is the ranger would lose his job.'

'So, there's nothing we can do?' asked Bright.

Alfie looked unhappy. His usually bright eyes were tired and despairing. 'The only thing that would expose Mr Rich is if we could find proof that he was involved in poaching,' he said. 'That way, the ranger could give the evidence to the police, and they could arrest him. Poaching endangered species in the National Park is forbidden by human laws, and humans punish people who break those laws. Unfortunately, their police system needs evidence to identify the guilty person, and we don't have any of that.'

'We can tell them he's guilty,' cried Dent, as if it were obvious. 'I know it was his scent!'

'I don't think they would listen to animals, Dent,' said Stella gently. 'They would only take notice of what other humans say.'

'What kind of evidence would we need?' Bright asked Alfie.

'Photographs or human witnesses to Mr Rich's poaching,' said Alfie after a moment's thought. 'Or for the police to catch him with a store of tusks, horns, or furs.'

'In that case, I don't see how we can do anything,' said Stella. She stamped one of her huge front feet in a rare display of annoyance. 'This is so frustrating!' she cried. 'We've finally found the poacher who killed my beloved father and Dent's mother, and it seems as if there's nothing we can do to stop him from doing the same to other animals.'

'I will try talking to the ranger,' Alfie said reluctantly. 'I suspect Mr Rich might be the chief poacher in charge of others. If the ranger believes me, he could tail Mr Rich and his fellow poachers and catch them in the act, although, even then, it would be his word against the word of an important man.'

It was almost dark by then, and the animals realised they felt tired.

'I think we should go back to the rest of the herd and find somewhere safe to pass the night,' said Stella, trying to return to normality. She looked down at Dent, who was still lying on the ground. 'Do you feel well enough to walk, Dent?' she asked the little rhino kindly.

Dent scrambled to his feet. 'Yes, I'm fine now,' he said. 'I think it was just the shock of realising who the leader was that made me faint.'

Stella noticed Felicity was standing next to Leader. 'Where is your mother, dear?' she asked her. 'Is she sleeping somewhere nearby?'

Felicity shook her head. 'I don't think so,' she said. 'She got angry with me when I said I wanted to stay with Leader and Dent, and she stormed off. Now I don't know where she is. I don't think she wants me to be friends with anyone except other rhinos.'

The other animals looked at Felicity's unhappy face and felt sorry for her. She was so friendly and kind and so different from Wanda.

'You stay with us, and she'll come and find you when she's ready,' said Stella, draping her trunk over Felicity's neck to comfort her.

'I think I'll stay with you tonight, too,' said Alfie, much to the others' surprise. 'The ranger had to drive the leader and his bodyguard back, and I wanted to see that you were okay, Dent, so he left me here. He said he'd come back tomorrow to pick me up if I didn't make my own way home.'

'Does the ranger live a long way away from here?' asked Bright.

'It's a long walk in the dark,' said Alfie, 'especially when you've got legs as short as mine.'

The animals broke into laughter, glad to relieve the tension a little.

'In fact, I think chimpanzees lose out in many respects,' said Alfie, breaking into his usual grin. 'What other species have legs as hairy as ours and such huge ears?'

'I'm sorry, but I don't think you're in a position to complain about the size of your ears,' said Stella with a twinkle in her eye.

'No,' added Bright, 'and I think your nose is rather delicate compared to ours.'

The friends laughed merrily and forgot their troubles for a while before wandering away from the valley in the direction of the elephant herd.

The sky was as clear as it had been during the day, and the moon and stars shone brightly. As he walked, Alfie looked up at the moon and remembered his conversation with Leopard. 'You can play the piano, you can fly to the moon, and you can certainly beat poachers,' he had said. 'You must never give up on anything, even when it seems impossible.'

The fight against the poachers was beginning to seem impossible now, even to Alfie. He suddenly felt extremely worried for the safety of the endangered species. If one of the humans responsible for their wellbeing was a poacher himself, what chance did they have? Mr Rich had everything in his favour whilst the animals could only rely on their instincts, with horns and tusks that could do nothing against guns. It seemed as if even the ranger might be of no help to them now.

He watched Stella and Bright as they walked and saw that determination had not left their eyes. Leader, Dent, and Felicity were chattering with excitement despite the day's events, and Alfie chastised himself. *These brave animals haven't given up*, he thought. *What am I doing, giving up so easily? I'm supposed to be here to help them.*

'We're not going to let the poachers win!' he vowed aloud. 'We're going to find a way to catch Mr Rich!'

Stella looked at him with a smile. 'Of course we are,' she said. 'I never doubted it for a moment. If Mr Rich thinks he can continue to get away with poaching, he has underestimated the animals of these plains.'

CHAPTER 30

Alfie Can't Sleep

THAT NIGHT, ALFIE FOUND it impossible to sleep. Once the elephants had settled down in a safe group of trees, the herd soon dozed off, leaving Bright on guard and Alfie tossing and turning in the prickly grass. The chimp had come to like his soft bed with its warm covers, and he found the grass very uncomfortable. The night was clear, but it was also cold. Alfie almost drifted off to sleep several times, only to wake and find himself shivering. To make matters worse, his mind raced with thoughts about the day's events as his brain went over the options left to the animals.

This is hopeless, Alfie thought as he gazed up at the blinking stars. *I'm no nearer going to sleep now than when I first lay down, and dawn can't be far away.*

Thoughts of Mr Rich crowded everything else out. He went over the problem again and again in his mind—what could the animals do to expose Mr Rich as a poacher? There were undoubtedly other poachers in the park, but Alfie suspected Mr Rich might be the man in charge of the gruesome operation. The ranger had told him what a wealthy businessman Mr Rich was, and Alfie knew enough of how humans operated to imagine that Mr Rich might easily persuade other humans to help him, either by threatening them or paying them money. Alfie suspected Mr Rich would also have connections with other wealthy humans to whom he could sell his poaching gains.

Alfie's thoughts turned to the ranger, and he wondered if the ranger would be brave enough to help the animals, no matter what it took. He remembered the ridiculous things the ranger had asked the animals to do to please Mr Rich, and the way the ranger had bowed to the leader and hung on his every word. Alfie decided that, sadly, his lovely ranger was probably too in awe of Mr Rich for him to believe the man was a cold-blooded poacher.

Alfie sighed and rolled over, trying to get more comfortable. There seemed to be sharp shoots of bush digging into his skin and stones everywhere, stopping him from finding a flat piece of ground. He opened one eye and squinted around at the herd. To his amazement, the elephants and the two rhinos were all sleeping peacefully. How did they manage it? Didn't they feel the cold? At least the elephants were sleeping standing up, so it wouldn't feel as if dozens of needles were being pressed into the tenderest parts of their skin.

As Bright stood on watch, listening for any sound that might mean danger, she heard Alfie sigh heavily again and mutter to himself. Bright stepped quietly around the other members of the herd to where the chimp was lying.

'Can't you sleep?' she whispered. Alfie nearly jumped out of his skin, so preoccupied with his thoughts that he hadn't heard her coming.

Alfie smiled a tired smile and shook his head. 'I'm trying to think how we can prove Mr Rich is a poacher,' he whispered back. 'The more I think about it, the more impossible it seems. I so want to help you all, but I'm running out of ideas.'

Bright smiled back at him. 'It isn't really your problem,' she said truthfully. 'We should be able to protect ourselves without needing to ask you or the ranger for help.'

'Yes, but you can't,' said Alfie, thinking again how brave and independent the elephants were. 'It's an unequal battle. You don't have any guns. The only way to stop Mr Rich is for him to be taken away by the human police—unless, of course, we somehow try to remove him ourselves.'

'We could never do that,' said Bright firmly. 'Unnecessary violence is completely against the principles of the savanna.'

'Then I don't see what we can do,' said Alfie.

'What about the ranger?' whispered Bright after a while. 'Don't you think he might help us?'

Alfie shook his head. 'I know him very well now,' he said. 'I don't think he will believe Mr Rich is a poacher unless he sees evidence.'

'Then we'll have to get him the evidence he needs,' replied Bright. 'Perhaps you could use one of those machines to take a picture of Mr Rich aiming his gun at an animal, or we could find his collection of poached items and take the ranger there.'

Alfie considered these ideas, and a spark of hope awoke in his mind, but it was quickly extinguished when he realised the difficulties.

'I don't have a phone or a camera, although I could probably borrow one,' he said, 'but how would we know when Mr Rich was coming, to make sure we got a video of him shooting at an endangered species like an elephant or rhino? We would need some poor creature to act as the target, and one of our friends might be killed. Even then, there is no guarantee we'd be able to get the endangered species and Mr Rich in the same video. It's not illegal for humans to hunt other animals, so unless an endangered animal were also clearly visible, it would be no kind of evidence.'

'It's still a possibility, though,' persisted Bright.

Alfie marvelled at her determination. 'Well, yes, it is a possibility,' he said, 'but it's a difficult one.'

'What about finding his store of tusks and horns?' whispered Bright. 'We could do that. Martial Eagle could follow Mr Rich away from the plains to find out where he lives.'

'Yes, but how would we get inside his house?' said Alfie. 'That's even supposing he keeps the store at his house.'

'You aren't being very positive tonight,' said Bright, a little impatient. 'I thought Leopard told me you believed anything could be done if you tried hard enough. It sounds to me like you have already given up.'

Alfie sat up, suddenly more determined. 'You're right!' he said, rather too loudly. Dent, who was sleeping nearest to the chimp, stirred slightly. The little rhino wriggled his feet, but his eyes remained tightly closed.

'It's no good, Felicity. I don't know how to fly,' Dent mumbled before falling silent and back into a deep sleep.

Bright giggled, and Alfie chuckled under his breath. 'That sounds like an interesting dream,' said the chimp with a grin.

'You should try to get some sleep, too,' whispered Bright after a while. She looked down at Alfie with concern. 'Please don't worry about us so much. We don't expect you to work miracles.'

'I'm completely wide awake now,' said the chimp, jumping to his feet and reaching over his shoulder to brush bits of grass from his back. He looked up at the big shadowy frame blocking out the moon above him.

'I'm going to go for a wander,' he told Bright. 'I think better when I'm moving around.'

'Well, be careful,' said Bright. 'You are rather vulnerable on your own.'

'I can take care of myself,' said Alfie, 'but thank you. I expect I shall be back soon but don't worry if I'm not. I've got a lot to think about.'

The elephant brushed the top of his head affectionately with her trunk. 'See you later,' she whispered.

'See you later,' Alfie replied, and he gave her a little wink.

Alfie wandered into the darkness, and Bright watched until she could no longer see his hunched figure. She thought about the dangers of the savanna at night and hoped he wouldn't meet with any trouble. At least he knew the animals in the group, and she knew they would never do him any harm, but there was no knowing who else might be out there.

Dent stirred again and opened his eyes. 'Who was that?' he asked, barely awake.

'Don't worry. It was Alfie,' Bright whispered. 'Be quiet and go back to sleep. We don't want to wake the others.'

CHAPTER 31

Kidnapped!

ALFIE STRODE THROUGH THE grass, up and down little hills and around termite mounds. The mounds looked like mysterious towers in the darkness, spreading long, black shadows away from the moon's light. The chimp liked to imagine they were alive, staring solemnly out across the plains, noticing everything going on there.

The savanna was quiet, with only the distant baying of hyenas breaking the silence. Alfie stopped to look around him and felt alone. The silent figure of an owl swept across the sky, and Alfie saw a darting movement in the grass as a mouse hurried by. The owl swooped but missed and returned to the air with empty talons, whilst the mouse kept quite still until the owl had flown away.

A small figure poked her head out from behind a baobab tree and quickly drew back again when Alfie looked in her direction. Alfie wasn't quite as alone as he thought.

The chimp found a fallen log and sat quietly, surveying the land around him. He could tell that dawn was not far off now, as the black of the horizon was just beginning to lighten in the east.

I've got to think of a way to catch Mr Rich, thought Alfie. *Otherwise, the endangered species are in terrible trouble. He'll kill them all in the end—what am I going to do?*

He gazed at the ground and drew a little pattern in the dust with a stick. For the first time, he found that he had no ideas at all, and it was a helpless feeling he didn't like. He ran over the suggestions Bright had made and realised that she was right: the only chance they had was for him to convince the ranger that Mr Rich was a poacher. The animals would have to find some way of making sure the ranger saw Mr Rich in action.

'I'll go home and speak to the ranger when he wakes up,' Alfie said aloud 'He's the only chance the animals have.'

The chimp stood up and yawned. He felt extremely tired and wondered if he could face the long walk back to the ranger's little house. However, he was also cold, and the prospect of a warm house with good food was a nice one, so Alfie set off with renewed determination.

He hadn't gone far when he spotted a familiar figure ahead, standing hock-deep in the grass. The big animal was quite alone and in a very open part of the savanna, a long way from any cover.

'Wanda,' Alfie called with some alarm, 'what are you doing out here on your own?'

The rhino lifted her head from grazing. She sniffed at the air in his direction, as she couldn't see who had called her. 'It's the chimpanzee, isn't it?' she said rather sourly.

Alfie hurried to where she stood and looked up at her. 'Yes, it's me,' he said. 'I'm just heading home.'

'Oh, good,' Wanda said. 'I don't like being bothered by other animals.'

'You should go nearer to cover, especially when you're on your own like this,' Alfie warned her. 'You're very vulnerable. You'd have nowhere to hide if poachers were to come. I'm sure they'd be delighted to get hold of horns as impressive as yours.'

'That's none of your business, really,' said Wanda. 'As for being on my own, I wouldn't be, except that Felicity has decided she would rather stay with an elephant herd than with her own mother.'

'She only wanted to see that Dent was all right,' said Alfie, cautious not to argue with the big, unfriendly animal.

Wanda opened her mouth to say that she thought animals were better off staying with their own kind when they both heard a noise. Alfie felt his heart jump, and he strained his ears to hear better. It sounded like an engine and one that wasn't too far away.

Alfie tried to think who it might be. He could hear that it wasn't the ranger's van as the engine sounded deeper, and he had never seen tourists in the savanna so early in the day. A feeling of apprehension came over him, and he looked at Wanda uneasily.

'Can you hear that noise?' he asked.

'Yes. It's a van, isn't it?' answered the rhino, and Alfie detected a note of fear in her voice.

'I'm afraid it might be poachers,' Alfie whispered. 'I think we should get away from here as quickly as possible. They could arrive here in no time in their van, and with the sun starting to rise, they would see us at once.'

'But we're so far from any cover. What can we do?' said Wanda. Now Alfie knew she was frightened, as her eyes were wide open.

'We might be lucky, and they'll turn off in another direction,' said Alfie, 'but we have to move fast. That van is getting closer all the time. Quick–come with me!'

Alfie scampered off, and Wanda followed him as fast as she could. They hurried over the rough ground, trying to put as much distance as possible between them and the van, but the drone of the engine remained steady as they ran. The chimpanzee and the rhino sprinted through the grass, and Alfie cursed Wanda silently for straying so far from cover. If he had been alone, he could have hidden in one of the little acacia bushes they bolted past, but now he had to help the rhino survive. Alfie glanced ahead, hoping to see some thicker bushes, but he saw only endless grassland with sparse trees that seemed to stretch out in all directions. He steeled himself to run for miles, if necessary, but Wanda had already begun to drop behind.

'I'm getting tired, Alfie,' the rhino cried desperately, 'and the van's getting closer–what are we going to do?'

Alfie slowed down to allow her to catch up, and Wanda promptly stopped running. She gasped heavily, trying to catch her breath.

'Don't stop!' Alfie shouted at her. 'Just catch up, and then let's go again. We'll try bending around those termite mounds and changing direction a little to see if we can lose them.'

'I can't,' said Wanda between pants. 'I can't carry on. That's all there is to it.'

'You've got to try!' shouted Alfie, struggling not to get angry with her. 'They'll be here any moment, and once they spot you, it will all be over. Think of Felicity. She needs her mother!'

The roar of the engine was coming closer all the time. Now Alfie could see the van's lights as little pinpricks through the acacias. He wondered at the van's accuracy—had it been luck that the driver was able to follow the animals so precisely? Perhaps they had a device that enabled them to track Wanda.

Alfie suddenly realised what it might be—he himself wore a tracking device around his neck so the ranger could always find him in the grasslands—perhaps the driver had been able to follow his own signal.

The chimp tore the device from his neck, threw it as far away as he could, and turned to look at Wanda again. He was frustrated to see that she hadn't recovered at all. There was no way the rhino could continue, and the van was bearing down on them fast. Alfie realised it was up to him to save Wanda's life. He looked at the van and then back to where the rhino was still heaving for breath.

'You stay here,' he ordered. 'When you feel better, run in the direction we've been going, and I'll go back and try to distract them.'

The rhino nodded, unable to say anything, and Alfie raced back the way they had come. Up ahead, the lights of the van came straight towards him, and for a moment, his courage almost failed. He would have to get close enough for the driver to see him so he could lead them in the wrong direction.

Alfie slowed for a moment and swung around to see if Wanda had moved. To his relief, she was trotting away, albeit slowly. However, the van was gaining rapidly, and he knew he had to stick to his plan.

The van came closer and closer until Alfie was almost blinded by the headlights. He stood directly in the vehicle's path and waited until he thought the driver had seen him. Time seemed to slow as the purr of the engine became louder, and the van bore down on him. Then, right at the last minute, when the vehicle was no more than twenty metres away, Alfie sprang to his right and raced across the grass. He listened for the van to change direction. If it didn't, his plan would fail, and Wanda would be killed.

Suddenly, there came a noise he hadn't anticipated. The sound of a gun exploded behind him, echoing around the distant hills, and every muscle in the chimp's body tensed.

They're after me! thought Alfie in horror.

The bullet missed. Alfie heard it whistle over his head. He forgot about Wanda and catching Mr Rich and instead devoted everything he had to trying to survive. The chimp saw a fleeting image of himself lying in the grass in a pool of his own blood, and he vowed that he wasn't going to die at the hands of poachers.

He darted from side to side to make it more difficult for the poachers to shoot him. Adrenaline flooded his body, and his legs moved faster than ever before. There came another enormous crack from behind him, and Alfie instinctively ducked. He was lucky—the bullet skimmed past his side, missing him by a tiny margin.

Alfie scuttled around rocks and little bushes, trying to take the most difficult path for his pursuers in their van. His heart thumped in his chest, and he felt the first indications that his body was getting tired. His arms and legs began to feel heavy, aching as he urged them to go faster. Alfie knew he was beginning to slow, and despite the rough terrain, the van was gaining on him.

Alfie didn't hear the last shot they fired. He felt dizzy, and all he heard was the sound of his heart echoing around in his head. There came a terrible pain as if somebody had kicked him exceptionally hard in his right shoulder, but it was brief, and he blacked out in an instant.

The chase over, the van drew up slowly beside the chimp's body, and two men jumped out. Some distance away, Wanda heard the noise of the engine drop, and she bit her lip, wondering if Alfie was safe, knowing he had put himself in great danger for her. She didn't like to think about what the other animals might say to her if Alfie had been killed. She knew she should never have been out in the open on her own. It was all her fault!

Meanwhile, two men bent down to pick up the chimp's body, which was now quite still. There was a gash on Alfie's shoulder where the bullet had hit him, and blood was pouring down his arm, making his black hair sticky. The men carried him to their van and threw his body on a rug in the back seat.

Alfie was bleeding badly, but he wasn't dead. In his semi-conscious state, he dimly recognised Mr Rich's voice.

'Good. That's gotten rid of the wretched chimpanzee,' said Mr Rich. He let out a cruel laugh. 'Now he won't be telling any stories to his ranger about who the leader of the poachers is.'

'He's a clever animal,' said Mr Rich's companion. 'I didn't know chimps could communicate in sign language.'

'There aren't many that can,' said Mr Rich. 'That will be useful. Such an extraordinary chimp will fetch an excellent price. I have several rich friends who I think might like a nice playmate for their children.'

Alfie stirred, feeling as though the conversation were a dream. He opened his eyes a tiny slit, enough to see the two men peering down at him, and immediately shut them again, hoping they hadn't seen.

'We'll have to get that bullet out,' said the second man, eyeing the wound uneasily. 'Otherwise, the only companion he'll make will be a rather silent, stuffed one.'

Mr Rich laughed again. 'Yes, we'll get it out, but we'll go back to the house first. I don't want the ranger turning up and seeing his little friend bleeding all over the back of the van. Let's go!'

Wanda heard the engine start up again, and she felt dreadful. She tried to put the growing feeling of anxiety out of her mind, but something inside her knew Alfie was in terrible trouble.

Meanwhile, unbeknown to Wanda, another creature had seen the whole episode, who trembled as she watched the van drive away. The secretary bird had been following her hero ever since the meeting with Mr Rich, although at a distance, so he wouldn't realise. She had settled down to roost for the night near to where the elephants were sleeping but had awoken at the sound of Alfie's voice. The secretary bird had watched him talk to Bright for a while, wishing she dared to join the conversation. Then, to her surprise, Alfie had walked off on his own, and the secretary bird had set off in quick pursuit. She had seen him meet Wanda and watched as Alfie had spoken to her.

Why is he wasting his time with that rude animal? the bird had thought to herself. *Why doesn't he talk to me instead?*

The secretary bird had been as alarmed as Alfie and Wanda to hear an engine coming. She had followed the pair as they ran away and perched on a nearby acacia branch while Alfie had tried to persuade Wanda to keep running.

Yes, come on, you awkward creature, she had thought when Wanda refused to continue. *You're putting Alfie in great danger*.

She had watched in horror when the chimp turned back towards the vehicle, and almost shrieked at him not to do it. The secretary bird found herself torn between trying to stop him from getting into trouble and not giving away the fact that she had been following him.

As Alfie got closer to the van, the secretary bird saw a gun barrel emerge through the window, and she almost had a heart attack. The lovely Alfie was going to be shot! In a rare display of bravery, she hovered in front of the van, determined to make things difficult for the poachers.

Although Alfie didn't realise it at the time, the men missed him twice because the driver had to swerve to avoid an annoying bird that appeared out of nowhere.

The secretary bird let out a little sob. 'This is terrible, quite terrible. Absolutely appalling, in fact,' she muttered to herself. 'Goodness me, what am I going to do? Oh, my goodness–what can I do?'

She watched the van disappear into the early dawn, and the secretary bird made the biggest decision of her life: she charged her wings and flew off after the van, where Alfie lay all alone.

'I'll rescue you, Alfie!' she twittered nervously. 'I've got no idea how, but I'll do it somehow, I promise!'

CHAPTER 32

Stella Takes Charge

WANDA FELT UTTERLY MISERABLE. She returned to where she had last seen Alfie and called out his name again and again. She picked up Alfie's scent and felt hopeful for a moment, following it to see if she could find him. She sniffed around, and his scent seemed to grow stronger. The rhino hurried her pace as she followed it around rocks and bushes. Alfie had taken a difficult route to follow.

At one point, Alfie's scent seemed to disappear without a trace. Of course, that was where he had been picked up and put into the van, but Wanda didn't know that. She wandered around with her head stooped in the grass and her powerful nose to the ground, hoping to find a clue to tell her what had happened.

It wasn't long before Wanda saw the pool of blood on the ground. It was still fresh. Her heart sank. Whatever had happened to Alfie, he must have been hurt.

The rhino stood rooted to the spot, not knowing what to do. A dreadful feeling of guilt overwhelmed her. Although she had always preferred to live a solitary life, she had begun to appreciate the friendly group of animals living on the plains. She could see they always tried to help each other and could be relied upon as friends in times of trouble. Then there was Alfie, who was trying so hard to help the animals, even though he stood to gain nothing himself. He wasn't threatened by the poachers. He could simply stay in his comfortable house and close his eyes to the problems of the animals if he wanted to, but he didn't. He did everything he could to help them, even when it meant putting himself in danger.

Wanda felt very small and very selfish. If Alfie had been killed by the poachers, she knew it would be because of her. The rhino tried to think what else she could do, but she realised it was hopeless. She didn't know where Alfie was or what had happened to him. Reluctantly, she decided she had to find Stella and tell her the dreadful news. She knew it would make her even more unpopular with the other animals, but it had to be done.

They're going to hate me even more for this! she thought, and she was surprised at how bad it made her feel.

Dawn arrived while Wanda trudged several miles to find the elephant herd. A beautiful, pale blue light spread gradually across the dark sky, and the early morning sun scattered its golden rays through the plains. Wanda shivered and welcomed the sun's warmth on her back, but even the lovely new day did nothing to lift her spirits.

The rhino found the herd quite easily, as she had recalled Stella mentioning where they were headed. She remembered how she had been supposed to find the herd, join Felicity, and stay with the elephants for the night. Why hadn't she done that? If she had spent the night with the herd, none of this would have happened. She had stupidly made a stand against the mixing of the species because it was strange to her.

♦♦♦♦♦

Stella had awoken early and was talking to Buffalo, whose herd was nearby as Wanda approached. There was no sign of Felicity, who had gone to the waterhole with Leader and Dent to have a water fight, and Wanda felt quite relieved as she didn't want her daughter to be there when she made her confession.

Wanda stepped nervously towards the herd, many of whom were still sleeping, and picked up fragments of what Buffalo was saying. She caught her own name several times and that of Felicity, and she realised Buffalo was talking about how she had left Felicity and not returned.

'I think it's appalling!' said Buffalo with his usual bluntness. 'That poor young rhino is constantly embarrassed by the rude things her mother says, and then the heartless animal just leaves her with no explanation or idea of when she will come back. What a terrible mother!'

As Buffalo finished, Stella saw Wanda creeping towards them with tears rolling down her cheeks, and she cleared her throat hurriedly. Buffalo had been about to launch into further examples of the rhino's inconsiderate behaviour when he caught the signal and stopped to look behind him.

'Oh, she's back. And about time, too,' he said, but Stella noticed the tears and the wretched expression on Wanda's face and hushed him.

'I'm so sorry. Buffalo didn't mean to say anything to hurt you,' she said, thinking Wanda had been upset by Buffalo's words. 'Please forgive us. It was quite wrong of either of us to sound critical.'

Stella looked at Wanda anxiously. The rhino had stopped a few metres away and was now sobbing as if her heart had broken. Stella gave Buffalo a stern look. He was always upsetting other animals with his big mouth.

Buffalo looked back indignantly. Surely it couldn't have upset her that much. She was going on as if the world were about to end.

'There, there,' said Stella, and she kindly brushed the tears from Wanda's cheeks with her trunk. 'Buffalo didn't mean to be rude. He can be a bit tactless sometimes.'

Buffalo couldn't believe his ears. 'You're calling me rude?' he spluttered. 'What about some of the things Wanda's been saying about everyone else?'

'Shut up, Buffalo,' said Stella very firmly, and Buffalo promptly did so, turning his back on her in annoyance.

'Now, Wanda, dry your eyes, and we'll go and find Felicity,' Stella comforted. 'She wouldn't want you to be so upset. She didn't mind staying with us last night.'

The elephant looked down at the rhino in alarm. She seemed to be sobbing even harder.

'It's not that!' burst out Wanda. 'It's Alfie! I've done a terrible thing, Stella, and everyone's going to hate me for it.'

The rhino collapsed into wails again, and to Stella's amazement, she even pressed her head against Stella's side.

'Wanda, you mustn't get yourself into such a state,' she exclaimed, gently rubbing the rhino's head with her trunk. 'Whatever it is, it can't be that terrible. You can tell me about it. I won't hate you. I promise.'

'Well, *I* might,' Buffalo couldn't help but say.

Stella looked at him furiously, but Wanda didn't seem to have heard.

'It's Alfie,' she said, although it was difficult to understand her through the sobs. 'I think he's been shot by the poachers and captured or even dead, and it's all my fault. He was trying to save me from being shot because I was so stupid and went out into the middle of the grasslands where there wasn't any cover, and the poachers came in their van and chased us, and we tried to run away, and—'

'Slow down!' said Stella, trying to work out what had happened from Wanda's heaving sentences. 'Take a big breath and tell me slowly—how did you get away from the poachers? Where is Alfie now?'

Wanda gulped her way through the story while Stella, Buffalo, and Bright, who had now joined them, listened in silence (other than the occasional sigh of disbelief from Buffalo). The rhino finished and stared down at the ground in front of her, expecting an angry outburst from the three animals, but to her surprise, it didn't come. All were far more concerned with Alfie's fate than with what Wanda might have done.

'So, you don't know what happened to Alfie?' queried Stella.

Wanda shook her head. 'There was a pool of his blood in the grass,' she said, starting to sob again, 'but that's all I could find. He didn't answer when I called his name, and there was no sign of his body. I think they must have taken him away with them in the van.'

The rhino looked heartbroken, and Stella didn't want to press her for any more details. The important thing for now was to try to find Alfie. Everything else could wait.

Stella decided to ask one last question: 'Was there anyone else around who might have seen what happened? Try to remember if you can. It might help.'

Wanda thought for a moment and shook her head. 'The plains were completely deserted,' she said. 'I saw Lion and his pride, although they pretended not to see me, but that was some time before I bumped into Alfie.'

'Never mind,' said Bright. 'There might have been somebody you didn't notice. What are we going to do, Mum?'

'Well, first we need to arrange a search party for Alfie where Wanda last saw him,' said Stella. 'I also want to find out if anybody saw what happened to Alfie after Wanda and Alfie parted. You never know; someone might have an idea about where to find him.'

'What if we can't find him and nobody saw what happened?' asked Bright.

'I'm not sure,' admitted Stella, 'but we'll deal with that if we come to it.'

'I think we should charge at every group of humans we see,' said Buffalo angrily. 'They shouldn't be allowed to come into our land and interfere with our lives in this way.'

'Yes, Buffalo, I'm sure you're right,' said Stella, who had heard it all before and wasn't thinking about what she was saying.

Buffalo looked surprised, and his heart gave a little skip. At last, Stella had agreed! He began to imagine how he might organise his herd to charge, while Stella continued with her own, rather different plans.

'Would everyone gather round, please?' Stella called to the rest of the herd. 'I have some very bad news, I'm afraid.'

The elephant leader told the herd what had happened, and some of the elephants cast shocked reactions and accusing glares at poor Wanda, who didn't know where to look.

'I knew that animal was trouble the moment I first set eyes on her,' Mabel whispered far too loudly to Ethel.

Wanda hung her head in shame, and Stella responded to Mabel at once. 'No one other than the poachers is at fault here,' she said firmly. 'All that matters now is for us to find Alfie, and as quickly as possible. He might be lying injured somewhere in the grass, alone and vulnerable. Ethel, Mabel, Maud—I want you to lead the herd back to Moonlight Plains and search the area thoroughly, please.'

'That shouldn't take too long,' said Ethel. 'There's nowhere to hide there, apart from a few sparse bushes.'

'Meanwhile, Bright, Buffalo, and I will spread the news and ask if anyone saw Alfie being shot at last night,' Stella continued. 'Now, get to work straight away—we haven't a moment to lose.'

The herd obediently hurried away in the direction of the open plains with Leader's three big aunts at the front.

'Wanda, I want you to go to the waterhole and make sure Felicity, Dent, and Leader are safe while we are gone,' Stella told the rhino, who managed a small, grateful smile. She didn't want to be involved in telling the other animals what had happened. 'At the first sign of any humans, get them to cover at once,' the elephant added, but Wanda didn't need to be told. She had well and truly learned her lesson.

'Yes, of course, Stella,' she said humbly, and she headed away towards the waterhole, feeling a tiny bit happier. Stella hadn't been too angry with her, or if she had, she hadn't shown it. She hoped against hope that the elephants might yet find Alfie and that he would be okay.

CHAPTER 33

Martial Eagle Has Some News

BRIGHT SOON SPOTTED MARTIAL Eagle hovering way up in the sky, and she waved her trunk to get his attention. Martial Eagle plummeted towards her at great speed, turning aside at the very last minute and making Bright's stomach jump in surprise.

The bird landed and perched on a nearby tree root that had come out of the ground. 'Good morning!' he said, looking cheerful. 'What a beautiful day it's going to be.'

'Unfortunately, it's not quite as beautiful as you think,' said Bright. 'It looks as though Alfie may have been taken away by poachers. I take it you didn't see it happen?'

Martial Eagle's smile vanished at once, and he looked grim. 'No, I didn't. When did this happen?'

'Just before dawn,' Bright told him. 'He was trying to get Wanda to cover when the poachers arrived. The silly rhino was on her own in the middle of Moonlight Plains at dawn.'

Martial Eagle shook his head. 'You know me,' he said. 'I'm not one to criticise, but Wanda seems to cause a lot of trouble.' He thought for a moment and said, 'Do you want me to ask around if anyone else saw anything?'

Bright nodded. 'That would be really helpful,' she said gratefully. 'Stella and Buffalo are doing the same as we speak, but a pair of wings would make things much faster. Alfie might be in more danger with every passing moment. We have to find out what happened and where he is. Of course, he may also be dead.'

'Let's hope not,' said Martial Eagle. He stretched and shook himself in preparation to fly. 'I'll hurry around the plains to see what I can find out,' he said, and with a powerful beat of his wings, he was off.

Meanwhile, Stella sought out the meerkat commander-in-chief. The meerkats on watch in the grasslands directed her efficiently to where the commander was carrying out her duties. She was in the middle of instructing a group of very young meerkats when the elephant found her. The elephant listened with some amusement to the commander, who was briefing the group on what she called 'The Snake Response'.

'I'm very sorry to interrupt,' Stella broke in, 'but I must ask if any of your troops saw what happened to Alfie early this morning. He seems to have been taken away by poachers, just before dawn.'

The young meerkats gasped simultaneously. They had heard about the incredible chimpanzee who could speak to humans. The commander ordered silence, her face remaining as inscrutable as ever.

'My troops reported a van driving across Moonlight Plains early this morning,' she answered briskly, 'but none of them mentioned Alfie's presence. Would you like a search party organised?'

'It's very kind of you to offer,' said Stella, 'but my herd is already busy looking for him now.'

'Hmm,' said the commander. Privately, she didn't rate the elephant herd as highly as one of her own search units. 'Well, let me know if you need any assistance. I should be only too willing to help.'

Stella thanked her and moved off, hearing the commander resume her description of snakes as being the greatest danger in the animal kingdom. She allowed herself a smile and thought how proud Puff Adder would have been to hear her words.

Stella hurried on and soon came across the lion pride. With luck, Leopard and her cubs were also nearby. Leopard was aghast to hear her friend had been hurt and possibly killed by poachers. She fought back tears and remembered how Alfie had told her the poachers could be defeated if the animals were just determined enough. It seemed terrible that the bright and fun-loving chimp might have met his end at their hands.

'What was he doing out on the plains?' Leopard asked.

Stella noticed a catch in her voice and knew Leopard was upset. 'Apparently, he couldn't sleep,' the elephant replied. 'He was worrying about what to do to stop Mr Rich, but then he came across Wanda and tried to help her escape from the van, and that is all we know.'

'He is always more concerned for our well-being than for his own,' said Leopard, looking unhappy. The cubs nudged their little heads against her side, trying to get her attention.

'What's happened to Alfie, Mum?' one of them asked in his high voice.

'Is he going to come and teach us some more acro... acro...acrobatics?' asked the other.

'I don't know,' said Leopard shortly. 'We don't know where he is.'

'You could ask the meerkats,' suggested Lioness. 'I'm sure if anyone saw what happened, they did.'

'Thank you. That's a good idea,' said Stella, 'but I've just come from the commander's headquarters, and none of her troops saw anything except the van driving away.'

'Well, let us know if there is anything we can do to help,' said Lioness, and she nudged her mate.

'Yes, yes, anything at all,' said Lion hastily. 'You know the lions are always willing to help... as long as we aren't too busy, that is.'

'I'm coming with you,' said Leopard suddenly. 'He is a wonderful friend, and I want to help you find out what has happened to him. Come with me, children, quickly!'

Between them, Stella and Leopard spoke to the baboons, the ostriches, and the leaders of the zebra, wildebeest, and antelope herds, but no one knew anything about the incident.

'None of us went anywhere near Moonlight Plains last night,' said Baboon apologetically.

'Sorry, but we were asleep,' said Ostrich, looking rather puzzled. 'That's what we always do at night.'

'No, we didn't see or hear anything,' said Zebra. Antelope shook his impressive horns at the same time. 'Sorry, but that goes for my herd, too,' he said, and Wildebeest nodded.

'Well, thank you anyway,' said Stella politely, and she and the leopards moved on to try to find someone who might know more.

'It occurs to me that Alfie might have been kidnapped to keep him quiet,' said Leopard suddenly. 'After all, that Mr Rich saw how he could communicate with us and the ranger. Mr Rich wouldn't want Alfie telling the ranger that some of the wild animals recognised him as a poacher.'

'Yes, you may be right,' said Stella. 'So, the poachers may not have been after Wanda at all. They may have come for Alfie himself last night.'

Yes, and by the sounds of it, Alfie put himself directly in their path by trying to save Wanda,' said Leopard rather bitterly.

'Don't blame Wanda,' said Stella, who felt sorry for the rhino. 'She is very upset about what happened.'

At that moment, Martial Eagle swooped down from the sky and made Stella jump by landing on her back. 'Hello!' he said.

'Bright told me what happened. Have you found anyone who saw it yet?'

Stella and Leopard shook their heads at the same time. One of the cubs cried, 'Have you found Alfie, Mr Eagle?'

'No, I haven't,' said Martial Eagle, smiling at the cub's little voice, 'but I do have some news.' He jumped down to the ground to address Stella and Leopard. 'I spoke to my friend, Owl, and he told me he did see Alfie last night. He also heard the poachers' van arrive and said there were three gunshots after that. Owl went to see what had happened, but he was too late to see anything except the van driving off. He said there was no sign of Alfie, although he could have been inside the van. The important thing is that he saw someone else follow the van away.'

'Who?' demanded Stella and Leopard at the same time.

Martial Eagle grinned. 'Have a guess,' he said, looking from one face to the other. 'Who beams every time she sees Alfie?'

'The secretary bird?' said Stella in disbelief. 'What was she doing up in the night? She's a day-bird.'

'I suppose she must have been following Alfie,' said Martial Eagle. 'Anyway, Owl said she followed the van for as far as he could see, so if Alfie was in that van, she might be able to tell us where the poachers have taken him.'

'It may be too late by then,' said Leopard. 'They might have killed him by the time she gets back.'

'Yes, but they might not have done,' said Stella. 'Thank you, Martial Eagle. This is most helpful. Now we just need to wait for the secretary bird to return.'

CHAPTER 34

Buffalo Gets His Moment

MEANWHILE, BUFFALO WAS HAVING his own adventure. He spoke to the giraffes, who hadn't seen or heard anything about Alfie, and then he stumbled across Puff Adder lurking in the grass. The snake was not pleased to be discovered. He had snuck silently away from his old home and set up in a new area some distance away from the troublesome meerkats. The last thing he wanted was for the meerkats to find out his new address.

'You'd better promise not to tell them where you found me,' he hissed at Buffalo, who was alarmed by the vehemence in the snake's voice.

'Of course, I won't tell them if you don't want me to,' said Buffalo. He changed the subject. 'Did you see what happened to

Alfie last night by any chance? He was out on Moonlight Plains and seems to have been taken away by poachers.'

The snake replied that he hadn't been anywhere near Moonlight Plains, and Buffalo felt disappointed. It was nearly time to meet up with the elephants again, and it looked as if he would have nothing interesting to tell them. He turned away from Puff Adder and began to wander back to the meeting place, wondering if Stella or Bright had found out anything useful. He was deep in thought, and it was a while before he noticed the noise of the engine.

Suddenly, Buffalo realised there was a van bouncing along on the nearby road. It was quite close and coming towards him. The big animal raised his head to look and stopped in his tracks, rage surging inside him. He didn't know if the humans in the van were poachers or not, but at that moment, he didn't care.

Buffalo breathed heavily. He drew himself up to his full height and stamped his hoof on the ground several times. These humans would regret trespassing on the savanna yet again! This time, he was going to charge at them. After all, Stella had said he could.

As he waited, his muscles tensed, ready to launch his body into action.

The van slowed and came to a halt on the road just beyond Buffalo. Although Buffalo didn't know it, the guide had asked the driver to stop to allow the tourists to take photographs of the buffalo behind them. It was a party of friends on a safari holiday, and they were keen to take pictures of as many different animals as possible.

Buffalo hesitated. He was starting to lose his nerve just a tiny bit. It seemed as if none of the humans were going to get out, and the van itself looked extremely solid. Perhaps he should wait for a better opportunity to charge at humans.

Unfortunately for Buffalo, at that moment, Puff Adder made his way through the grass. The snake had seen the big animal glaring at the van, and he knew exactly what was on his mind.

'Well, go on, then,' said Puff Adder. 'What are you waiting for? You're always saying how you want to charge at all humans. Here are your first targets.'

Buffalo felt irritated and wished he hadn't bumped into the snake that morning. After all of his boastful claims, Buffalo knew he couldn't back out now, or Puff Adder would never let him forget it.

'I'm just preparing myself,' he growled in what he hoped was a fiery way.

Puff Adder pretended to look impressed, although he knew very well what Buffalo was thinking.

'Now's your chance,' said the snake innocently. 'If you wait too long, they might drive away again.'

'I know,' said Buffalo, rather too loudly. Puff Adder grinned silently to himself – Buffalo was afraid.

The unfortunate Buffalo lowered his head, and an angry voice inside him urged him on. He tried not to listen to another voice telling him not to be so stupid. Meanwhile, the tourists in the van admired the enormous bull and his magnificent horns. It was as if the animal were trying to give them the best view of his horns. However, it wasn't long before the tourists gasped. The guide looked round to see what had made them react as Buffalo hurled himself towards the van at break-neck speed. His hooves kicked up enormous clouds of dust, making Puff Adder cough and turn his head. The snake looked back again to see that Buffalo had reached the van in no time and was just a few metres away. Even from his distant observation point, Puff Adder heard the people inside the van screaming for their lives.

The guide watched in amazement. He had never seen such an aggressive buffalo in his whole career.

Buffalo hesitated ever so slightly as he neared the van, but then he gritted his teeth and summoned up his determination. He bent his head almost to the ground and rammed into the back of the van at full speed, making it shake violently. The tourists screamed even louder.

Puff Adder cackled in delight whilst the driver turned on the engine and drove off at a tremendous speed, taking the hysterical party with him.

Meanwhile, poor Buffalo lay on the ground with a blinding headache. His head was pounding so much that he could hardly bear to move. The impact against the van came back to him repeatedly, and he shuddered and shut his eyes. His neck felt as if it had been shortened, whilst his head felt as though his horns had been forced into his skull and his brain might burst out. Buffalo murmured in confusion.

To make matters worse, Puff Adder's familiar lisp came from nearby, although, to Buffalo, it sounded like a thousand Puff

Adders. 'Congratulations!' the snake hissed. 'A very impressive display of head-butting, I'm sure.'

Buffalo groaned and wished Puff Adder would go away.

'I fear your horns may never be the same again, however,' said the snake, choosing his words carefully. He wasn't about to tell Buffalo that his horns were a little bent. He would let him find that out for himself.

'What do you mean?' demanded Buffalo, sitting up and forgetting about his headache for a moment. A searing pain shot through his head when he moved, and he immediately remembered why he had been lying down.

'Well, I'm not sure how to describe them,' said Puff Adder, bobbing his head and pretending to look at the horns from all angles. 'Let's just say they don't look quite as symmetrical as they did before.'

Buffalo scrambled to his feet and lowered his head, trying to see the ends of his horns. A lump came to his throat, and he blinked back tears. Surely, his horns weren't too badly damaged. Try as he might, he couldn't see what had happened to them, and Puff Adder laughed in a rasping tone as Buffalo turned his head in all directions.

'It's not funny!' Buffalo shouted. 'It's no good. I'll have to look in the waterhole.'

'You do that,' said Puff Adder, 'although you might not like what you see. I must say, the others will be amused to hear about your heroics. And they were such dangerous humans, too: little old men in their colourful clothing and women clutching their bags. Buffalo, you've saved the animals of the savanna from a terrible enemy.'

The snake cackled again, and Buffalo's face took on a huge frown. 'Don't you dare tell anyone about this,' he roared. Now it was Puff Adder's turn to feel alarmed. The snake stopped laughing at once and assessed the anger on Buffalo's face—the big animal was clearly furious.

'If you tell anyone, I'll go straight round to the commander and give her detailed directions to your new home,' said Buffalo, suddenly thinking of a useful bargaining tool.

Puff Adder considered his options while Buffalo glared straight into his round eyes. It would be tremendous fun to tell the other animals how silly Buffalo had been; however, he was genuinely anxious about the meerkats finding out where he lived. The snake sighed. 'All right,' he agreed. 'I won't mention this to anyone if you keep my secret for me.'

'It's a deal,' Buffalo growled, and relief swept over him. He shook his head gently to cast off the dirt and pieces of grass and grimaced at the shooting pain. The thought of Stella hearing about his moment of madness was more than he could bear. He spent his time copying her in the hope that he would, one day, be as respected a leader as she was, but Buffalo was suddenly quite certain the elephant would never do anything as idiotic and undignified as charging into the back of a van. He wondered what had possessed him to think it was a good idea.

Buffalo tried to focus on the horizon to get his balance, but it seemed to swing wildly. He racked his brain to think which direction he had come from, as he thought it was probably time to meet back with the elephants. Unfortunately, he had no idea, and he realised he had little option but to ask Puff Adder.

'Could you tell me which direction I came from?' he asked, aware of how stupid he must sound. 'Normally, I've got a good sense of direction,' he added, 'but I seem to have a headache, and it's making it more difficult to think clearly.'

'Oh dear,' said Puff Adder, pretending to be concerned. 'Perhaps it's the sun. It is rather strong this morning.'

'Very funny,' snapped Buffalo. 'Now, would you kindly tell me which direction I need to go in?'

For a moment, Puff Adder considered sending Buffalo in the wrong direction, but his conscience pricked him, and he realised he felt a bit sorry for Buffalo. The big animal was full of good intentions, but he didn't always pick the best way to carry them out. 'Yes. Back towards the sun,' said the snake with a little nod of his head.

Buffalo looked at him suspiciously. 'Are you sure?' he asked, and Puff Adder almost wished he had sent him the wrong way.

'Yes, I am sure,' the snake told him crossly. 'Now, be off with you, and leave me to have some peace.'

Buffalo headed towards the sun, which had now put a large gap between itself and the horizon. His legs felt as if they didn't belong to him, and he had difficulty maintaining a straight course.

'Tell Stella I hope she finds Alfie,' Puff Adder called after him. 'I should hate to think something awful has happened to him.'

CHAPTER 35

The Secretary
Bird Returns

MEANWHILE, THE ELEPHANTS HAD returned to the meeting place and were awaiting Buffalo's return. Led by Mabel, Ethel, and Maud, the group had searched meticulously in the area where Alfie had last been seen. They found the patch of his blood in the grass, which was now dark and dried up, but, of course, there was no sign of the chimp anywhere, and it was a solemn group that returned.

Stella and the leopards soon joined, with Martial Eagle flying high above them. Bright arrived after a brief conversation with a hyena. The animals usually avoided the hyenas as they were not to be trusted, but Bright thought this was enough of an emergency to overcome social tensions. However, the hyena hadn't been able to tell her anything at all.

Wanda, Felicity, Leader, and Dent had come back from the waterhole eager for any news of Alfie, and they were bitterly disappointed to find there was none. Martial Eagle's news that the secretary bird had followed the van away did little to raise their hopes. Alfie might not have been in the van, and even if he had been, he might now be dead. The gathering stood there looking glum as they waited for Buffalo. Nobody spoke except the leopard cubs to tell their mother they were hungry.

The sun crept above the two old baobabs, which the animals called the Grandfather Trees. For a few minutes, it seemed to hover there and then gradually slipped behind the second tree. Some while later, Buffalo had still not returned, and the animals began to fidget.

'Perhaps he's found Alfie, Mum!' said Leader.

'Yes, maybe he's taking so long because Alfie is injured and he can't walk very fast,' suggested Dent, not knowing this was quite close to the truth.

'Don't get your hopes up,' warned Bright. 'No one has seen Alfie anywhere. It's very unlikely Buffalo has found him.'

'On a different note, has anyone seen Cheetah?' asked Leopard. The animals all shook their heads.

'Oh dear,' said Stella. 'I hope he hasn't hidden himself away again to practise retracting his claws. He is so worried about that.'

The animals were silent again as they peered into the distance, wondering if Buffalo might soon be in view, but there was still no sign of him.

'I think we've all had enough waiting,' said Stella. 'Anyone who wants to bathe, please do so now,' she said, addressing the herd, 'and Leopard, Martial Eagle, Wanda—please don't feel as if you have to wait for Buffalo to get back. If he has anything to report, I shall come and find you at once, although I doubt we'll have any positive news.'

The animals nodded rather dejectedly before going their separate ways. Stella and Bright stood side by side, watching them.

'This really is the worst thing that could have happened,' said Bright. 'I don't know how we are going to manage without Alfie. I can't see any way to defeat Mr Rich without him. I just hope he is okay.'

Stella didn't respond. She wanted to say something uplifting, but she couldn't think of anything. 'You're right,' she said at length. The elephant stared into the distance and frowned.

'What's the matter?' asked Bright, following her gaze. 'Is Buffalo returning? Wait!' she cried. 'It's the secretary bird, isn't it?'

And it was! A very tired, very bedraggled secretary bird was flying towards them so slowly that Stella thought she might be about to drop to the ground. The departing animals heard Bright's cry and stopped in their tracks. The two elephants swung their trunks as they watched the secretary bird approach, and Stella felt her heart miss a beat. What would she tell them? Would she know where Alfie was?

The poor secretary bird was utterly worn out. She had seen the elephants and the buffalo herd from some distance away, but it had taken her a long time to reach them, and the final few metres seemed almost impossible. She willed her wings to last for a few more strokes, flying so low that the grass tickled her stomach. The elephants watched in alarm as she flopped to the ground and lay quite still.

Martial Eagle rushed over to her and peered at her anxiously. 'She's quite exhausted,' he pronounced, as if he were a doctor. 'Somebody–get some water. Quickly!'

Bright rushed off towards the waterhole to fill her trunk and carry water back for the poor bird.

'What's happened to Alfie?' demanded Leopard. 'Do you know where he is?'

'Wait, Leopard,' said Stella gently, 'she's very tired. I'm sure she'll tell us when she's ready.'

'Just tell me if he's still alive,' begged Leopard, unable to contain herself. She looked down hopefully at the little heap of feathers.

With a huge effort, the secretary bird opened her eyes a tiny crack and croaked, 'I think so. He looked like he was still breathing when I saw him taken inside.'

Several voices fired questions at the poor secretary bird at once–Were the men poachers? Where had they taken Alfie? Was he badly hurt?–and she felt quite overwhelmed. She shut her eyes again, and Stella realised she was too tired for so many questions.

'Shh!' said Stella. 'We must give her a chance to get her strength back. She's obviously flown a very long way.'

'Just tell us where Alfie is,' pleaded Leopard.

The secretary bird inhaled deeply and forced the words to come out of her beak. 'He's at a house in the park,' she said. 'It's surrounded by an enormous wall with big dogs inside, and I think it belongs to Mr Rich. It was certainly Mr Rich who took Alfie away.'

A gasp went around the group.

'It's as I feared! He's been kidnapped by Mr Rich,' cried Leopard in dismay.

From her position on the ground, the secretary bird nodded slowly, and Stella saw that her cheeks were wet with tears. There was a stunned silence that was broken by the elephant leader.

'Well, there's nothing for it,' she said determinedly. 'We shall have to rescue him.'

CHAPTER 36

Imprisoned!

THE ROOM WAS COLD and dark. There were no windows to allow the sun's warm light to enter, other than the tiniest of round windows high up on one side. The room was in the basement of Mr Rich's house, and mostly it was empty, but under the window there was a big pile of strange objects.

Alfie was lying stretched out on the stone floor of the room. The chimp had a steel collar around his neck, with a chain attaching him to a metal ring mounted on the wall.

After several hours, Alfie gradually regained consciousness, and his eyelids flickered. Very slowly, his eyes opened, and for a few minutes he lay quietly, feeling dazed and confused. He had only the vaguest memory of leaving the elephant herd to go back home to find the ranger. What was he doing in this dark room that was so cold he found himself shivering? Why was his shoulder so sore?

Alfie twisted his head to look at his shoulder and was shocked to see a deep, stitched wound, and around it fur that was matted and stained with blood. The bullet had been removed, but it was obvious to the chimp what had caused the injury.

He gradually started to remember what had happened. He recalled running with Wanda to escape from something and the purring noise of a van that seemed to gain on them all the time. Alfie sat up slowly and tried to concentrate. He felt sure Wanda had stopped running, and they had separated, but what had happened then?

The memory of the van's bright headlights came back to Alfie, and he remembered that he had run towards the vehicle. He frowned as he tried to think why he might have done such a dangerous thing, and he realised it must have been to save Wanda. He had the feeling he had swerved aside and changed direction, and then ... BANG!

The memory of the sound of the gunshot was so powerful that Alfie couldn't help instinctively ducking. He trembled as he relived the chase in his mind. He remembered a second explosion and how he had panicked and not known which way to run. Then he recalled the sudden pain in his shoulder when the bullet tore into his flesh.

Alfie whimpered and threw himself on the floor, covering his eyes with the palms of his hands. He lay still for a moment and tried to think what had happened after that but found he had no memory at all beyond that point. He realised he must have lost consciousness.

The chimp breathed heavily for a few minutes before summoning the strength to sit up again. He felt strangely weak from the loss of blood and found it difficult to concentrate. His shoulder throbbed continually, and he was desperately thirsty.

Alfie looked around to see if there might be some food or at least some water for him on the floor, but there was nothing. He surveyed the room and peered through the shadows, trying to decipher the curious shapes. The dim light from the little window made it difficult to see anything clearly, but as his eyes adjusted, Alfie could make out that the room was long and narrow, with a low ceiling. Alfie moved closer in the dark to work out what the objects in the big pile were, and the chain pulled at his neck. For the first time, he realised that he was trapped. He tugged against the chain in dismay, but he was firmly bound to the wall, and no amount of effort would allow him to move any further.

The chimp stared at the pile curiously. There seemed to be long, white, curved things, then several heavy rugs. A little farther along the wall, there was what appeared to be a pile of broader, white objects with pointed ends. Alfie gasped at the sight once he understood. The objects stored in his cell were poaching gains—elephant tusks, rhino horns, and the furs and skins of several different animals. He was being kept prisoner in a poacher's storeroom!

Alfie looked around the rest of the room to see that it was otherwise empty. There was a solid-looking wooden door in the diagonal corner from where he was chained to the wall. A set of stone steps led up to the door. It looked to be the only way in or out except for the tiny window, which would barely have allowed a bird to enter.

Alfie felt panic well up inside him. Perhaps the poachers were going to leave him there alone to die of thirst. He might never see the ranger or any of his friends in the wild again, and they might never find out what had happened to him. The ranger would come to the agreed-upon meeting place to collect him and wait in vain, wondering why he wasn't there. The animals might think the chimp had simply deserted them in their time of need to live his own life in the forest.

Another whimper escaped from his throat, and Alfie thought of some of the things he would have said to them all, if only he had known it would be his last chance.

The chain prevented Alfie from moving beyond a small semi-circle, so he couldn't get anywhere near the door. He threw himself down on the hard floor again, feeling completely helpless, then scrambled to his feet, and pulled at the chain and then the collar with all his might, but the collar was tight around his neck and didn't budge. It was impossible to pull himself free, and it only hurt for him to try. Alfie hurried over to examine the metal ring on the wall more closely but, to his bitter disappointment, found it was far too solid to pull out. He could not help himself from trying, though. With both hands, he yanked at the ring as hard as he could, but it didn't move at all. He was completely trapped.

Alfie sat down with his back to the wall and stared miserably across to the other side of the room. A tiny shaft of light from the little window crossed his gaze, reminding him of the glorious sunshine and fresh air of the wild. He had to swallow hard to stop a few tears when he realised he might never have the chance to watch the sun rise or set again. He shut his eyes and tried to think of a plan, but he was weary and couldn't seem to think clearly at all.

Alfie realised he must have drifted off to sleep again as he awoke with a start when somebody unbolted the door with a loud clang. The chimp sat up breathless, hardly daring to imagine who was about to enter—would it be a poacher with more goods to store, or perhaps another prisoner to join him? He would not have wished imprisonment on another animal, but he desperately wanted some company.

Alfie's fur prickled when he heard a human voice shouting on the other side of the door. There was a creak as someone pulled the heavy wooden door open and the figure of a man appeared, silhouetted against the light. The man snapped a switch on the wall and Alfie bent his head and covered his eyes when the room was suddenly illuminated. Having been in darkness, the light made his eyes hurt terribly.

'Well, then,' said a familiar, unpleasant voice, 'I hope you're enjoying your stay as my guest. That's what happens to chimpanzees who are too clever for their own good.'

Alfie recognised the voice at once. He squinted through his fingers to see that it was Mr Rich. The man was standing at the top of the steps, leaning against the frame of the door with a smug smile across his face. He held the door open with his right hand and had what Alfie hoped might be a bowl of water in his left. He was immaculately dressed in a suit and tie, and his moustache looked as though it had just been trimmed.

Alfie looked at him for a moment and then turned his back in a defiant gesture.

'You won't be running to the ranger with any fairy tales now that you're stuck in here, will you?' the man gloated. 'In fact, you won't be going anywhere at all. Well, that is, until my lovely new client comes to collect you.'

Mr Rich let the door swing shut, making Alfie jump. The chimp heard Mr Rich walk down the steps towards him, his shoes sounding loud on the stone floor. Alfie held his breath as the man came closer.

Mr Rich stopped and placed the bowl on the ground, so it was just within Alfie's reach, and backed away quickly. Still Alfie refused to look at his kidnapper. He thought furiously about who Mr Rich's client might be, but he didn't have to wonder for long.

'You see, you're going to join a circus!' said Mr Rich, sounding very pleased with himself. 'Audiences love clever animals who can communicate with humans. They love them so much that my client is prepared to pay a ridiculous sum of money for you, and I'm very happy about that.'

Some humans will do anything for money, thought Alfie bitterly when he heard this. *They don't care who gets hurt as long as they get really rich.* He turned around to face the man and snarled at him, making Mr Rich lose his smile and jump backwards.

'You know, I think you really do understand what I'm saying, don't you?' the man sneered while Alfie glared into his eyes.

'Well, if you can understand, understand this,' said Mr Rich, 'you are never going to see the ranger or any of your savage animal friends again.' He stopped and laughed. 'Having said that, you might yet see parts of your friends again when they join my money-making piles over there.' Mr Rich pointed at the tusks, horns, furs, and skins with an outstretched hand, and Alfie couldn't help looking at them. The chimp felt sick to think of all of the animals that had died for the awful collection. He tried not to listen to anything else the horrible man was saying.

'Now that I've got you here, there's no way anyone will ever find out that I'm behind the poaching in this area of the National Park,' continued Mr Rich with a smile that made Alfie want to hit him. 'Your ranger will never think of me when he wonders why his precious chimpanzee has disappeared, although he's going to be far too busy with poachers to worry about you for too long. You see, I've just landed a deal to supply a very generous new client with all the rhino horns and cat furs he wants. I've got another client who is demanding huge amounts of ivory, and he's prepared to pay almost anything for it. I'm going to be the richest man in the country soon, and all the other poachers will answer to me.'

Alfie looked at him in utter disbelief. The man couldn't care less about the animals he killed, let alone their devastated families. The only thing he cared about was how much money he had to count. Alfie would have given anything to lock him away for the rest of his life.

Mr Rich made for the door again. Talking about money had reminded him about a telephone call he needed to make. 'See you later,' he called back, as if to a friend. 'I've got other things to do besides talk to you, although I have enjoyed our little chat.' He stopped for a moment and looked at Alfie, who glowered back at him.

'Oh, you might also like to know what is going to happen to your ranger,' said Mr Rich, as though he had just remembered. 'One day soon, he is going to be arrested for poaching. You see, one of my men is going to find evidence in his garden shed that he has been killing endangered species. It's very sad, but nobody will believe the honest little ranger over a very important man like me. I just thought you might like to know.'

Alfie waited until the man had left, slamming the door behind him, before he hurled himself to the floor and cried angry, helpless tears. Mr Rich was going to do all of these terrible things, and there was nothing he could do to stop him. The animals would try their best, but what could they do against the poachers' guns? If the ranger were arrested and the animals left without any protection, they would be completely defenceless. Unbearable images hurried into the chimp's mind as he imagined what might happen. Cold, miserable, and ravenously hungry, Alfie sank into a fitful sleep, disturbed by frightening dreams that twisted from one scene to the next, always dominated by Mr Rich's self-satisfied smile. First, he saw the animals being hunted down, one by one, and then the ranger being roughly dragged into a police van by an officer in uniform, while Mr Rich stood by, pretending to be sad as he shook his head. In the dream, the policeman got into his van and the engine started up, sounding distressingly loud.

Alfie awoke with a jump, and it took a moment for him to realise that the sound was real—somebody was starting an engine just outside his cell.

He hurried under the window and stopped to listen. There was no doubt that a vehicle was leaving. The chimp wondered if the driver was Mr Rich. Perhaps Alfie was all alone in the house now. He waited until he could no longer hear the engine's roar and shouted up at the window in the hope that somebody might hear him. He thought his only chance was if a friendly creature might take a message to the park animals to tell them where he was. If he could just send a message to Leopard, she might be able to bring the ranger to rescue him. The ranger would recognise Leopard, who might remember her way to the ranger's house.

'Help!' yelled Alfie as loudly as he could. 'If anyone can hear me, help me, please!'

He waited for a response, but there was only silence, so he tried again. 'Help! I'm a prisoner! Help! Help!'

Again, he waited, desperately hoping that someone might hear him. Unfortunately for Alfie, the animals outside couldn't hear him shouting, as his voice barely carried through the little window with its thick glass. However, the man in the next room heard what sounded to him like a chimp roaring in distress. Shortly, the door was unbolted, and Alfie jumped in fright when he saw it pulled open.

CHAPTER 37

Alfie Meets Mr Rich's Housekeeper

'WHAT'S ALL THIS NOISE?' demanded the man.

To Alfie's relief, it was not Mr Rich but a smaller, humbler-looking man who appeared to be in the middle of cleaning. He wore glasses and a white apron and carried a duster in his hand. He had spoken harshly, but Alfie could see that he had a kind face, and the chimp wondered if the man might be willing to help him.

He whined pitifully and gazed at the little man, trying to look sad while rattling his chain to draw attention to it. As he had hoped, the man stepped forward into the room, wearing a sympathetic expression.

'You poor chimp, here all alone and away from your friends,' said the man, switching on the light and closing the door gently behind him. 'I think it's wrong to keep an animal locked up like this, I do, although don't tell Mr Rich I said so. Not that you could, of course. Chimpanzees can't talk.'

No, but I really wish I could right now, Alfie thought. He watched the man edge closer rather nervously and realised the man was afraid of him. Suddenly, a thought occurred to Alfie: he wondered if the man might understand sign language.

Alfie waved his hands and signed a few simple sentences to the man, very slowly. 'Please help me. I need to escape,' he said. 'I'm a prisoner here, and I want to go home.'

The man stared at him, and for a moment, Alfie thought he saw a glimmer of comprehension on his face, but then it faded, and the chimp realised it had simply been interest.

'You're trying to tell me something, aren't you?' asked the man, shaking his head. 'Well, I never believed animals could talk until now, but I'm sorry – I just don't understand what you are saying.'

Alfie looked around in frustration, wondering how else to convey his message to the man. He instinctively knew he was a kind man, and he suspected he might be persuaded to help him if only he could make him understand.

The man turned to look sadly at the pile of poached animal parts against the wall. He shook his head again. 'I think it's dreadful,' he said. 'I don't think it's right to kill all those animals, and just for money, too. My employer, Mr Rich, is already one of the richest people in the country. I don't know why he thinks he needs any more money.' He looked at Alfie with an apologetic smile. 'Of course, you mustn't tell him I said that either. I am just his housekeeper, and I'd lose my job.'

As soon as the man looked back at him, Alfie waved his arms frantically and pointed up at the window. *Please help me to escape!* he thought as hard as he could, hoping to somehow communicate telepathically.

The man looked at him and at the window with a puzzled expression. 'Now, what is it you want?' he asked. 'I can't help you escape if that's what you mean. It's more than my life's worth. Mr Rich would be furious with me if I released one of his valuable animals.'

Alfie was crestfallen. He sank to his knees, realising that although the housekeeper was kind, he was too scared of his boss to do anything to help. The little man watched him with concern, knowing that the chimpanzee was extremely unhappy. It made him feel wretched to see a wild animal cooped up against its will.

'I can't set you free,' he said after a while, 'but I could let you into the study while Mr Rich is out. I could even give you some nice food if you wanted. I'm sure Mr Rich wouldn't miss it. Would you like that?'

There was no mistaking Alfie's comprehension abilities. The chimp jumped up and down excitedly and nodded his head, shaking the chain with his hands to make as much noise as possible.

The housekeeper smiled cautiously at his reaction, but then he looked doubtful. 'You mustn't tell my boss I did this, though,' he warned. 'Do you promise to keep the secret?'

Alfie had no intention of going back to his hateful prison cell, but he knew he had to make the little man trust him, so he nodded vigorously and adopted a solemn face, hoping he would believe him.

'I'm sure you can't really understand me,' said the housekeeper with a laugh. 'I must have imagined that you seemed to nod your head. Anyway, this will be our little secret.'

He came towards the chimp, and for the first time, Alfie noticed the small ring of keys hanging from his belt. The man twisted to look down at the keys, sorting through them until he found the one he wanted. 'Here we are,' he said brightly. 'I think this might be the key to your chain.'

He bustled over to the ring on the wall and bent down to unlock a tiny lock Alfie hadn't noticed. The housekeeper turned his back to the chimp as he struggled with the lock, and Alfie thought how trusting he was. Alfie knew he could easily have overpowered the man, grabbed his keys, and locked him in the room that was Alfie's prison, but he hadn't the heart to betray him. He also thought the housekeeper might tell him some useful things about how to get out of the house, so Alfie waited patiently until he finally managed to unlock the chain.

'Come on, then,' said the housekeeper, as though speaking to a very small child. He pulled gently on the chain, leading Alfie towards the door. 'Come with me.'

Alfie followed him as slowly as he could manage, not wanting to arouse suspicion by hurrying. He pretended to be quite nervous, and the man began to feel less worried about letting him out.

'That's right. Keep following me,' he encouraged the chimp, pulling again on the chain. Alfie wondered why the man bothered to talk to him if he thought he didn't understand.

Alfie followed the housekeeper up the stairs to the door and stepped gratefully out of the basement into the next room, which he looked around in relief.

The room in which he found himself was clearly a study, and he realised the housekeeper had been working there when he had heard Alfie's cries for help. There was a can of polish on the big desk by the window, and a vacuum cleaner stood at the edge of the richly carpeted floor. On the other side of the room was another door, which was shut.

The room also contained a tall bookcase next to the desk, but it held no books. Instead, several files stood neatly side by side on the shelves, all unlabelled. Alfie wondered if they contained the secret details of Mr Rich's poaching deals.

On the desk, Alfie saw a computer with a printer next to it, a telephone, and a big lamp. The desk was immaculately tidy, without a scrap of paper in sight. Evidently, Mr Rich didn't believe in cluttering his surroundings.

The housekeeper carefully shut the door to Alfie's cell behind them and let Alfie's chain drop on to the floor in the room. The chimp watched the man, wondering if he would take him anywhere else.

'Well, I don't think I ought to take you out of this room,' said the housekeeper, as if he had heard what Alfie was thinking. 'Mr Rich wouldn't like it if he found out I had let you explore the house. Not that he'd like it if he found out I'd let you out at all, of course.'

The man laughed nervously, and Alfie realised he was enjoying disobeying his boss. The chimp suspected, correctly, that Mr Rich was a hard and unforgiving man who frightened his employees.

Alfie looked hurriedly around for possible ways to escape from the study. The housekeeper watched him with an expression of wonder on his face, and Alfie hoped the man wouldn't realise what he was doing.

'Is that better, then?' the housekeeper asked kindly. 'At least there's more light in here, not like the basement with that tiny window.

'Would you like something to eat?'

Alfie realised this might be his best chance, and he nodded as hard as he could. He made a grunting noise and rubbed his hairy stomach with one hand, trying to sound as encouraging as possible.

The man beamed at him. 'All right, then,' he said. 'I'll go and see what I can find. Do you like salmon? Or caviar? I know there are some leftovers that Mr Rich won't eat himself.'

The housekeeper made for the door on the other side of the study. He unlocked it with a key from the inside, took the key, and disappeared into the next room. Alfie heard him lock the door behind him on the other side, and he sprang into action.

Alfie raced across to the desk with the chain dragging behind him. He jumped up on the desk to examine the window more closely. To his bitter disappointment, there were heavy iron bars across the window, and they were far too thick for him to bend. He thought how determined Mr Rich must be that no one came into his study.

Alfie hurried back to the door and grasped the handle with both hands, hoping he might be able to wrench it open. Unfortunately, it was a strong lock, and the door didn't move, not even slightly. However, Alfie wasn't about to give up that easily. He realised there was a small gap between the bottom of the door and the carpet, so the chimp rushed over to the desk and pulled open each of the drawers. At last, he found one with a neat pile of white paper and another with several perfectly sharpened pencils. He took what he needed and slammed the drawers shut before hurrying back to the door. He prepared to do a little trick the ranger had taught him during a moment of play. Alfie had never imagined he might one day need to use it in a real emergency.

CHAPTER 38

Trying to Escape

ALFIE PUSHED A PIECE OF paper under the door until only a tiny bit was left on his side, reached up to the keyhole, and pushed the pencil in. Luckily, it was slim enough to fit into the keyhole, and he poked it through as far as it would go. To his delight, he felt the pencil push the key out on the other side of the door and heard it land on the floor with a bounce. Alfie's hand trembled as he pulled the paper carefully under the door, watching for the key to appear.

Now the whole piece of paper was in view, but the key wasn't on it. Without meaning to, Alfie cried out in disappointment. The trick had failed, and he was still a prisoner. He thought for a moment, and a new idea came to his mind. His heart beat madly and his legs were like jelly as he ran over to the desk again and rummaged through the drawers for a ruler. In the bottom drawer, he came across what he was looking for and snatched up the ruler without bothering to shut the drawer this time.

Alfie lay on his side, pushed the ruler under the door and slid it around to see if he could locate the key and pull it towards him. To his frustration, he couldn't find the key anywhere, and he realised it must have bounced well away from the door when it landed.

He froze. There were footsteps coming from the next room! Quick as a flash, Alfie whipped the ruler out from under the door, put the ruler, pencils, and paper back into the right places and closed the drawers. He looked around quickly, relieved to see there was no sign of what he had done.

Alfie recognised the housekeeper's shuffling steps as they came towards the door. There was a pause during which the chimp realised it probably looked as if the key had mysteriously jumped out of the lock all by itself. He cringed, hoping the housekeeper would think nothing of it, and waited for the man to find the key and unlock the door.

'Here we are, then,' said the housekeeper, entering the room with a big smile. He laughed a little mischievously. 'I've got the best of everything for you. I don't think Mr Rich would be very pleased. I expect he planned to give you the food the dogs get.' The man came into the room with a silver tray balanced on his left arm. Much to Alfie's disappointment, he locked the door behind him with his other hand.

Alfie eyed the tray in astonishment. The housekeeper had not exaggerated. There was a huge plate of pink salmon complete with a slice of lemon, a separate plate of black caviar with some carefully buttered brown bread, and to finish, a big bowl of chocolate mousse. Normally, Alfie would have preferred simpler, less extravagant food, but he was famished and would have eaten anything. He looked up at the housekeeper gratefully and made what he hoped sounded like an appreciative noise. The man laughed again, and he laid the tray down on the floor in front of him. There was even silver cutlery for Alfie to use and a serviette to wipe his mouth. The chimp knew how to use cutlery as the ranger had taught him, but unless the ranger had company, he generally used his fingers.

Alfie hesitated. The sight of the food was appealing, and he didn't know when he might be offered another meal, but his main concern was to escape. He could see the key still in the door and wondered whether to push the housekeeper over and charge for it, but Alfie didn't want to hurt the man who had shown him such kindness.

I'll eat the food quickly, and when he takes the tray back to the kitchen, I'll make my escape, he decided. *That way, I don't need to frighten him. I only hope I can find my way out.*

Alfie wolfed the food down at a rate that quite alarmed the watching housekeeper. 'You must have been really hungry,' he commented. 'Would you like some more?'

Alfie danced around and nodded his head. The man grinned, picked up the tray, balanced it back on his arm, and headed for the door. Alfie watched and waited until he was securely locked in again, and the sound of the footsteps had died away. Then, the chimp darted to the desk and brought out the pencil and paper again. He was about to go back to the door for a second attempt when the telephone on the desk caught his eye, and he had a great idea: he could phone the ranger!

Telephones were difficult for Alfie. Although he could understand human language, he couldn't speak it. The problem would be to make the ranger understand where he was being held. At least Mr Rich had a landline, so no code was needed to make the phone work.

Alfie picked up the receiver with difficulty. It was impossible to stop his hand from shaking so much that he could hardly control it. He dialled the ranger's mobile number with his free hand and waited with a huge knot of anxiety in his stomach, praying the ranger would have his phone with him.

Meanwhile, a car drew up in the front drive of Mr Rich's house, although Alfie was too preoccupied to hear it. There were footsteps on the gravel outside, and somebody let himself in through the front door. Alfie was so focused on the call that he didn't realise Mr Rich had returned home.

CHAPTER 39

Caught!

THE RANGER'S MOBILE PHONE rang several times, and Alfie bit his lip. He knew the ranger sometimes took a while to answer his phone when he was out and about in the van or busy with an animal.

Answer it, please! he begged silently. He heard a small beep, and his heart leapt. The ranger's familiar voice said hello to him on the other end, and Alfie prepared to make the noises he knew the ranger would immediately recognise, but to his horror, the receiver was snatched from his hand, and he was roughly pushed off the desk and on to the floor.

Mr Rich glared at Alfie as he spoke calmly into the phone: 'Hello. I am sorry. I think I may have the wrong number,' he said. 'I do apologise. Goodbye.'

Mr Rich replaced the receiver and paused for a moment before turning back to face Alfie. The chimp saw that he had a gun in his other hand, and he knew he was caught. Alfie trembled, wondering what Mr Rich might do to him and to the poor housekeeper.

'Back!' roared the man, and he aimed the gun at Alfie's head. 'Get back in your cell, you interfering animal! I don't know how you got out, but you're going straight back to where you belong!'

Alfie scuttled towards the door to the dreaded basement, hardly daring to turn his back on Mr Rich. The man was so angry that the chimp was afraid he might shoot him in a fit of rage. He pressed himself against the wall, allowing Mr Rich to unbolt the door, and tried to look pleadingly at the man. He couldn't bear the idea of being in the basement again.

Mr Rich shouted at him to go down the steps. Alfie hesitated for a split second, but Mr Rich was still aiming his gun at him, and the chimp had no doubt he was prepared to use it.

Alfie rushed through the doorway so fast that he lost his footing, and tumbled down the steps towards the hard, stone floor. Mr Rich threw the chain in behind him, which landed in a pile by his face. The door slammed violently, and Alfie lay on the ground, feeling bruised and utterly dejected. He had been so close to communicating with the ranger. If only Mr Rich hadn't arrived back when he had.

The chimp listened for the unfortunate housekeeper to return to the study, knowing he would be in terrible trouble. Within a few minutes, there was another angry roar, and Alfie could hardly bring himself to listen. He heard Mr Rich shout at the top of his voice, and the frightened housekeeper try to give some kind of explanation. Shortly, he heard a door slam, and there was quiet again. Then, the hoover started up, and Alfie guessed the housekeeper had been ordered back to work. He hoped it meant the little man had been given another chance and wasn't going to lose his job because he had tried to help him.

Alfie lay still on the cold stone floor, thinking he might die of despair. There was no hope of escape now, of that he felt certain. Mr Rich would make sure he was firmly locked in and would probably chain him to the wall again. He turned his head slowly and stared at the big pile of poaching gains, standing ghost-like in the shadows. It was difficult to believe that pile was the reason he was a prisoner, the reason he might never see the ranger again, and the reason his friends' lives were being threatened. Alfie thought about the animals in the National Park. He had so wanted to help them avoid a terrible fate, but now it seemed there might be nothing he could do.

Alfie looked up at the tiny window to see that it was now dark outside. After a while, the hoover stopped, and he could hear nothing from the house. He suspected, correctly, that Mr Rich might be having dinner, and he hoped the man would leave him alone for the rest of the evening. At least, thank goodness, he wasn't chained to the wall any longer.

He looked around, barely able to make out anything now that it was dark. The only light came from the moon's rays shining faintly through the window, illuminating the pile of poaching trophies and making their shapes visible. Alfie stared at the pile and realised there *was* something he could do. He might not be able to stop any more animals from being killed, but he could do his best to wreck Mr Rich's current store.

He bounded across to the pile to examine the horns and tusks. They looked solid, and Alfie suspected they might be difficult to break. He touched the furs and skins, and a shudder went down his spine. These had been real leopards, cheetahs, lions, and antelopes once, until they had fallen prey to Mr Rich's gun.

Alfie set to work. He hurled the horns and tusks against the stone walls with all his might and was overjoyed when some of them shattered into fragments. Horn after horn, tusk after tusk, he demolished as much as he could, hoping it would make them useless to Mr Rich. He worked his way through the pile for what seemed like ages, until nothing remained but thousands of broken pieces of horn and ivory spread across the room. Alfie felt himself glow with satisfaction.

He turned his attention to the furs and skins across the floor. There were four leopard furs, two cheetah furs, the heads and manes of three male lions, and several antelope hides. Alfie didn't think he had ever seen as many as four leopards in the ranger's area of the National Park. Now he understood why their numbers were falling.

The chimp took hold of one of the leopard furs and tried to tear it apart, but despite using all his strength, it was too tough for him. After several attempts with his hands and teeth, Alfie threw the fur down and admitted defeat.

He consoled himself with the fact that he had at least managed to ruin some of the stock. Mr Rich would regret keeping him prisoner in that horrible room. Alfie didn't know how much money Mr Rich would get for selling him to the circus, but he felt sure it wouldn't be anything like what he would have received for the pile of horns and tusks Alfie had just smashed to pieces.

Alfie lay down on the leopard fur, deciding he deserved some comfort. The chimp thought Mr Rich would probably kill him for what he had done, but he suddenly didn't care. At that moment, damaging Mr Rich's business seemed far more important than his own life. Alfie didn't want to belong to a circus anyway.

He relaxed into the comfortable fur and soon fell into a deep sleep filled with pleasant dreams about his friends in the wild. However, in all his dreams, he never guessed how nearby his friends truly were.

CHAPTER 40

Buffalo Tells a Story

THE ANIMALS HAD BEEN extremely busy since the secretary bird's return.

Stella had tended to the poor bird, making sure she had plenty of food and water. The elephant leader moved her to the shade of a broad acacia tree, where she would be protected from the sun's fierce rays, and the secretary bird gradually recovered. It wasn't long before she was frantic to tell her story.

Her eyelids flickered open. 'We have to rescue him!' she cried at once.

Stella smiled down at the little bundle on the ground. 'Are you feeling better?' she asked.

'Yes, yes, I think so!' twittered the bird, beginning to recover to her usual nervous state. 'Stella, we have to rescue Alfie straightaway,' she said. 'Mr Rich might do something terrible to him. We must go! Let's hurry!'

The secretary bird struggled to her feet and raced around the tree, making Stella smile despite herself.

'We most certainly will go to rescue him,' said the elephant. 'The others are rounding up everyone as we speak. All we need now is for you to tell us where Alfie was taken.'

'Mr Rich's house, Mr Rich's house,' warbled the secretary bird, and Stella could see the worry in her eyes.

'Yes, but where is Mr Rich's house?' Stella asked, trying to sound patient.

'I can take you there,' replied the bird, almost in hysterics. 'Let's go right away! We mustn't waste any time!'

'We are going to wait until dark,' said Stella firmly. 'It is safer for a big group to travel at night. I think we shall also have a much better chance of rescuing Alfie when Mr Rich is asleep.'

The secretary bird ran back and forth. 'I suppose so,' she said. 'I suppose so. I just hope Mr Rich doesn't hurt him.'

The animals assembled quickly. Between them, Leopard, Martial Eagle, Wanda, and the rest of the elephant herd rounded up the other species in no time and the news they brought shocked everyone. As Stella had hoped, every creature was determined to join in the rescue attempt and soon the different species were gathering around her.

One of the first animals to slink up to where Stella and the secretary bird were waiting was Buffalo. When the secretary bird had returned, Stella had been so preoccupied with her news that she had completely forgotten about Buffalo. She watched him as he approached, a forlorn-looking figure whose head drooped almost to his chest. *Whatever's the matter?* she wondered, and then she saw his mangled horns.

'Buffalo, what on earth has happened to your horns?' she cried out. 'You look as if you've had an argument with a tree trunk.'

Buffalo looked at her dismally. 'Are they that bad?' he asked.

'Well, no,' said Stella, peering at him, 'but they are a little crooked, and you look slightly lopsided.' The elephant chose her words carefully as she didn't want to make him think she was laughing at him. 'What happened to you?' she repeated. 'You didn't have a brush with the poachers, did you?'

Buffalo had spent quite some time deciding what his story was going to be and he had perfected it. He adopted a solemn expression. 'While I was asking if anyone had seen Alfie, a van appeared across the plains,' he said. 'It came closer and closer until I could see that the men inside were carrying guns. Then I knew they must be dangerous. It was my duty to stop them from harming one of our friends, so I waited until the van came near before ramming into the back of it as hard as I could.'

Buffalo paused for a moment, allowing for the extent of his bravery to sink in. Stella gasped as if on cue, and a wide-eyed secretary bird flapped her wings in alarm. Buffalo felt pleased and he continued. 'The men inside were terrified. The whole van was thrown to one side by my weight, and it nearly fell over. Once the driver had regained his balance, he drove away at an incredible speed, back in the direction the men had come from.'

Buffalo tried to look brave. 'I know my horns will never be the same,' he said, 'but if I have saved the life of just one of our friends or family, it will have been worth it.'

'We shall never know,' murmured Stella.

She realised Buffalo was waiting for praise, and she hurried to give it to him. After all, he had acted extremely courageously. 'You truly are a brave animal,' she said with a smile, 'and all of the hunted species will greatly appreciate what you have done. I shall make sure your selfless act is known to everyone.'

Buffalo tried to seem humble. 'Oh, I don't think that will be necessary,' he began to say, but Stella interrupted.

'No, it is quite necessary,' she said firmly. 'Any animal who puts his or her own life at risk for the sake of others deserves recognition.'

Buffalo did his best to look pleased, although he began to feel anxious. The animals would hail him as a hero, but he was afraid Puff Adder wouldn't be able to keep his mouth shut.

'Well, I should go back to my herd,' he told Stella, trying to find some reason to escape.

'Oh, but you don't need to,' said Stella, realising she hadn't explained what was happening. 'The secretary bird told us that Alfie has been kidnapped by Mr Rich.

Leopard, Martial Eagle, Wanda, and the elephants are busy collecting everyone so we can try to rescue him this evening. Your herd is being rounded up, too, so you can wait here.'

A sudden thought came to Stella's mind. 'Was Mr Rich one of the poachers you frightened away?' she asked.

Buffalo hesitated, wondering if it wouldn't be better to tell the truth. Puff Adder would surely betray his trust. At least if he were honest now, only Stella and the secretary bird would have heard the lie. He looked at the lovely elephant but couldn't bring himself to tell her there hadn't been any poachers in the van. He admired her so much that he didn't want her to think badly of him.

Unfortunately, Stella took his hesitation as modesty. 'You're too shy to admit it, aren't you?' she said, beaming. 'Well, you've done a wonderful thing, Buffalo. It was extremely brave of you to tackle Mr Rich like that. Well done!'

Buffalo cringed inwardly and realised there was no way out now. He wandered away, pretending to look out for the arrival of the other animals, leaving Stella feeling a little confused. She had thought Buffalo would welcome praise for his deed.

A little while later, nearly all of the animals had arrived. Buffalo was the object of much attention, with his newly bent horns, and everyone was most impressed to hear his story. Poor Buffalo could see the other animals' estimation of him going up, and he wished it had been strictly true. Somehow, it wouldn't have sounded the same to tell them the van had been full of harmless tourists.

'Thank you so much, Buffalo,' Leopard told him gratefully.

'We could have been lying there dead by now,' exclaimed Mabel, and Ethel nodded in agreement. 'You're a proper hero, that's what you are,' she said, tickling Buffalo under his chin with her trunk.

'I can't believe the poachers came back again,' said Wanda when she heard the story. She was, at last, beginning to understand the value of the union between the animals. She could see they really did care for and protect each other.

Wanda made a point of going to speak to Buffalo. 'I really appreciate what you did for us all,' she told him a little awkwardly. 'I think I can learn a lesson from your willingness to help others. You were very brave to tackle Mr Rich.'

'Yes, incredibly brave!' came a sarcastic voice, making Buffalo jump in dismay. It was Puff Adder. 'Who knows what Mr Rich might have done otherwise,' continued the snake, delighting in making poor Buffalo feel uncomfortable.

Buffalo caught his eye, pleading, and Puff Adder decided to say no more. The meerkats still hadn't found his new home, and he was keen for it to stay that way.

Soon, all of the animals had arrived except for Cheetah. It was Leopard who noticed his absence, and she pointed it out to Stella. 'I haven't seen him recently,' she said, shaking her head. 'I hope he isn't hiding again.'

'I'm afraid we can't wait for him, Leopard,' said Stella. 'The sun is close to the horizon now, and it will soon be dark. The secretary bird says it will take us some time to reach Mr Rich's house.'

Leopard nodded her agreement, although she felt worried as Cheetah was a good friend.

Stella turned to face the hundreds of animals who were now waiting in front of her. 'Is everyone ready?' she asked them, and the roar back was deafening. Stella looked flushed and excited. 'Good, well, let's go,' she cried.

'Secretary Bird, please lead the way.'

CHAPTER 41

The Animals Set off to Mr Rich's House

MEANWHILE, CHEETAH HAD, INDEED, been keeping himself to himself in one of his hiding places, some distance away from where the animals were setting off. Nobody had found him to tell him about the rescue attempt, and when he came out of hiding, he realised that none of the others seemed to be around. Stella, Leopard, Buffalo, Giraffe, and even the herds—where were they all? They had all mysteriously disappeared. For a terrible moment, Cheetah wondered if they had all been caught and taken away by Mr Rich, but then he realised how ridiculous that was—that would mean hundreds of animals had been taken all at once—but otherwise where could they have gone?

'I suppose it's my own fault for hiding,' he said aloud in a gloomy tone. 'They've probably all agreed to move to another area and just left me here alone. Poor Cheetah.'

'Poor Cheetah, indeed!' said a sympathetic voice softly at his side. Cheetah jumped in fright, having been unaware of the other animal's presence. He stood in astonishment when he saw who had spoken and caught her delicious scent.

'Who has left you all alone?' asked the female cheetah, looking deep into his eyes.

Cheetah completely lost his voice. Somehow, he couldn't seem to think of anything to say, and he felt quite dizzy. For a dreadful moment, he thought he was going to faint. Meanwhile, the female cheetah smiled pleasantly at him, waiting for an answer.

'Errr... my... errr... my... my... my...' said Cheetah, feeling her eyes fixed on his face. 'My friends have left me at the moment, it seems.'

He looked down, feeling stupid for all his stuttering. He felt quite sure the female would move swiftly on, thinking him a nervous idiot, but to his surprise, she didn't move at all. She even sat down next to him as if ready for a long conversation. 'And who, exactly, are your friends?' she asked lightly. 'Another female cheetah, perhaps?'

'No, no!' said Cheetah, startling his companion and himself with the force of his reply. 'No, I haven't seen a female cheetah for ages. I was beginning to think there weren't any left.'

'And you're the first male I've come across in a long time, too,' said the female with that deep gaze that made Cheetah shift awkwardly. Surely, this pretty female with her soft voice wasn't interested in him. 'I think we should get a little better acquainted, don't you?'

♦♦♦♦♦

Meanwhile, some distance away, the animals set off with the secretary bird flying proudly at the front of the enormous gathering. The animals all had determination in their strides as they knew what they were there to do.

Early on in the journey, Stella slowed and waited for the lion pride to catch up with her so she could speak to Lion himself. 'I wonder if you might do something very important for us, Lion,' she said with an engaging smile.

'Well, of course,' said Lion, much to Lioness's surprise. 'What is it?'

'The secretary bird tells me that Mr Rich's house is surrounded by several large and unfriendly dogs,' Stella explained. 'I expect they are there to protect the property from all strange animals or humans. Unless we do something to distract them, they might bark and give us away, or even attack some of our group.'

'I hope you aren't suggesting that I try to distract them?' said Lion, already wishing he hadn't agreed to help.

'You know I wouldn't want you to put yourself in danger,' said Stella. 'No, I think the best means of distraction would be a gift for them, something tasty to take the dogs' minds off their duties and help them to see us as friends.'

Lion suddenly understood what the elephant might have in mind. 'Oh, no,' he said. 'You don't mean I have to go and find meat to give to the dogs, do you?'

Stella looked at Lion pleadingly. 'We all have to help in whatever way we can,' she said. 'Surely, it's a small sacrifice if it means rescuing Alfie so he and the ranger can help us defeat the poachers once and for all. For a few pieces of meat, we might regain our freedom and the peace we used to enjoy.'

Lioness chose that moment to interrupt. 'I will help,' she said, and she shot her mate a meaningful look. 'Alfie has done his best to help us, and it might be because of us that he has been kidnapped. I think it's the least we can do—don't you, Lion?'

Lion nodded his head at once, although the dismayed expression on his face gave his thoughts away. Stella had to try very hard not to laugh. She thought it was unlikely Lion had ever given away any morsels of food, however small, in his entire life.

'You go on with the group, Stella,' said Lioness, taking charge. 'I shall organise the lions to find some meat and we shall catch up with you all.'

'Thank you, Lioness,' said the elephant leader gratefully. 'Could I also ask you not to tell the herd animals what you are doing? I don't want them to think they are in any danger.'

'Of course,' agreed Lioness.

The female lion looked at her mate, who was still imagining the awful prospect of having to give away some food. 'Come on, Lion,' she teased. 'A little bit of exercise won't hurt you.'

The lion pride parted from the group, with Lion trailing miserably at the back, whilst the rest of the animals continued on with their steady walk. Night was just beginning to fall, and hyenas howled in the distance. The secretary bird and Martial Eagle flew together at the front, flying a little way and then stopping and waiting for the slower land animals to catch up. There was a great deal of chatter about what was going to happen.

'How are we going to rescue Alfie?' Felicity asked Dent and Leader excitedly.

'I don't think my mum knows yet,' said Leader, 'but she'll think of something. She always does.'

'I hope we can do something to help,' said Dent, with a fierce expression on his face. 'I want to make sure Mr Rich never kills another animal like my mum in his whole life.'

Felicity rubbed her shoulder against him. 'You still miss her enormously, don't you?' she said.

'Of course, I do,' said Dent, and Leader's face fell slightly, 'but I'm lucky enough to have a wonderful new family and a great pair of friends,' the rhino added. Leader beamed in delight.

Meanwhile, the older elephants struggled bravely to keep up. Stella was focused on reaching the house as quickly as possible, and she was setting a tremendous pace.

'I'm too old for racing across the plains like this,' Mabel said between pants.

'Perhaps we should stay behind,' agreed Ethel. 'I'm not sure how much longer I can keep going.'

'You two can stay behind if you want,' said Maud, 'but I'm not missing out on all the excitement. How often do you try to rescue someone who's been kidnapped? This will be talked about for many seasons to come!'

'Do you really think so?' asked Mabel.

'Undoubtedly,' said Maud. 'Our story will be passed on from generation to generation.'

'Well, in that case, I'm definitely coming,' declared Ethel. 'I've always wanted to be famous.'

The animals walked on. Puff Adder made his way through the grass, careful to avoid the clumsy hooves all around him, as well as the meerkats, who were marching in perfect formation at the head of the group. The snake knew the commander-in-chief was frustrated that he had moved to a new and unknown place. She had even excused some of her troops from their normal duties to send them on a special mission to find the snake's home, but to no avail.

For once, the baboon family were all on good terms. They always stuck together when there was a common enemy, and they now bounded along quietly as a troop. The baboons were eager to join the rescue attempt as they all liked and admired Alfie. They also felt passionately on behalf of their other distant cousins, the mountain gorillas, as the baboons knew that they, too, had suffered at the hands of poachers.

The ostriches hurried along with Stella, although for them, the pace was far too slow. They would have preferred to stretch out their legs and run. Leopard made sure her cubs were to one side of the group as she didn't want them getting crushed under the herd animals' hooves. Giraffe and his family stood out in the middle of the group, and the herd animals brought up the rear. There were literally hundreds of buffaloes, wildebeests, zebras, and antelopes, and those at the back were now a long way behind Stella and the meerkats.

The animals marched on through the night, their route illuminated by the silvery light of the moon. From time to time, a cloud scurried across the moon, and the world was suddenly plunged into near-total darkness.

'The secretary bird says we're nearly there,' whispered Stella to the animals just behind her. 'Pass it on to the others.'

There was hurried and excited whispering as the message was transmitted through the group. Although there was no real need to whisper, the animals instinctively spoke in low voices.

'Thank goodness for that,' said Mabel rather loudly when she heard there would not be much more walking to do.

'Shhhhh!' warned Ethel and Maud at the same time.

'You never know who might hear us,' added Ethel.

'Don't be ridiculous,' said Mabel. 'There is nobody around except for us.'

Just then, Giraffe twisted his head around and whispered another message: 'Apparently, the house on the hill over there is Mr Rich's house. Stella says everyone should be extremely quiet—we don't want him to hear us coming.'

The elephants stopped talking, and the animals peered at the house ahead of them. The keen-eyed creatures could see that it was a huge, white building surrounded by strangely green trees, despite the dryness of the plains. The shapes of the trees were unfamiliar to the animals, and Stella correctly guessed they had originated from outside of the park. There was a large stone wall running all around the house and garden, and Stella eyed it with concern, wondering how difficult it might be to topple. Total silence fell as the animals approached the house and imagined how they might rescue Alfie.

At that moment, the lion pride came bounding back towards the group. They had been lucky and found a half-eaten carcass, and three of the lionesses carried big pieces of meat in their mouths. Stella was pleased to see they hung slightly away from the herd animals, knowing how distressed they would be to see it.

When the group was no more than a hundred paces from the house, Stella called as quietly as she could for the secretary bird to stop. She turned to face the group, and the animals stopped to listen.

'Well, everybody can see where we are heading,' she whispered as loudly as she dared. 'The house seems to be surrounded by a wall. I don't yet know whether it goes all around the grounds, but I suspect it does. Obviously, our first problem will be to get inside.'

'Well, we can't, can we?' said Ethel, her face looking blank. 'We might as well go back.'

'Don't be stupid,' said Buffalo before he could stop himself. 'Elephants can push down walls.'

'And Baboons can climb over them,' added Baboon.

'Birds can fly over the wall quite easily, too,' said Martial Eagle.

'And my troops are exceptional diggers,' pointed out the commander-in-chief. 'We could have a tunnel under that wall in no time.'

Stella felt pleased and excited. 'Excellent!' she whispered. 'Once we are inside, the first thing we need to do is placate the dogs. Although dogs are animals like us, we know that, for some reason, they feel great loyalty to their owners. If we offer them the meat, hopefully in return they will agree not to warn Mr Rich. Lion, you are in charge of talking to the dogs.'

Lion nodded rather mournfully. He wasn't looking forward to giving away the juicy chunks of meat.

'We need to locate Alfie as quickly as possible and decide how we can rescue him,' Stella continued. 'It looks like there are glass openings to the house, known as windows. Meerkats, you can look through the windows at ground level, and the birds can fly up to look through the windows at the higher levels. Giraffe, you can also help here. Obviously, it is vital that we don't attract attention to ourselves. Mr Rich may suspect that we will try to rescue Alfie. He may even have guards watching out for us.'

'I think we should take Mr Rich prisoner as well as rescue Alfie,' declared Zebra. 'Then, hopefully, the other humans will do something to stop him.'

'I agree. We should do exactly that,' said Stella, 'and that is where Leopard comes in.

'Leopard, do you think you can remember your way to the ranger's house? I know you have only been there once.'

Leopard felt anxious. Her leg had been in great pain when the ranger had driven her to his house, and it had been dark when he had brought her back to the waterhole. 'I think so,' she said. 'I know which direction it is in, but it might take me some time to reach it. I think it's quite a long journey.'

'Well, I want you to set off for his house straightaway,' whispered Stella. 'You must somehow persuade the ranger to accompany you back here. I think we may need his help later.'

'Suppose he won't come with me?' asked Leopard, her voice growing louder in alarm. 'I can't talk to him and tell him what is happening like Alfie can.'

'No, but he'll recognise you,' said Stella, 'and he might suspect Alfie has sent you. I think you'll be able to persuade him to follow you.'

'Would you look after the cubs, then?' Leopard asked. 'I'll be much quicker alone.'

'Of course,' said Stella. For once, the cubs didn't argue. They knew it wasn't the time to complain that they didn't want to be left behind. Besides, they were going to look for Alfie.

Leopard bounded away and was soon lost to sight in the darkness.

'Stella, what should we do?' asked Zebra, who was keen to play a part in Mr Rich's downfall. 'I'm sure we can help in some way.'

'All of the zebras, buffaloes, wildebeests, and antelopes should surround the house,' Stella told him. 'Mr Rich may try to escape if he sees what is going on, and we don't want him going anywhere.'

'Suppose he shoots at us?' asked Antelope, looking horrified. 'I don't want any of us to stand in the way of his gun.'

'I know,' said Stella, nodding her head slowly. 'I'm asking you to be very brave. Of course, there is a risk that he might shoot at us. I just hope that with so many animals around him, he will realise it is hopeless to try to shoot us all.'

The herds shifted uneasily, and a murmur ran through the group. This was not the reassuring answer they had sought.

'What can I do, Stella?' asked Wanda humbly. She still felt as if Alfie's capture was her fault, and she was keen to help with his rescue.

'Yes, and what about us?' cried Leader rather too loudly, while Dent and Felicity looked at the great elephant leader in anticipation.

'Hush,' whispered Stella. 'Don't worry—I have a very important job for all of you. Now, is everyone ready?'

There came the strange sound of all the different voices whispering in reply. Stella glanced around the group and saw that everyone was eager to begin. 'Right—let's go,' she whispered excitedly. 'Alfie is depending on us.'

CHAPTER 42

The Animals Encounter the Dogs

THE GROUP FOLLOWED AS the secretary bird flew steadily towards the house, and the secretary bird felt herself grow breathless as she neared the wall. She hoped her hero was still alive.

The animals had been travelling for several hours when they reached Mr Rich's house. However, they were too excited to think about how far they had walked. The elephants stopped at the gates and looked up at them in awe. They were a pair of enormous black gates with strong iron bars but no obvious handles or knobs to turn. Stella nudged them with her head and found they didn't move at all. She was puzzled and wondered how they might be opened and closed.

'The gates are locked,' she whispered to the hundreds of animals behind her. 'We'll have to find another way in.'

Stella looked at the secretary bird and Martial Eagle. 'Would you fly around the wall and see if there is another way to enter, please?'

The birds did so quickly, although the secretary bird was in such a state of nerves that she wondered how she could fly at all. They returned after a couple of minutes, both shaking their heads.

'The wall runs right around the garden,' gabbled the secretary bird, 'and the only break in it is this gate.'

'There seems to be no way of opening the gate from the other side either,' said Martial Eagle. 'It must open from inside the house somehow.'

'There are five dogs in the garden,' added the secretary bird. 'They seem to be asleep at the moment, but they are very big.'

'And there is a car by the house,' said Martial Eagle, 'so somebody is at home.'

'Thank you,' said Stella. 'Now, how do we get inside?'

'We shall dig a tunnel at once,' said the commander-in-chief, trying to take control, but Stella stopped her quickly.

'Thank you, but let's go farther along, where we will be out of sight of the house,' she said. 'Then we elephants shall see if we can push down the wall. I think it might take too long to dig a tunnel large enough for all of us to get through.'

The commander-in-chief nodded her acceptance, and the group followed Stella as she led them around the garden wall. Many of the animals looked nervously up at the dark windows. For all they knew, Mr Rich himself could be watching them at that very moment.

Stella took them right to the end of the long garden, as far as possible away from the house. She didn't want Mr Rich to be awakened by the sound of his wall falling in. Although the animals were trying to walk quietly, the hundreds of hooves sounded loud to her in the still of the night, and she hoped desperately that they wouldn't be heard.

Eventually, Stella stopped in front of the tall stone wall and faced the rest of the group. 'Bright, Mabel, Ethel, Maud – would you come forwards, please?' she whispered. 'We need as much strength as possible for this.'

'The buffaloes can help too,' offered Buffalo, and, to his delight, Stella nodded her agreement. Several large buffaloes stepped through the group, and the other animals moved aside a little to give them room.

'On the count of three, I want everyone to put their weight against the wall and push with all their might,' said Stella, who was having difficulty keeping calm. 'Ready? One, two, three! Push!'

The animals leaned against the wall and drove forwards with all the power they could muster, while the watching group encouraged them in whispers. At first, it seemed the wall was not going to give way. The elephants and buffaloes heaved against it, but the wall remained solid and didn't move even slightly.

'Come on!' Stella said, panting. 'Try harder. I think we can do it if we give it just a little bit more effort.'

The animals summoned up everything they had and pushed hard again. They felt heat build up inside them, and Mabel thought her legs were going to buckle underneath her. Then, a part of the wall suddenly gave way with a mighty crash!

The watching animals cheered in delight. Even Puff Adder looked pleased.

Stella stepped back from the wall and waved her trunk at them frantically. 'Be quiet. Be quiet,' she whispered. 'We mustn't wake anyone in the house.'

'I think it might be too late for that,' said Ostrich in alarm, noticing that the dogs had jumped up from their sleeping positions and were now charging across the lawn towards the animals, barking loudly. They were huge Alsatians, and they looked extremely threatening.

'Lion, quickly, bring forward the meat,' called Stella, and the lions pushed their way through the group.

'We bring this meat as a gift,' Lion called to the dogs as they approached. 'Quiet your barking. Your master is holding one of our friends prisoner and we have come to rescue him. We mean you no harm.'

The lions threw the meat down in front of the dogs, who gathered around it, sniffing suspiciously.

'Do you mean the chimpanzee?' asked one of the Alsatians in an unfriendly growl.

Stella nodded. 'Your master has kidnapped him because he was trying to stop your master from poaching wild animals. Your master is responsible for the deaths of some of our friends and family.'

'But the numbers of wild animals have to be kept down,' replied another of the dogs. 'We have heard there are too many elephants, rhinos, and other species. The numbers need to be controlled.'

The animals couldn't believe their ears. 'That's rubbish,' spluttered Wanda. 'There are hardly any white rhinos left in the park, and I haven't seen a black rhino for many seasons now.'

'We are the only female elephant herd, as far as we know,' added Bright.

'Leopard hasn't met another leopard since she last mated,' continued Stella, 'and the only cheetah we know has disappeared. It is more than possible that your master has killed him.'

The dogs looked uneasily at each other. They had never heard the story from the mouths of the park animals before. Their information came from hunting dogs who had told them they were employed by their masters to stop the wild animals from becoming too numerous.

Lion couldn't believe the way the dogs were all just ignoring the meat, which was lying untouched on the ground in front of them. They looked extremely well-fed, and he supposed they had never gone in fear of missing a meal.

'I think the chimpanzee may be dead anyway,' said a third dog rather dismissively.

A horrified gasp went around the group, and the dogs looked quite surprised.

'Why do you say that?' demanded Stella.

'We saw him being carried out of the van, and he was quite limp,' explained the first dog. 'We tried to talk to him, but he gave no response.'

'Is he still in the house somewhere?' asked Bright.

'Well, we haven't seen him being taken out,' answered the third dog, 'but we aren't always here. It's possible his body was taken away during one of our walks.'

There was a terrible silence as the animals tried to digest this information. The dogs stared at the hundreds of creatures in front of them and saw how worried their expressions had become.

'You really do care about him, don't you?' exclaimed the second dog. 'How strange that you should be so concerned for a member of another species. The hunting dogs have always told us that wild animals are completely selfish and live only for themselves.'

'The hunting dogs don't seem to know much about us,' said Buffalo, looking annoyed.

'These animals are not selfish,' interrupted Wanda suddenly, much to everyone's surprise. 'I used to live alone with my daughter until I joined this group. It is wonderful how all the species band together to help each other in the fight against the poachers. Don't ever think these animals are selfish. I owe my life to them.'

The rhino looked at Leader with tears in her eyes, and the little elephant felt as if he would burst with pride. Wanda still remembered his bravery.

Meanwhile, the dogs were also affected by her words. The other four looked at the first dog, who was evidently the leader, and waited for him to speak.

'Is it true there are very few of some species left?' asked the first dog.

Stella nodded seriously. 'And soon there may be none at all.'

'And this chimpanzee has done no harm to anyone?' continued the dog.

'Of course not,' said Bright rather impatiently. 'And his closest friend is the ranger of the National Park. The ranger's job is to protect the endangered species.'

'We've met the ranger,' said the fourth dog suddenly. She looked at her companions. 'Do you remember, the very friendly man who spoke to each of us in turn? Our master certainly called him the ranger. I think he came to ask our master to attend a meeting.'

'That was a meeting with us..,' began Giraffe excitedly, but the first dog interrupted him.

'Yes, I remember,' he said slowly. 'He seemed very humble and a little afraid of our master. I wanted to tell him that he had nothing to fear.'

'But now you say our master is a poacher who kills animals, even though there are few of their species left,' surmised the second dog, looking at Stella for confirmation.

The elephant leader nodded sadly. 'Yes,' she said. 'I'm afraid there is no doubt of it. He killed my father.'

'In that case, we shall help you to rescue your friend,' said the first dog. 'I'm appalled if that is what my master has been doing. We didn't know. Come in! Come in!'

The dogs stepped aside to allow the animals to pour into the garden. To Lion's disappointment, three of them picked up the meat in their jaws before they moved away. He had hoped to snatch one of the bigger chunks when nobody was looking.

The animals looked around the garden in amazement. Even in the dim light of the moon, they could see it was beautifully kept, with exotic, colourful flowers and neatly trimmed trees and shrubs. The green lawn felt soft under their feet compared to the rough stubble of the plains. In the centre of the grass stood a huge fountain with stone figures holding large water jars. Water spouted from their mouths and from the jars they held and tumbled into a big pool around the statues.

'My master is very wealthy,' said the dog leader, seeing the elephants staring at the fountain with wide eyes. 'He makes his money doing very clever business deals.'

Buffalo was just stepping through the hole in the wall when he heard this remark, and he snorted in disgust. 'Your master makes his money by killing endangered species and selling parts of their bodies,' he said.

The dogs looked quite distraught. 'I can hardly believe it,' the leader said, shaking his head sadly. 'Well, do whatever you need to. We won't get in your way.'

CHAPTER 43

Searching for Alfie

IT TOOK SOME TIME for the animals to enter the garden. Stella watched them anxiously, aware that time was ticking by. She didn't know how early Mr Rich would get up, but she suspected they didn't have very long before dawn, and they might be in trouble once the light came.

'Hurry along,' she whispered, encouraging the few antelopes who had not yet entered the garden. 'Now, Martial Eagle, Giraffe, Secretary Bird—I want you to scout around the upper windows to see if you can find Alfie. Meerkats, please follow me, and we shall look into the lower windows. Look out for Mr Rich, as well. Wanda, Leader, Dent, Felicity—you know what I want you to do. Zebras, antelopes, buffaloes, and wildebeests—please make a circle around the house several animals thick. Lions, guard the front gate—we don't want Mr Rich to escape. Lioness, please look after Leopard's cubs. Ostriches, keep a watch for any sign of movement in the house. Puff Adder, scorpions, baboons—please come with me; you will be needed shortly. Be careful, everyone.'

'What do you want us to do?' asked Mabel, looking a bit crestfallen. All of the animals seemed to have an important job except for the adult elephants.

Stella heard the disappointment in her voice and tried to think of something the rest of the elephant herd could do. 'You have already been invaluable,' she said. 'Nobody else would have had the strength to knock down that wall.'

'We must hurry, Mum,' Bright murmured.

Stella looked around. Her eyes swept across the beautiful garden, and an unusually mischievous smile spread over her face. 'I know what I need you to do,' she told the elephant herd. 'This garden looks far too nice for a human who makes his money by killing endangered species. You have my permission to eat whatever you fancy as quickly as possible.'

Mabel, Ethel, and Maud looked delighted. Not only would they be destroying Mr Rich's garden, but they could have a feast. They hurried off into the flowerbeds and were soon lost to their task.

'Right—let's go,' Stella whispered urgently to the others. 'We have to hurry now!'

The animals dispersed around the big house, and the meerkats hurried to spread out and peer into all the ground floor windows. The commander-in-chief organised her troops neatly around the house so they could cover every angle. Stella's heart beat faster than she had ever felt it before, and she prayed that nobody would see them. Meanwhile, the dogs looked on, feeling rather confused. They had never doubted their master until then. The night had come as an unwelcome surprise.

'Have you found him?' Stella whispered repeatedly as she went from one meerkat to the next. They all shook their heads in disappointment. Each of them had hoped to be the one to discover where Alfie was being kept. Unfortunately, no one had noticed the tiny window just above the ground that provided the only light into the chimp's cell, as it was well hidden behind a bush.

Stella felt her hopes begin to fade. Perhaps Mr Rich had killed Alfie, and they were too late. However, something inside her couldn't believe that was true. She felt certain that Alfie was alive in the house somewhere. They just had to find him. Across the sky, a gradual lightening was starting to show, and Stella realised that dawn was not far away. They didn't have much time.

'Keep looking,' she told them all, and the meerkats continued their hunt around the ground floor. Meanwhile, the herds had obediently formed a large circle and had the house completely surrounded.

Martial Eagle softly called Stella's name, and she raced around the corner of the house to where he was hovering. 'I think I've found Mr Rich,' he whispered. 'It's dark inside, but I'm sure it's him asleep in this room.'

The elephant felt a shiver run down her spine. She was standing just metres away from a man who would shoot her without even thinking.

'Well done,' she whispered. 'Now, come away from the window in case you wake him.'

Martial Eagle dropped down to perch at the same moment that Giraffe approached them. 'There's an unidentified human asleep in the room through the upper window just there,' Giraffe whispered, indicating with his head.

'And I've found another window open high up,' twittered the secretary bird, who was almost hysterical with excitement.

'Excellent,' said Stella, realising this was a great piece of luck. 'Martial Eagle, please find Baboon and his family and bring them here immediately. Giraffe, wait here with me.'

The baboons soon appeared from the other side of the house, and Stella quickly explained what she wanted them to do. They understood at once, and the secretary bird pointed at the open window she had spotted high up near the roof.

Giraffe and Baboon hurried over to stand beneath the window. Giraffe set apart his front legs and bent his long neck, so his chin rested on the grass. Baboon wasted no time clambering up his neck and on to his back, and Giraffe stood upright again, pulling his front legs up next to each other.

'Ready?' whispered Baboon, and the animals watched as Giraffe raised his head up to the window and rested it on the narrow ledge outside.

'Go for it,' he encouraged Baboon.

Giraffe held his breath as Baboon swung his way up his neck, and was quickly at the top, clinging on beneath Giraffe's head.

'Hurry up,' gasped poor Giraffe, whose face was beginning to turn red. 'I can hardly breathe!'

Stella found herself unable to watch as Baboon stretched himself across from Giraffe's neck to the open window. He reached out with both hands, grabbed the window frame, and with the style of a true climber, swung himself neatly into the room inside, where he was lost from view. A muffled cheer ran through the watching herd animals, and the secretary bird felt so dizzy she thought she might faint.

Inside his cell, Alfie stirred at the slight noise, and he opened his eyes. Was that Ostrich's voice he had heard?

Meanwhile, Baboon found himself in a small bedroom, which was, fortunately, empty. He took a quick look around to see that it was elaborately furnished, with a red velvet cover on the bed and a mirror opposite it. To his disgust, he saw the head of a mountain gorilla hanging over the mirror, clearly another of Mr Rich's trophies. He thought of his poor cousins suffering in the forests and vowed he would make sure Mr Rich was stopped from ever poaching again.

Baboon crept across to the door and grasped the handle. The door opened without the slightest noise, and he found himself on a long landing with several other doors, from where he could see two floors below through the staircase bannisters. Baboon made his way to the stairs at the end of the landing and tiptoed down them, watching the row of doors for any movement.

There were two flights of stairs to go down. Once at the bottom of the stairs, Baboon was in a large hall with a chandelier hanging down from the painted ceiling. Four more stuffed heads were framed on the walls, this time of various types of antelope, and a huge, stretched-out leopard skin took up much of the marble floor. Baboon tried not to look at it as he made his way to the big front doors, which looked to be made of solid wood.

He paused as he wondered how to open the doors. There was a chain across them, which he quickly removed. There was also a key sitting in the lock, which he pulled right and then left until it turned. Baboon yanked at the doors, but still they wouldn't open, and he began to feel anxious. What would he do if he couldn't open them?

Fortunately, he noticed the doors seemed to be stuck at the top. He glanced upwards and realised there was a bolt lying across them. Baboon jumped up and pulled the bolt from its catch, and to his delight, he was able to pull the doors open.

The animals outside saw him appear in the doorway, and they cheered softly, barely able to contain their excitement.

'Is there any sign of Alfie?' called Zebra in a low voice.

'Have you found Mr Rich?' Wildebeest hissed.

'No,' answered Baboon, 'but I haven't looked yet.'

As Stella had planned, the rest of the baboon troop, Puff Adder, and a nest of scorpions had assembled by the front doors, waiting for Baboon. They scuttled inside the house, and the baboons split up at once. The hunt for Alfie was on!

Baboon shut the doors gently behind them, as he didn't want the wind to rush through the house and wake Mr Rich. However, he didn't bolt them, knowing they might need to get out quickly later.

The baboons hurried around the house, trying to pick up Alfie's scent. Each baboon scampered to a different room, opened the door silently, and sniffed to work out if Alfie might be inside. Finding no luck in the rooms on the ground floor, a few of the baboons headed softly up the stairs to look inside the rooms on the first floor, starting with the open doors. Meanwhile, Stella and the other animals waited outside, wondering what was happening.

Baboon himself eventually found Alfie. He had hunted around the ground floor and found the office where the housekeeper had taken Alfie to give him some food. Alfie's scent was strong, and Baboon knew the chimp had been there recently. However, he didn't notice the door to the basement, which was cleverly designed to camouflage with the wall.

Baboon sniffed the wall, feeling puzzled. He knew he was close.

Alfie heard Baboon sniffing. He had been sitting upright on a leopard skin ever since hearing the noise outside. He wondered if, by any chance, the whispered voices might be his friends coming to rescue him. It was too early for the humans in the house to be up, and the voices hadn't sounded like the dogs he had heard before.

Alfie had rushed over to stand beneath the window and shout to the animals outside, hoping they would hear him. Unfortunately, the window was so tiny and the glass so thick that his voice had barely reached the outside world. All the nearby animals heard was a faint hum as it reverberated around the cell. It was no louder than the wind blowing gently across the plains, and nobody had realised it was Alfie.

The chimp had thrown himself down in frustration. He suspected the animals were near, yet he couldn't communicate with them. He glared at the window, wishing it were lower so he could bang on the glass.

It wasn't long afterwards that he heard what sounded like somebody moving furniture around in the adjacent room. Alfie sat quietly for a moment, listening for any voices, but there was silence except for the opening and closing of cupboard doors. He wondered if his friends had somehow managed to get inside the house and were looking for him, but he was afraid to shout in case it was Mr Rich.

He changed his mind when he heard the sound of Baboon sniffing around at the door. Then he knew for certain it must be an animal.

Alfie ran up the steps and called out softly for fear of disturbing anyone else in the house.

Baboon heard him and quickly realised there must be an entrance. He spotted the bolts on the door in no time and kicked himself for not having noticed them before. Baboon rammed the bolts back, pulled the door open, and Alfie danced into his arms in delight.

CHAPTER 44

Mr Rich with a Gun

'BABOON! HELLO! HELLO! THANK you! Thank you!' cried Alfie. 'I thought I would never see any of you again. How did you find me here?'

'I'll explain later,' whispered Baboon. 'We need to get out of the house and quickly.' He looked with disgust at the collar around Alfie's neck and the chain hanging from it. 'That thing looks awful. We need to get you out of that, too.'

'Yes, definitely,' Alfie said. 'Let's go. You've saved me from a life in the circus or worse. I dread to think what Mr Rich would have done to me if he had seen this mess.' He pointed down the stairs and into the cell, where Baboon could just make out the fragments of tusks and horns in the gloom.

He looked at Alfie with wide eyes. 'Are they–'

'Elephant tusks and rhino horns?' Alfie finished for him. 'Yes, indeed, they are, and leopard, cheetah, lion, and antelope furs and skins too. Mr Rich has clearly been busy recently.'

'I can't believe it,' said Baboon. White shards of different shapes and sizes covered the floor, and Baboon thought quietly about the number of animals who must have died to make that pile.

Alfie fidgeted while Baboon gazed at the floor. 'Let's go,' he urged. 'We need to get away before they wake up.'

'Sorry,' whispered Baboon, and he closed the door without making a sound. He turned to face Alfie. 'Of course, we'll get out of this place as fast as we can,' he said, 'but we also need to capture Mr Rich.'

Alfie looked terrified. 'You don't know how dangerous he is,' he whispered back. 'How can we capture him? He carries a gun, even in the house, and the ranger is nowhere near to help.'

'Hopefully, the ranger is already on his way,' replied Baboon. 'Leopard has gone to fetch him. Everyone is outside, surrounding the house until the ranger gets here.'

'How did you find me here?' Alfie asked again. 'I was all alone on Moonlight Plains when they shot me down. Wanda might have seen me fall, but she wouldn't have known where the men had taken me.'

'Somebody followed you,' said Baboon with a big grin. 'Somebody who follows you everywhere because she thinks you're amazing.'

'Who do you mean?' Alfie asked. 'One of Leopard's cubs, perhaps?'

'No, try again.' Baboon laughed. 'Someone you noticed was late to the meeting the time we all first met, and you were so nice to her that she positively swooned.'

'The secretary bird!' exclaimed Alfie, rather too loudly.

'Shh!' whispered Baboon with a little smile. 'Yes. You owe everything to her. She followed the van all the way here, and then flew all the way back again to tell us what had happened and where you were.'

'What a kind thing she is,' said Alfie with tears in his eyes. 'I am so grateful to her.'

Now it was Baboon's turn to be impatient. 'I must tell the others I've found you,' he whispered. 'My troop is busy searching the rest of the house.'

'They might wake Mr Rich,' said Alfie. 'Let's hurry!'

Alfie scooped up his chain in his arms, and the two animals tiptoed into the hall. Alfie felt relief flood over him at being able to leave the study. A few of the other baboons were waiting in the hall, and they were delighted to see Alfie. They exchanged rapid hugs and whispered greetings while Baboon counted them up.

'Where is Bibi?' he hissed. 'Has she gone back outside?'

Nobody had a chance to answer before there came a sudden shriek from one of the bedrooms upstairs, and the animals stood still. Somebody was screaming for help, and Alfie recognised it as the voice of Mr Rich's housekeeper.

A door was flung open, and Baboon's daughter, Bibi, came charging down the stairs in a panic. 'He woke up!' she cried. 'I was looking under the bed when he woke up. Alfie! You're here! Thank goodness!'

The screaming continued, and Alfie took charge. 'You all go back outside,' he ordered. 'I'll go to the man and stop him screaming. It's not Mr Rich. It's his housekeeper. He's a nice man. He will recognise me.'

Before anyone realised this was a mistake, the baboons raced out of the front door, while Alfie charged up the stairs and headed for the noise, still carrying his chain. He swung open the bedroom door and looked across the room to where the housekeeper was standing with his back to the wall, his eyes wide in terror.

Alfie smiled at him and brought his fingers to his lips. 'Shh,' he said gently, imitating the sound he had heard the ranger make before. 'Shh.' The chimp stood just inside the door, not daring to approach the housekeeper in case he frightened him even more.

The man stopped screaming, pointed at Alfie, and a sudden smile spread across his face. 'Of course, it was you,' he said, looking as though he felt silly. 'I thought you were a wild baboon. You looked like one when I caught you peering under my bed.'

Alfie beamed at him again, hoping the man might settle back into bed and forget about him. He brought his hands together and pressed them to the side of his face in a gesture the ranger had used to tell Alfie it was time to go to sleep before Alfie could understand human language.

'Zzzzzzzzz,' he said, sounding rather like a motorbike driving into the distance. *Go back to sleep*, he thought.

'Yes, I'm tired, too.' The man laughed. Alfie watched with relief as he slid under the covers on his bed. The housekeeper seemed to be on the verge of settling down when it occurred to him that Alfie shouldn't be out of his cell, and he sat up straight to look at the chimp.

'How did you get out?' he asked.

A voice behind him echoed the same words. 'Yes, it's a good question,' said Mr Rich's sneering voice from the doorway. 'How did you get out? You are just too clever for your own good, aren't you, you horrible animal?'

Without turning around, Alfie heard Mr Rich come towards him and the chimp felt something cold and hard being pressed against his back. He shivered when he realised it must be a gun.

CHAPTER 45

Panic!

'THIS IS THE LAST chance you'll get, chimpanzee,' threatened Mr Rich while the housekeeper looked on. 'Get back to your cell at once, or I'll have to get rid of you for good.'

Alfie turned around slowly. Mr Rich was standing in the doorway in his dressing gown, pointing his gun straight at Alfie. He looked furious, and Alfie knew he was in big trouble. Alfie dropped to all fours and hurried through the bedroom door to the landing, looking back at Mr Rich all the time. He hardly dared to turn his back on the man in case he changed his mind and shot him.

Mr Rich was suddenly distracted by the sight of an elephant through the landing window, and he looked out in astonishment.

Alfie realised this was his chance to escape, and he bolted towards the stairs, his chain dragging behind him.

Mr Rich gasped as he saw the huge gathering of animals in his garden through the window. He turned to face Alfie, and their eyes locked for a moment before the chimp began bounding down the stairs as fast as he could manage. Though Alfie would ordinarily have been able to outrun Mr Rich, his chain caught around the bannister and slowed him a little. Mr Rich charged after him with surprising speed, grabbing at the end of the chain with his left hand to pull Alfie back. He walloped Alfie on the back of his head with the gun in his other hand, and the poor chimp collapsed midway down the stairs, tumbled down the remaining stairs to the lower landing, and lay there, still.

Mr Rich raced past him down the rest of the stairs, intending to check that the front doors were locked, and the animals couldn't get in.

He hesitated for a second at the bottom of the second flight of stairs, horrified to see that the doors weren't bolted. Were the animals already inside?

It was the moment Puff Adder and the scorpions had been waiting for. Stella had told them to hide in the hall for exactly this reason. Puff Adder waited until Mr Rich was directly between him and the front doors and then hissed loudly, uncoiling his body and flicking his tongue at the man. Puff Adder eyed Mr Rich's bare feet and legs as the man stood frozen to the spot in his velvet dressing gown. Puff Adder was delighted to realise the poacher's exposed legs would make him more vulnerable.

Mr Rich heard him and turned around in alarm—the snake was only a few paces in front of him. The entire floor also seemed to be covered in scorpions coming towards him, their dangerous stingers raised. He looked back up the stairs behind him to see that more scorpions were gathered there, too. He was surrounded!

He could shoot the snake with his gun, but he couldn't shoot all the scorpions. There were hundreds of them, crawling all around him! Where had they all come from? Just one sting could be deadly, let alone dozens.

For the first time in his life, Mr Rich realised what it must be like for a wild animal to feel trapped and helpless. The only choice left was to go outside and face the animals waiting for him there.

Meanwhile, Puff Adder made his way towards the poacher, forcing him back in the direction of the front doors. The scorpions followed, scuttling rapidly along, and Mr Rich made a hurried decision: he raced for the front doors, snatched them open and ran outside, turning to pull the doors shut behind him. In his panic, he dropped his gun as he shut the doors, and a quick-thinking baboon charged in and picked it up before Mr Rich could reach for it. The man watched in horror as his gun disappeared. He was now alone and defenceless with hundreds of wild animals!

The animals outside stood in absolute silence. Stella had warned them this might happen, and she had ordered everyone to stay quite still.

Mr Rich stood in front of the doors, clearly having no idea what to do. He eyed the huge collection of animals in fear, noticing first the baboons, the elephants, and the rhinos, then the lions, two small leopards, and then seemingly hundreds of buffaloes, wildebeests, antelopes, and zebras standing behind them. He supposed these were the animals he had met at that wretched meeting. If only he hadn't gone, the animals might never have realised he was a poacher.

The animals stared back at him nervously, wondering what the horrible man was about to do. It was obvious he was terrified, but Stella was thankful to see that he was unarmed and hopefully no longer a threat to the animals.

Mr Rich hesitated, then whistled twice for his dogs, hoping they might help him. To his surprise, they didn't come, so instead he made a dash for his car, which stood just along from the front doors. Before any of the animals had a chance to react, he was inside, placing a sheet of glass between him and the watching group.

'Ha ha!' he shouted. 'You can't get me now!' He pulled out a key from under the seat, put it into the ignition and turned the engine on. He didn't care where he was going as long as he could escape from the hundreds of frightening animals. Mr Rich might be a bully, but without his guns, he was a coward.

The man pointed a remote-control device at the gates, and they slowly opened, prompting Lion and Lioness to move hurriedly. He turned on the car engine, gave the animals a gloating laugh and a wave of his hand, pressed on the accelerator, and got a dreadful shock when the car didn't move at all.

A determined little group had ensured that Mr Rich couldn't escape. Wanda, Dent and Felicity had taken great care to puncture the tyres with their horns, and they were now completely flat. At the same time, Leader had managed to open the bonnet and had reached in and plucked out as many important-looking wires and bits of metal as he could find.

Mr Rich trembled as the realisation struck him. He was surrounded by animals who could trample him to death or tear him apart if they chose. He looked around at the different species through the car windows and in his terror, he saw only sharp teeth and bloodthirsty expressions. After a nod from Stella, the animals closed in around the car, with the elephants leading the way. Soon, all Mr Rich could see were thick, grey elephant legs everywhere, and to his dismay, they began rocking the car gently back and forth between them. The poacher grabbed hold of the steering wheel in a frantic attempt to stop himself from sliding around as the animals laughed in relief.

They had done it! Mr Rich was caught, and he couldn't escape. Baboon had already shared the news of the tusks and horns he had seen in Alfie's cell. All they needed now was for the ranger to arrive and take Mr Rich away.

Stella stood back from the crowd for a moment to watch with satisfaction. It had been her dream to avenge her father's death one day, but she had never truly believed she would catch the very poacher who had killed him. It was all thanks to her wonderful group of friends and the lovely Alfie.

Alfie!

CHAPTER 46

Arrested!

STELLA REALISED ALFIE MUST still be in the house somewhere. In their delight at capturing Mr Rich, the animals had forgotten about the poor chimpanzee. Stella felt her heart sink. Supposing Mr Rich had killed Alfie!

Baboon saw her worried expression, and he bounced across to her, knowing what she was thinking. 'Let's go and find him,' he said urgently. 'Something must have happened, or he would have joined us by now.'

'Yes, you're right,' said Stella unhappily.

The secretary bird appeared at her side. 'Where is Alfie?' she asked in a small voice. 'Has something terrible happened?'

'We're just going to find out,' said Stella.

The three figures hurried to the doors, afraid of what they might find. The other animals were so focused on Mr Rich that they didn't notice them leave. Stella paused at the doors and addressed her companions with a serious expression.

'I think we should all be prepared for what we might find here,' she said. 'It is quite possible that Mr Rich has hurt Alfie very badly, and perhaps even killed him.'

Baboon and the secretary bird nodded in silence.

'Stand back a little way, and I shall break down the doors,' ordered the elephant, and the other two obeyed at once. Stella settled her head against the double doors and braced herself for the jolt. She closed her eyes and took a deep breath. To her enormous amazement, the doors fell inwards before she had even started to push.

Baboon and the secretary bird shouted in delight when a cheery face greeted them from the hall. 'Alfie!' cried the secretary bird, and she rushed towards the chimp to nuzzle his arm with her beak.

'I'm so glad you're all right!' added Baboon, looking relieved. He bounded through the doors and hugged his cousin warmly.

Alfie looked from one animal to the next. 'I thought I would never see any of you again,' he cried. 'Thank you so much for rescuing me. I owe you my life, especially you, dear Secretary Bird. Thank you! You have all been so brave!'

The secretary bird beamed from ear to ear and went slightly pink. She felt as if this was the best day of her life. 'It's my pleasure. It's my pleasure,' she said in delight. 'I wanted to help you.'

'You are a true friend, and I will never forget it,' said Alfie, giving her wing a gentle stroke, and the secretary bird thought she might explode with happiness. She had always felt a little shy and not very popular, but now the wonderful Alfie had called her a friend.

'Where is Mr Rich?' asked Alfie anxiously.

Stella nodded towards the car, almost completely hidden from view by the animals. Alfie peered out of the front doors and caught glimpses of Mr Rich's face inside the car, looking extremely green as the animals heaved the vehicle back and forth with such fervour that the wheels even tipped away from the ground.

'Hooray!' shouted Alfie ecstatically, and he punched a fist in the air and did a backward somersault into the hall. 'We've got him at last! And if he is the chief poacher, the others may well disappear too.'

The animals beamed at each other, and Alfie couldn't stop himself from jumping up and down on the spot for sheer joy. The chimp caught sight of the housekeeper trembling on the stairs and felt sorry for him. The housekeeper looked very scared, especially of Puff Adder and the scorpions, who were still gathered in the hall.

Alfie moved towards him and beckoned as he had seen the ranger do to other humans. 'Come here,' he wanted to say. The man seemed to understand him, but he hesitated nervously. Alfie beckoned slowly again, and the housekeeper plucked up the courage to shuffle down the stairs towards him. The chimp stretched out a hand of encouragement, and, to his amazement, the housekeeper reached out and took hold of it. Alfie led him slowly down the last few stairs, taking care not to rush him.

'This is Mr Rich's housekeeper,' he explained to Stella, Puff Adder, Baboon, and the secretary bird as he guided the man towards them and out of the front doors. 'He is a very nice man. He risked getting into terrible trouble with Mr Rich to let me out and give me some food.'

Stella nodded her head politely at the man, who, of course, hadn't understood his introduction. Baboon patted him on the arm, making him shrink away in fear, and the secretary bird gabbled off three different forms of greeting.

'What happened to your head?' asked Baboon, noticing the gash where Mr Rich had dealt him a blow. Alfie reached up to feel the back of his head, realising, for the first time, that it was bleeding.

'Mr Rich hit me with his gun,' he said, shaking drops of blood from his fingers. 'He panicked when he saw you all outside, and I was in his way at the time.'

There came a loud, sudden shout above the noise the animals were making: 'Quiet!' It was Lion's powerful roar. 'The meerkats have spotted a van coming towards the house. They think it's the ranger!'

Attention turned away from Mr Rich, and the animals looked eagerly across the plains for the arrival of their friend. It was, indeed, the ranger, and he was not alone. Leopard was sitting in the front seat, from where she was directing him. Throughout the journey, she had put her paws up on the dashboard and nodded her head to indicate which way he should go. Following the ranger, in a second van, were two large men wearing identical uniforms. To his delight, Alfie realised that the ranger had brought the police with him.

'How did Leopard communicate with the ranger?' he wondered in amazement.

The ranger stopped his van abruptly at the gates and got out rather cautiously, holding his gun close to him. He wasn't afraid of the animals when Alfie was there to translate for him, but he felt a little nervous now. The chimp quickly pushed his way through several sets of hooves and ran up to the ranger. Stella was delighted to see how happy they were to see each other.

The ranger hugged the chimp for some time, and Alfie mischievously tweaked the ranger's nose with his hand. The ranger looked with dismay at the gash on Alfie's head, and at the collar and chain still attached to his neck. Meanwhile, Leopard jumped out of the van to greet Alfie with a friendly pat of her paw.

'I'm so glad you're okay,' she said. 'Thank goodness—I was so worried.'

Alfie hugged her around her neck. 'Thank you, dear Leopard,' he said with tears in his eyes. 'Thank you for all your help. It is wonderful that you brought the ranger here.'

Alfie hurried to explain to the ranger what had happened. 'Mr Rich is a poacher,' he signed to him, nodding his head emphatically. He pointed towards the car, and the animals stepped aside so the ranger could see their prisoner.

Mr Rich stared sullenly out through the window, not daring to risk getting out of the car. The ranger's astonished eyes met his, and the poacher hung his head in shame.

'We've got evidence, too,' Alfie signed when he got the ranger's attention again. 'There is a room in the basement where he stores the horns, tusks, furs, and skins from his poaching. I can show you. I smashed up a lot of the rhino horn and ivory so it couldn't be sold.'

The ranger looked shocked. He shook his head and gazed at Alfie and at the gathering of species before him. He couldn't believe how clever the animals were. Questions swam into his mind: How had they found out where Alfie was? How had they managed to trap Mr Rich in his own car? Who was that man standing at the front door, looking scared? And why were Mr Rich's dogs nowhere to be seen?

'I'll explain everything later,' Alfie signed to him. 'Now, please arrest Mr Rich.'

The ranger beckoned to the two policemen, who were still waiting in their van, peering through the windows. The men hesitated and glanced at each other. Neither looked keen to get out. Eventually, one of the men cautiously opened the van door as if expecting the wild animals to descend upon him at once. The pair got out, holding their guns tightly. The ranger hurried over to them and quickly explained about the poaching evidence in the basement and that they needed to arrest Mr Rich. The two policemen stood warily behind the ranger, eyeing the animals in fear.

'You'd better move away from them,' Alfie told the animals, laughing at the timidity of the policemen. The animals stepped back, creating a path to the car from where Mr Rich looked out at them.

At last, the policemen stepped forward and went about their duty. Mr Rich scowled when the policemen escorted him out of his car and one of them handcuffed Mr Rich's right hand to his own. As they led Mr Rich towards their van, he shook his other fist at the animals and made a point of glaring at Alfie for a long time. 'I won't forget this, you horrible chimpanzee,' he threatened, although his voice sounded weak, and he knew the fight was over.

The animals cheered, making the policemen almost run back to the van with their prisoner. It sounded to them as if the hundreds of animals were about to attack, but the animals were simply overjoyed. None had ever dared to believe they would really catch Mr Rich.

The engine started up, and the policemen drove away. The animals watched until they could no longer see the poacher's cruel face through the windows of the van, and then the celebrations began for real.

CHAPTER 47

Standing Together

LEADER, DENT, AND FELICITY danced around in a circle, while the ostriches seized the opportunity to sprint around the garden. The older elephants returned from their task in the back garden, and Ethel, Maud, and Mabel proudly told anyone who would listen how they had destroyed the strange plants.

'They really were very tasty,' said Maud, who was now uncomfortably full.

'Some of them had a lot of spikes, though,' Mabel pointed out. 'They pricked my tongue!'

Buffalo was so excited that he boasted about how he had charged at Mr Rich, half-forgetting that the story wasn't actually true. Puff Adder made a point of appearing and catching his eye, and Buffalo quickly changed the subject.

Leopard found her cubs, who had been keeping out of danger with Lioness. They curled themselves around her in delight, and she nuzzled them back.

The baboons chattered away to each other, and an argument looked likely to break out. Stella watched them all with a faraway smile, and Bright knew she was thinking of her father, Bright's grandfather.

Meanwhile, Alfie had quickly recovered his energies and was bounding around from species to species, patting the animals on their backs or hugging them. 'Thank you for all your help,' he said as he politely shook the commander-in-chief's little paw.

'My pleasure, sir!' said the commander, saluting at once.

'Thank you. Thank you all for coming to rescue me,' the chimp cried to the zebras, antelopes, wildebeests, and giraffes. 'And thank you, scorpions,' he added, seeing the tiny creatures disappear into the garden as he waved to them.

'Alfie!' The chimp looked around in surprise. He had half-forgotten the ranger in his excitement at seeing his friends again. The ranger was waiting by his van, with Mr Rich's housekeeper already sitting in the back seat.

'Come here,' said the ranger firmly. 'We need to look after this poor man, and I think that wound on your head needs attending to. We need to get rid of that awful chain, too.'

'But I haven't finished saying thank you,' Alfie protested through signing.

'Okay, but hurry up, please,' said the ranger with a knowing look. 'I'll give you a few more minutes, and then we must go. You need to get everyone out of Mr Rich's garden too, please, so I can close the gates. More police will be coming this afternoon to investigate the evidence and take it away. We don't want any of it disappearing in the meantime.'

Alfie nodded and called to the animals that they needed to go out of the front gates. Stella realised what he was doing and asked for everyone to follow her. The commander-in-chief engaged the meerkats to help get the message around to all of the animals in the garden.

As the chimpanzee and the elephant leader together led the way out of the front gates, they heard Martial Eagle suddenly cry from overhead. 'Alfie, Stella—look! It's Cheetah...with another cheetah!'

The animals all turned to look, and sure enough, there was Cheetah with his new friend, looking happier than the animals had seen him for a long time. He ran across to see them all. 'Thank goodness, we've found you!' he exclaimed. 'I was starting to get really worried about what had happened to you all, so we followed your scents and came to see if you needed our help. This is Amber, by the way.'

The female cheetah nodded her head and smiled. She had a kind face and beautiful markings.

'Delighted to meet you,' said Stella, and Alfie bounded over to say hello to them both.

'Well, blow me down with a feather,' whispered Mabel from the back of the elephant herd, making Leader burst into giggles at the image this conjured up. 'I've known Cheetah for years, and he's always been on his own as far as I can remember.'

'I can't believe it,' agreed Maud. 'I'd have thought he'd be a quivering wreck if he had to talk to a female of his own kind.'

Stella heard them and turned around, looking directly at Mabel and Maud. 'Well, he's obviously found a good friend now,' she said, with a warning in her voice. 'I don't think any of us should offer our opinions.'

Ethel whispered something, but Stella told her off at once. 'I mean it,' she said, and the old elephant fell silent and waited until Stella's back was turned again.

'I knew Stella when she was just a little thing with downy hair,' Ethel whispered to Mabel indignantly. 'Now she's telling me off about my manners.'

The day was beautiful now. Not a cloud was in the sky, and the temperature was pleasantly warm as the remaining animals poured out of the gates from Mr Rich's garden.

Alfie stood and watched the animals with affection: Stella looking around her herd and checking everyone was present, Wanda now a part of the herd and visibly grateful for being so. Leader, Dent, and Felicity standing close together, talking happily. Buffalo, slightly unsteady under his wounded horns, but still full of determination. Lion and Lioness standing with their backs to each other, not looking on the best of terms. The baboons starting to argue amongst themselves, and the meerkat commander-in-chief looking displeased to see her troops somewhat out of position, Puff Adder watching with a gleeful expression. Martial Eagle flying off to catch the first rays of the sun, and the secretary bird chatting to the nearby ostriches. The herd animals gathering with their own species in preparation to gallop away, Giraffe and his family towering above them all. Cheetah and his new mate nuzzling each other warmly. Leopard watching rather forlornly as her now bigger cubs began to wander off into the distance. She knew this moment would come, but she was going to miss them.

Alfie suddenly realised there was something important he still had to do. 'Wait!' he called after the animals. 'Wait! There is something I want to say to you all.'

The animals stopped in their tracks and turned to listen to him. Alfie looked around at the watching faces, taking in their expressions as he paused until silence fell.

'We beat him,' Alfie said determinedly, 'and that was a huge triumph, but friends, there will be other poachers like Mr Rich out there, and we must always be on our guard. Our strength is standing together and giving each other unwavering allyship, friendship and support. We must never let arguments or frustrations drive us apart as some humans do. We are the incredible animals of the African savanna, and together, we will survive!'

The animals felt their hearts uplifted. They looked warmly at each other; the baboons having forgotten their argument. Lion and Lioness eyed each other in an affectionate truce. Puff Adder did his best to smile at the meerkat commander-in-chief, although somehow it came out as a strangled leer, and the nearby meerkats backed away in alarm.

'Three cheers for us, the animals of the savanna!' yelled Dent. The noise was tremendous as every animal joined in enthusiastically. Several animals looked at the secretary bird, who beamed with joy.

'And three cheers for Stella,' cried Wanda, to everyone's surprise. 'We would never have all come together like this without her.' The cries and stamping of hooves thundered again, and Stella looked quietly delighted. Bright rested her trunk against her mother with pride.

The sound gradually faded. Then, to Alfie's enormous pleasure, Cheetah, who had never been sure about the chimp, called out, 'And three cheers for Alfie, who's saved us from Mr Rich!' Cheetah's mate smiled tenderly, thinking how much more confident he seemed already.

This time, the cheers were even louder, and they rang out across the plains and echoed through the valley. At that moment, the morning wind blew with a gentle hum as if Nature herself were adding her support.

Alfie had never been lost for words before, but now he stood looking faintly pink, quite unable to think of anything to say. The ranger clapped and smiled as if he somehow understood what was happening.

'Thank you,' said the chimp at last, although his words were drowned out by the happy noise. 'You're wonderful animals, all of you. Don't you ever forget it.'

Alfie leapt into a backwards somersault and went tumbling over and over towards the ranger; it was time for him to go home.

Acknowledgements

A big thank you to the brilliant Daniella Blechner, whose advice, wisdom, and guidance have been invaluable from the moment I first met her. As well as publisher and mentor, she has also acted as co-editor of the book and encouraged me all the way through a new process, thank you.

Thank you, too, to my other excellent editor, Elise Abram, whose thoroughness, patience, and advice have also been invaluable. I have learnt a great deal from her, and the book is very much better for her input.

Thank you to my wonderful illustrator, Laura Liberatore, whose incredible illustrations always bring a smile to my face. She depicts the characters just as I see them, even though we live thousands of miles apart on different continents!

Thank you to my lovely husband, Chris, for your love and support and for putting up with me endlessly disappearing during evenings and weekends to finalise this book.

Thank you, too, to my beloved Mum and sister, Jeanette, for being readers of the first manuscript and for encouraging me throughout.

Thank you to my talented god-daughter, Bethany Phillips, who read an earlier version of the book and gave me very helpful feedback from a young reader's perspective.

Thank you to Catherine McDonald at the World Wildlife Fund for signposting me to resources on threats to wildlife from the illegal wildlife trade. The WWF is doing amazing work to help protect species across the world. Please do look at their website for more information: *www.wwf.org.uk.*

Thank you to Bradley, the blue-coated, orange-eyed cat who regularly comes to visit me at the window outside my writing room. His determined miaows usually get him the stroking and fuss he is after. He is a fine example of never giving up!

In a similar vein, thank you to little Isla, who is a clever and fiercely affectionate schnocker, and Truffle, an exuberantly joyful cockapoo, who both make me incredibly happy whenever I see them.

Finally, thank you to our darling Dad, who always encouraged me to write and who shared his brilliant imagination and humour with such love and kindness. We miss you, Dad.

About the Author

Carolyn May was born in Surrey in the UK and lived for a long time in South West London, but now lives in Cardiff with her husband, Chris. She works in healthcare and writes about animals in her spare time. Carolyn wrote the first version of this book shortly after university some 25 years ago, edited it, and brought it up to date for publication. She had thought the book was lost as the disk on which it was saved became corrupted, but when she and Chris were clearing out a garage in 2018, she came across a copy she had printed out!

Carolyn is totally passionate about preserving the beautiful species of our world and raising awareness of the challenges they face for survival. When she was a little girl, she and her sister, Jeanette, raised money for the David Shepherd Wildlife Foundation. Their approach included washing neighbours' cars, sponsored activities and—to the slight dismay of their parents—selling items they had been given for Christmas at car boot sales! Carolyn hopes this book will encourage young readers to get involved in helping to protect and safeguard wildlife throughout the world, and she would love to hear about the activities they are doing!

Conscious Dreams
PUBLISHING

Transforming diverse writers
into successful published authors

www.consciousdreamspublishing.com

authors@consciousdreamspublishing.com

Let's connect

Milton Keynes UK
Ingram Content Group UK Ltd.
UKHW051128180624
444338UK00009B/252